PENGUIN CLASSICS

THE WAR OF THE WORLDS

H. G. WELLS, the third son of a small shopkeeper, was born in Bromley in 1866. After two years' apprenticeship in a draper's shop, he became a pupil-teacher at Midhurst Grammar School and won a scholarship to study under T. H. Huxley at the Normal School of Science, South Kensington. He taught biology before becoming a professional writer and journalist. He wrote more than a hundred books, including novels, essays, histories and programmes for world regeneration.

Wells, who rose from obscurity to world fame, had an emotionally and intellectually turbulent life. His prophetic imagination was first displayed in pioneering works of science fiction such as *The Time Machine* (1895), *The Island of Doctor Moreau* (1896), *The Invisible Man* (1897) and *The War of the Worlds* (1898). Later he became an apostle of socialism, science and progress, whose anticipations of a future world state include *The Shape of Things to Come* (1933). His controversial views on sexual equality and women's rights were expressed in the novels *Ann Veronica* (1909) and *The New Machiavelli* (1911). He was, in Bertrand Russell's words, 'an important liberator of thought and action'.

Wells drew on his own early struggles in many of his best novels, including *Love and Mr Lewisham* (1900), *Kipps* (1905), *Tono-Bungay* (1909) and *The History of Mr Polly* (1910). His educational works, some written in collaboration, include *The Outline of History* (1920) and *The Science of Life* (1930). His *Experiment in Autobiography* (2 vols, 1934) reviews his world. He died in London in 1946.

PATRICK PARRINDER took his MA and Ph.D. at Cambridge University, where he held a Fellowship at King's College and published his first two books on Wells, *H. G. Wells* (1970) and *H. G. Wells: The Critical Heritage* (1972). He has been Chairman of the H. G. Wells Society and editor of the *Wellsian*, and has also written on James Joyce, science fiction, literary criticism and the history of the English novel. His book *Shadows of the Future* (1995) brings together his interests in Wells, science fiction and literary prophecy. Since 1986 he has been Professor of English at the University of Reading.

BRIAN ALDISS has been writing for half a century. He is best known for his science fiction novels and stories, but has also written many novels on contemporary subjects, poetry and non-fiction. Aldiss was born in Norfolk in 1925. He soldiered in the Far East, chiefly Burma, Sumatra and Hong Kong, during and after the Second World War. In 2000 he was made Grand Master of Science Fiction by the Science Fiction Writers of America and given an Honorary D.Litt. by the University of Reading. His history of science fiction, *Billion Year Spree* (1973), is generally considered to be the best and wittiest survey of the field.

ANDY SAWYER is the librarian of the Science Fiction Foundation Collection at the University of Liverpool Library, and Course Director of the MA in Science Fiction Studies offered by the School of English. He also teaches a science fiction module for undergraduates. He has published widely on science fiction and related literatures, and co-edited the collection of essays *Speaking Science Fiction* (Liverpool University Press, 2000). He is also Reviews Editor of *Foundation: the International Review of Science Fiction* and Associate Editor of the forthcoming *Encyclopedia of Themes in Science Fiction and Fantasy* (Greenwood Press).

H. G. WELLS

The War of the Worlds

Edited by PATRICK PARRINDER
With an Introduction by BRIAN ALDISS
and Notes by ANDY SAWYER

PENGUIN BOOKS

PENGUIN BOOKS

Published by the Penguin Group
Penguin Books Ltd, 80 Strand, London WC2R ORL, England
Penguin Group (USA) Inc., 375 Hudson Street, New York, New York 10014, USA
Penguin Group (Canada), 10 Alcorn Avenue, Toronto, Ontario, Canada M4V 3B2
(a division of Pearson Penguin Canada Inc.)
Penguin Ireland, 25 St Stephen's Green, Dublin 2, Ireland
(a division of Penguin Books Ltd)
Penguin Group (Australia), 250 Camberwell Road,
Camberwell, Victoria 3124, Australia (a division of Pearson Australia Group Pty Ltd)
Penguin Books India Pvt Ltd, 11 Community Centre,
Panchsheel Park, New Delhi – 110 017, India
Penguin Group (NZ), cnr Airborne and Rosedale Roads, Albany,
Auckland 1310, New Zealand (a division of Pearson New Zealand Ltd)
Penguin Books (South Africa) (Pty) Ltd, 24 Sturdee Avenue,
Rosebank 2196, South Africa

Penguin Books Ltd, Registered Offices: 80 Strand, London WC2R ORL, England

www.penguin.com

First published 1898
This edition first published in Penguin Classics 2005
10 9 8 7 6 5 4 3

Text copyright © the Literary Executors of the Estate of H. G. Wells
Biographical Note, Further Reading, Note on the Text copyright © Patrick Parrinder, 2005
Introduction copyright © Brian Aldiss, 2005
Appendix and Notes copyright © Andy Sawyer, 2005
All rights reserved

CONTENTS

Biographical Note

Herbert George Wells was born on 21 September 1866 at Bromley, Kent, a small market town soon to be swallowed up by the suburban growth of outer London. His father, formerly a professional gardener and a county cricketer renowned for his fast bowling, owned a small business in Bromley High Street selling china goods and cricket bats. The house was grandly known as Atlas House, but the centre of family life was a cramped basement kitchen underneath the shop. Soon Joseph Wells's cricketing days were cut short by a broken leg, and the family fortunes looked bleak.

Young 'Bertie' Wells had already shown great academic promise, but when he was thirteen, his family broke up and he was forced to earn his own living. His father was bankrupt, and his mother left home to become resident housekeeper at Uppark, the great Sussex country house where she had worked as a lady's maid before her marriage. Wells was taken out of school to follow his two elder brothers into the drapery trade. After serving briefly as a pupil-teacher and a pharmacist's assistant, in 1881 he was apprenticed to a department store in Southsea, working a thirteen-hour day and sleeping in a dormitory with his fellow-apprentices. This was the unhappiest period of his life, though he would later revisit it in comic romances such as *Kipps* (1905) and *The History of Mr Polly* (1910). Kipps and Polly both manage to escape from their servitude as drapers, and in 1883, helped by his long-suffering mother, Wells cancelled his indentures and obtained a post as teaching assistant at Midhurst Grammar School near Uppark. His intellectual development, long held back, now progressed astonishingly. He passed a series of examinations in science subjects and, in September 1884, entered the Normal School of Science, South Kensington (later to become part of Imperial College of Science and Technology) on a government scholarship.

Wells was a born teacher, as many of his books would show, and at first he was an enthusiastic student. He had the good fortune to be taught biology and zoology by one of the most influential scientific thinkers of the Victorian age, Darwin's friend and supporter T. H. Huxley. Wells never forgot Huxley's teaching, but the other professors were more humdrum, and his interest in their courses rapidly waned. He scraped through second-year physics, but failed his third-year geology exam and left South Kensington in 1887 without taking a degree. He was thrilled by the theoretical framework and imaginative horizons of natural science, but impatient of practical detail and the grinding, routine tasks of laboratory work. He cut his classes and spent his time reading literature and history, satisfying the curiosity he had earlier felt while exploring the long-neglected library at Uppark. He started a college magazine, the *Science Schools Journal*, and argued for socialism in student debates.

In the summer of 1887 Wells became science master at a small private school in North Wales, but a few weeks later he was knocked down and injured by one of his pupils on the football field. Sickly and undernourished as a result of three years of student poverty, he suffered severe kidney and lung damage. After months of convalescence at Uppark he was able to return to science teaching at Henley House School, Kilburn. In 1890 he passed his University of London B.Sc. (Hons.) with a first class in zoology and obtained a post as a biology tutor for the University Correspondence College. In 1891 he married his cousin Isabel Wells, but they had little in common and soon Wells fell in love with one of his students, Amy Catherine Robbins (usually known as 'Jane'). They started living together in 1893, and married two years later when his divorce came through.

During his years as a biology tutor Wells slowly began making his way as a writer and journalist. He wrote for the

Educational Times, edited the *University Correspondent*, and in 1891 published a philosophical essay, 'The Rediscovery of the Unique', in the prestigious *Fortnightly Review*. His first book was a *Textbook of Biology* (1893). But no sooner was it published than his health again collapsed, forcing him to give up teaching and rely entirely on his literary earnings. His future seemed highly precarious, yet soon he was in regular demand as a writer of short stories and humorous essays for the burgeoning newspapers and magazines of the period. He became a fiction reviewer and, for a short period in 1895, a theatre critic.

Ever since his student days Wells had worked intermittently on a story about time-travelling and the possible future of the human race. An early version was published in the *Science Schools Journal* as 'The Chronic Argonauts', but now, after numerous redrafts and much encouragement from the poet and editor W. E. Henley, it finally took shape as *The Time Machine* (1895). Its success was instantaneous, and while it was running as a magazine serial Wells was already being spoken of as a 'man of genius'. He was celebrated as the inventor of the 'scientific romance', a combination of adventure novel and philosophical tale in which the hero becomes involved in a life-and-death struggle resulting from some unforeseen scientific development. There was now a ready market for his fiction, and *The Island of Doctor Moreau* (1896), *The Invisible Man* (1897), *The War of the Worlds* (1898), *When the Sleeper Wakes* (1899; later revised as *The Sleeper Awakes*, 1910), *The First Men in the Moon* (1901) and several other volumes followed quickly from his pen.

By the turn of the twentieth century Wells was established as a popular author in England and America, and his books were rapidly being translated into French, German, Spanish, Russian and other European languages. Already his fame had begun to eclipse that of his predecessor in scientific romance, the French author Jules Verne, who had dominated the field since the 1860s. But Wells, an increasingly self-conscious artist, had larger ambitions than to go down in history as a boys' adventure novelist like Jules Verne. *Love and Mr Lewisham* (1900) was his first attempt at realistic fiction, comic in spirit and manifestly reflecting his own experiences as a student and teacher. By the end of the Edwardian decade, when he wrote his 'Condition of England' novels *Tono-Bungay* (1909) and *The New Machiavelli* (1911), Wells had become one of the leading novelists of his day, the friend and rival of such literary figures as Arnold Bennett, Joseph Conrad, Ford Madox Ford and Henry James.

But Wells was never a devotee of art for art's sake; he was a prophetic writer with a social and political message. His first major non-fictional work was *Anticipations* (1902), a book of futurological essays setting out the possible effects of scientific and technological progress in the twentieth century. *Anticipations* brought him into contact with the Fabian Society and launched his career as a political journalist and an influential voice of the British left. During his Fabian period Wells wrote *A Modern Utopia* (1905), but failed in his attempt to challenge the bureaucratic, reformist outlook of the Society's leaders such as Bernard Shaw (a lifelong friend and rival) and Beatrice Webb. Wells's Edwardian scientific romances such as *The Food of the Gods* (1904) and *The War in the Air* (1908), though full of humorous touches, are propagandist in intent. In other 'future war' stories of this period he predicted the tank and the atomic bomb.

Success as an author brought about great changes in his personal life. Ill-health had forced him to leave London for the Kent coast in 1898, but in the long run the only legacy of his footballing injury was the diabetes that affected him in old age. He commissioned a house, Spade House, overlooking the English Channel at Sandgate, from the architect C. F. A. Voysey, and here his and Jane's two sons were born – George Philip or 'Gip', who became a zoology professor and collaborated with his father and Julian Huxley on the biology encyclopedia *The Science of Life* (1930), and Frank, who worked in the film industry. Wells gave generous support to his parents and to his eldest brother, who was a fellow-fugitive from the drapery trade. Increasingly, however, he looked for emotional fulfilment outside the family, and his sexual affairs became notorious. He had a daughter in 1909 with Amber Reeves, a leading young Fabian economist, and in 1914 the novelist and critic Rebecca West gave birth to his son Anthony West, whose troubled childhood would later be reflected in his own novel *Heritage* (1955) and in his biography of his father.

As Wells's personal life became the gossip of literary London, his roles as imaginative writer and political journalist or prophet came increasingly into conflict. *Ann Veronica* (1909) was an example of topical, controversial fiction, dramatizing and commenting on such issues as women's rights, sexual equality and contemporary morals. It was the first of Wells's 'discussion novels' in which his personal relationships were often very thinly disguised. His later fiction takes a great variety of forms, but it all belongs to the broad category of the novel of ideas. At one extreme is the realistic reporting of *Mr Britling Sees It Through* (1916) – still valuable and unique as a portrayal of the English 'home front' in the First World War – while at the other extreme are brief fables such as *The Undying Fire* (1919) and *The Croquet Player* (1936), political allegories about world events each cast in the form of a prophetic dialogue.

Wells was by no means an experimental novelist like his younger contemporaries James Joyce and Virginia Woolf, but he was often technically innovative, and in some of his books the boundaries between fiction and non-fiction begin to break down. Sometimes he would take a classic from an earlier, premodern epoch as his literary model: *A Modern Utopia* (1905), for example, refers back to Sir Thomas More's *Utopia* and Plato's *Republic*. His bestselling historical works *The Outline of History* (1920) and *A Short History of the World* (1922) break with historical conventions by looking forward to the next stage in history. These works were written in order to draw the lessons of the First World War and to ensure that, if possible, its carnage would never be repeated; Wells saw history as a 'race between education and catastrophe'. The same concerns led to his future-history novel *The Shape of Things to Come* (1933), later rewritten for the cinema as *Things to Come*, an epic science-fiction film produced in 1936 by Alexander Korda. Both novel and film contain dire warnings about the inevitable outbreak and disastrous consequences of the Second World War.

By the 1920s, Wells was not only a famous author but a public figure whose name was rarely out of the newspapers. He briefly worked for the Ministry of Propaganda in 1918, producing a memorandum on war aims which anticipated the setting-up of the League of Nations. In 1922 and 1923 he stood for Parliament as a Labour candidate. He sought to influence world leaders, including two US Presidents, Theodore Roosevelt and Franklin D. Roosevelt. His meeting with Lenin in the Kremlin in 1920 and his interview in 1934 with Lenin's successor Josef Stalin were publicized all over the world. His high-pitched, piping voice was often heard on BBC radio. In 1933 he was elected president of International PEN, the writers' organization campaigning for intellectual freedom. In the same year his books were publicly burnt by the Nazis in Berlin, and he was banned from visiting Fascist Italy. His ideas strongly influenced the Pan-European Union, the pressure group advocating European unity between the wars.

But Wells became convinced that nothing less than global unity was needed if humanity was not to destroy itself. In *The Open Conspiracy* (1928) and other books he outlined his theories of world citizenship and world government. As the Second World War drew nearer he felt that his mission had been a failure and his warnings had gone unheeded. His last great campaign, for which he tried to obtain international support, was for human rights. The proposal set out in his Penguin Special *The Rights of Man* (1940) helped to bring about the United Nations declaration of 1948. He spent the war years at his house in Hanover Terrace, Regent's Park, and was awarded a D.Litt. by London University in 1943. His last book, *Mind at the End of Its Tether* (1945), was a despairing, pessimistic work, even bleaker in its prospects for mankind than *The Time Machine* fifty years earlier. He died at Hanover Terrace on 13 August 1946. He was restless and tireless to the end, a prophet eternally dissatisfied with himself and with humanity. 'Some day,' he had written in a whimsical 'Auto-Obituary' three years earlier, 'I shall write a book, a *real* book.' He had published over fifty works of fiction and, in total, some 150 books and pamphlets.

Patrick Parrinder

Introduction

In the middle of the seventeenth century, the Dutch son of a basket-maker made an alarming discovery. His name was Antony van Leeuwenhoek. He ground his own lenses and constructed a microscope. Whereas Galileo had been surveying the stars and Isaac Newton was measuring the Moon's orbit, van Leeuwenhoek looked in the opposite direction, into the very small.

Observing a drop of water from a lake, he found it full of living things, of 'animalcules': 'On these last I saw two little legs near the head, and two little fins at the hindmost end of the body . . . And the motion of most of these animalcules in the water was so swift, and so various upwards, downwards, and round about, that 'twas wonderful to see . . .'

At last, someone had discovered alien life!

Long before the seventeenth century, the human mind was amply populated by hobgoblins of all kinds, and indeed still continues to be. Ghosts and vampires abound there. But to discover these minute, hidden, seemingly hostile 'animalcules' in a drop of water was a new and disquieting thing. Water! Water, the symbol of purity, infested with unimagined creatures! Peace of mind departs and one more step towards our neurotic modern world is taken.

The young Mr H. G. Wells attended the biological laboratory of what was in 1884 known as the Normal School of Science. An echo of his learning experience sounds in the opening lines of his story 'The Stolen Bacillus': ' "This again," said the Bacteriologist, slipping a glass slide under the microscope, "is a preparation of the celebrated Bacillus of cholera – the cholera germ." '

The ubiquity of 'germs' as an idea took hold on Wells's mind.

Herbert George Wells was born in 1866, of lower-middle-class parents. The parents ran a china shop in Bromley, in Kent. At the age of seven, young Bertie broke his leg and was laid up for weeks. Sympathy and books came his way. He said, 'This fall was one of the luckiest events of my life.'

Although the population of Bromley increased from 20,000 to 50,000 in the decades of the sixties, seventies and eighties, it seems that none of the new inhabitants wanted to buy any china. The shop closed amid an increased urban sprawl which continues today.

Wells's education included a spell under the great scientist and humanist, Thomas Huxley. Huxley, in his vigorous defence of Darwin's evolutionary theory, became known as 'Darwin's Bulldog'. His grandsons included Julian and Aldous Huxley. Once Wells had won his hard-earned freedom, he moved ever onwards; through over a hundred books, we see him struggling with questions of evolution, over-population, education, and the betterment of mankind.

He became a leading contributor to the Sankey Declaration of the Rights of Man, which later formed part of the charter of the United Nations. When the UN General Assembly held its first session in London in January of 1946, Wells was in his last months of life. He died peacefully on 13 August of that year.

His creative powers had waned as his strength as a polemicist grew. In his early novels, these aspects are in balance: and never more so than in this present novel, *The War of the Worlds*. The novel's thrilling and horrific theme aims to puncture mankind's pretensions. As the 1930s dawn, novels give way to treatises such as *The Way to World Peace* (1930), *The Work, Wealth and Happiness of Mankind* (1932), *World Brain* (1938), and *The Fate of Homo Sapiens* (1939).

It was a part of Wells's genius that he could invent things never before imagined. A character in one of Chekhov's plays says, 'We should show life neither as it is nor as it ought to be, but as we see it in our dreams.' It is the Surrealists' prescription

and one at which Wells was good in his early days, until he
began desiring to change the world – by force if necessary. We
see a foreshadowing of this wish at the conclusion of the present
volume, when the narrator tells us that the Martians have
done much to 'promote the conception of the commonweal of
mankind'.

But to say this is to begin at the end. To begin at the beginning, and at that magnificent paragraph with which *The War
of the Worlds* opens, here we find mention of 'a man with a
microscope' who might scrutinize 'the transient creatures that
swarm and multiply in a drop of water'. We shall find that this
first reference, hardly cordial, to mankind as a whole is to be
followed by many another unflattering description.

I first came upon this novel at a youthful age, when I was not
unfamiliar with the more conventional novels to which the
term 'classic' was applied. Among such novels were *Robinson
Crusoe*, *Oliver Twist* and *Jane Eyre*. But I do not recall any
sentence which ever had such awesome effect on me as one
sentence in that first paragraph of *The War of the Worlds*: 'Yet
across the gulf of space, minds that are to our minds as ours
are to those of the beasts that perish, intellects vast and cool
and unsympathetic, regarded this earth with envious eyes, and
slowly and surely drew their plans against us.' Had there ever
been such an opening statement, labyrinthine yet pellucid,
before? No latinate long words here, designed to impress; the
longest word is that readily comprehensible understatement of
an adjective, 'unsympathetic'.

So the curtain comes up on the drama, and already the seeds
of Wells's clever denouement have been planted.

The novel was published in hardcover in 1898, having been
serialized in a popular magazine in 1897, the year of a second
Victorian jubilee and much British self-congratulation.

The later decades of the nineteenth century had seen the
popularity of the sensation novel, 'read alike in drawing-room
and kitchen'. Such novels might concern adultery or bigamy,
famous examples of both being *Lady Audley's Secret* and *East
Lynne* (wherein the famous line occurs, 'Dead – and never
called me mother!'). Something of the ubiquity of these novels

was owed to the 1871 Bill to provide public elementary education for all. The Education Act marks the first time that the state assumed direct responsibility for general education. A new readership developed, open to the wonders of Mr H. G. Wells.

There are sensations more overwhelming than adultery, more terrible than bigamy. The sensations of warfare and societal change in which Wells trafficked also emerge in the late decades of the nineteenth century. The year 1871 alone brought Bulwer Lytton's *The Coming Race*, Samuel Butler's *Erewhon* and Colonel George Chesney's *The Battle of Dorking*. The latter pamphlet describes a German invasion of England. England, unprepared, is defeated by Germany.

Chesney's story created an immediate effect, popular and political. The device of future war and sudden invasion, which exposes the unprepared nation to inevitable defeat, aroused fears and imitations everywhere. As Professor I. F. Clarke puts it in his invaluable book, *Voices Prophesying War 1763–1984*, 'Between 1871 and 1914 it was unusual to find a single year without some tale of future warfare appearing in some European country.'

But it is Wells's master-stroke to have the invaders arrive from another planet! No communication, no truce, is possible. The appearance on the stage of the hideous Martians, with their bad habits, decidedly raises the stakes and gives the novel an almost mythopoeic strength.

The War of the Worlds opens with portents in the sky above a peaceful England, with people going about their daily business. What some believe to be a meteor lies half-buried in a pit on the sandy common near Woking. Some people have a look. They are mistaken. The supposed meteor is a cylinder, the top of which slowly unscrews.

Onlookers gather. In Chapter 4, something emerges from the cylinder, something which 'glistened like wet leather'. Wells makes sure we understand how repulsive the Martians are, without going into detail at this juncture.

A delegation waving a white flag approaches the cylinder. The men are determined to communicate with their alien visitors. The Martians turn a heat-ray on the delegation. All are killed. Now we understand how remorseless the Martians are, lacking the qualities of emotion and empathy.

The narrator of the story is at first alarmed; but when he gets home and sits down to a good meal, his mood improves. He believes the Martians are terrified, and says, 'Perhaps they expected to find no living things – certainly no intelligent living things . . .'

People talk about the unusual event, but it does not make 'the sensation that an ultimatum to Germany would have done'. By similar touches, Wells brings verisimilitude to his tale.

A second cylinder arrives.

Soon the peaceful English countryside is burning. The Martians use their heat-ray. Perhaps with a nod towards *The Battle of Dorking*, the military are slow to get into action. Things go steadily and satisfyingly from bad to worse. Church steeples tumble down. People hide in trenches and cellars. While composing this story, Wells was cycling round the area. 'I completely wreck and sack Woking – killing my neighbours in painful and eccentric ways,' says he, with a certain sadistic relish.

It is destructive. However, destruction was modish. The taste of ruination was not in the mouths of the home population. The Edwardians were merely the children of a century in which a hideous adulthood was yet to come. So D. H. Lawrence exclaims, 'Three cheers for the man who invented poison gas.' And 'Let all schools be closed at once,' while T. S. Eliot regrets the spread of education, which is 'lowering our standards . . . destroying our ancient edifices . . .'

So why did Wells not call his novel, 'The War of Woking'? Because his intentions were more grandiose than merely the destruction of Woking, desirable though that might be.

The nameless narrator also witnesses the destruction of Weybridge and Shepperton. Always, the machines are contrasted with that essentially English invention, the countryside. 'The armoured Martians appeared, far away over the little trees, across the flat meadows that stretch towards Chertsey, and striding hurriedly towards the river.'

And these machines take no more notice of the humans than would the humans of 'a confusion of ants'.

The narrator meets a curate. The curate, like the artilleryman we meet later, is there merely to express a viewpoint; this is not really a characterization. But to my memory, the world of fiction was once populated with chinless wonders of vicars and curates; they were popular Aunt Sally figures – Aunt Sallys being popular recreational dummies in public-house gardens, designed merely to have wooden balls shied at them.

Wells's curate is there to express the helplessness of organized religion when faced with the invaders. ' "All the work – all the Sunday-schools – What have we done?" ' . . . ' "The end! The great and terrible day of the Lord!" ' . . . "Be a man!", said I.'

We learn that the narrator has a brother in London. The scene is thus enabled to shift to the city. Everything is calm there, a calm giving way gradually to excitement and anxiety. Fugitives begin to pour in from West Surrey. The Martians advance, and by Chapter 16 panic and disorder – how Wells hated disorder! – take over. There is 'a swift liquidation of the social body'.

We may ask ourselves today if something similar would take place, supposing Al-Qa'ida launched bombs containing anthrax upon the capital. I asked myself a similar question when, visiting the bookstall on Paddington station in the Second World War, I came upon a reprint of Wells's novel; the jacket showed search-light beams in the sky and flames arising from the destroyed city. Some fears remain ever topical.

The Martians are as remorseless as was the Luftwaffe.

It is not necessary to relate what happens next; we can safely leave that to Mr Wells. The question arises as to what was going on in the capacious mind of the author when he wrote about this wholesale destruction. The subject of colonialism emerges; the cruel treatment of the Tasmanians is mentioned. Wells was not the only one in reflective mood. Rudyard Kipling's poem 'Recessional' was published in 1897. ('Lo, all our pomp of yesterday / Is one with Nineveh and Tyre . . .')

More constantly on Wells's mind was the question of over-population – long before this became a subject for common discussion. Thomas Malthus's 'Essay on the Principle of Population' was published in the last years of the eighteenth century.

Malthus points out that whereas population increases in a geometrical ratio, subsistence increases only in an arithmetical ratio. An increasing number of people will go hungry. Such is a rule of nature. 'And the race of man cannot, by any efforts of reason, escape from it. Among plants and animals, its effects are waste of seed, sickness, and premature death. Among mankind, misery and vice.'

Although this stern judgement has been somewhat ameliorated by crop development and improved agricultural methods, Malthus still rules. And, as John Ruskin says in *Unto This Last*, 'In all the ranges of human thought, I know none so melancholy as the speculations of political economists on the population question.'

Later, when his amazing creativity was on the wane, Wells in his didactic mode devoted whole books to the question of over-population. In his *A Modern Utopia* 'degenerates' are prevented from breeding. The idiots, drug addicts, drunkards and violent men are exiled on various islands, and carefully policed.

Wells is, of course, one of the most prodigal producers of utopias. In book after book, society is overturned, eventually to develop a better and more orderly world. Perhaps we find such themes less convincing nowadays, after the ghastly regimes established in the early to middle decades of the last century. In 1910, some years after the publication of *The War of the Worlds*, Wells published the charming *History of Mr Polly*. While embodying many aspects of Wells's own earlier life, most notably Mr Polly's escape from drapery shops, the novel also contains a dream shared by many men of that time: escape from the captivity of shops to becoming a casual worker in a rural inn, owned by a pleasant woman and situated on the banks of an unsullied river. It is a form of one-man utopia, where Mr Polly finds happiness at last.

A pleasant variant on this scenario is played out in *Nineteen Eighty-Four*, where Orwell's humble notion of utopia is a private room and a girl to love. Mr Polly's utopia is of longer duration than that of Winston Smith. The mood had darkened by the 1940s.

This is a convenient place in which to say a word concerning some of the films and radio programmes made from Wells's book. In October 1938 a radio play based on *The War of the Worlds*, starring Orson Welles, was broadcast in the United States (and re-broadcast much later on BBC radio). It was produced in documentary form, the setting transposed to the eastern seaboard of the United States. Many people fell into a panic, believing they were actually being invaded by Martians, and headed for the traditional hills. It is difficult to see today how listeners could have been so gullible, but learned universities have written about, and a film studio made a movie about, what happened that night.

The War of the Worlds was filmed by George Pal/Paramount Productions and released in 1953. The opening is impressive. Sir Cedric Hardwicke, eminent member of the British contingent in Hollywood at the time, narrates much of the first paragraph of the novel against a starry background.

England gives way to Southern California. Woking gives way to Los Angeles. A square-jawed actor and a blank-faced actress provide a love affair. While the dialogue is plodding, the boomerang-shaped Martian war machines are attractive. It is a noisy film, full of destruction.

As we have seen, Wells's cleric is contemptible. Director Byron Haskin transforms him into an heroic figure. Advancing towards the Martian front-line, the heroic vicar chants, 'Yeah, though I walk through the Valley of Death, I will fear no evil' – when *Pow!* – he is wiped out.

An American TV series based on the Wells novel arrived on the small screen in 1988 and ran for forty-two episodes.

These films and others, such as *Kipps* and *The History of Mr Polly*, bear witness to a difference in British and American temperaments. The British like – or certainly did like – a pinch of melancholy to their dish, for flavour's sake. The Americans prefer triumphant individualism, such as was propagated in science fiction by the Robert Heinlein/Isaac Asimov/John Campbell group of writers. This preference was shown even more clearly by the fate of *The War of the Worlds* in the USA.

The novel was run as a pirated serial in an American newspaper. Americans were not going to take the Martian invasion lying down. A journalist by the name of Garrett P. Serviss wrote a kind of sequel to Wells's novel, entitled *Edison's Conquest of Mars*. Thomas Edison invents anti-gravity and a disintegrating ray, and sets off with a whole fleet of spaceships to pulverize Mars. The evil Martians are wiped out. As is Wells's lesson in humility.

There were reasons other than Malthus's essay on population to make a thinking man of Wells's time somewhat down in the mouth. There was, for example, William Thomson, Lord Kelvin's remark on entropy: 'Within a finite period of time past, the earth must have been, and within a finite period to come, the earth must again be, unfit for the habitation of man as at present constituted.'

Wells had already reported on those bleak last days of the human race in *The Time Machine*. Now he was commenting on other theories, such as the theory of Laplace and his nebular hypothesis, that Mars was an older world than ours.

In an article in a review published in 1896, Wells discusses the possibility of intelligent life on Mars, and states, 'There is no doubt that Mars is very like the Earth.' The statement was plausible before various NASA fly-bys had shown Mars to be a barren and inhospitable rock, bereft of life, bereft certainly of anything approaching intelligent bipeds or the umbrella-bearing public of Wells's day.

Wells was labouring under an illusion shared by many who took an interest in matters astronomical at that period. We now know Mars to be not senile, merely inclement. But Wells's view of Martian life is cleverly linked with that other great nineteenth-century discovery which preoccupied Wells and others (as it still preoccupies us in our century) – Charles Darwin's theory of evolution.

Wells reserves a close description of Martian anatomy until Book II, Chapter 2. There we are treated to three pages of exposition, following the opening sentence, 'They were, I now saw, the most unearthly creatures it is possible to conceive.' After we have become thoroughly and scientifically disgusted, comes the cool remark, 'To me it is quite credible that the

Martians may be descended from beings not unlike ourselves.'
After all, who knows what we may become? As Wells says, 'We
men ... are just in the beginning of the evolution that the
Martians have worked out.'

Moreover, another nasty trait of the alien invaders, to be
revealed later in the book, has perhaps been developed from
Darwin's statement in *The Origin of Species*. In the chapter
entitled 'The Struggle for Existence' Darwin states, 'The action
of climate seems at first sight to be quite independent of the
struggle for existence; but in so far as climate chiefly acts in
reducing food, it brings on the most severe struggle between
the individuals ... which subsist on the same kind of food.'
Undoubtedly, the colder climate of the Red Planet would
intensify this struggle, as Wells understood.

We can see that *The War of the Worlds* is a compendium of
many nineteenth-century concerns. Of course it is more than
that, for those concerns are woven into an extraordinary and
fascinating tale. It is the foundation stone for all alien invasion
stories, whether in print or in the cinema. Following Wells's
example, many other stories were to come where the world, or
England at least, is laid waste. Among these are Conan Doyle's
The Poison Belt, John Wyndham's *The Day of the Triffids*,
John Christopher's *The Death of Grass*, J. G. Ballard's *The
Wind from Nowhere*, Aldous Huxley's *Ape and Essence* and
my own *Greybeard*. The danger and interest in writing of such
things is that, in defying 'common sense', one does not fall into
common idiocy. Wells is adroit in such matters.

But of this sub-genre of catastrophe, it is the unsympathetic
Martians who wear the laurel crown.

Scientific romances and science fiction are generally considered to be remote from the author's experience. That can
never be the case; what we are fills the fictions we tell, often
without our realizing it. What lurks as fugitive in the mind
comes out clearly on paper. As Mary Shelley says in her introduction to *Frankenstein, or the Modern Prometheus* (1818),
'Invention, it must be humbly admitted, does not consist in
creating out of the void, but out of chaos; the materials must

in the first place be afforded: it can give form to dark, shapeless substances, but cannot bring into being the substance itself.' This was true in Wells's case; he had an ample stock of dark, shapeless substances.

We see this clearly in two instances. When the narrator is trapped with the curate in a ruined house, we find theirs is a filthy semi-subterranean entrapment. They are confined to the scullery of the half-destroyed building. We have here, unmistakably, a reconstruction of the scullery of Atlas House in which, when Bertie Wells was a lad, his mother slaved away years of her life. The squalor and discomfort of that room remained with Wells. Wells, like Orwell after him, knew that dirt has political significance. We find that scullery described again in the novel *In the Days of the Comet*, in Section III, Chapter 4 – described with sorrow.

He depicts it there in part as 'a damp, unsavoury, mainly subterranean region . . . rendered more than typically dirty in our case by the fact that into it the coal-cellar, a yawning pit of black uncleanness, opened, and diffused small crunchable particles about the uneven brick floor.' There his mother works, 'a soul of unselfishness'. 'And while she washes up I go out, to sell my overcoat and watch in order that I may desert her.'

This sad place is employed in *The War of the Worlds* as a symbol, for kitchens are places where things are prepared for eating. As the curate discovers.

The Martians have invaded Earth for a good meal. The narrator/storyteller sits down to a good meal before getting into his tale. Wells had an obsession with food – with both eating and being eaten. You can, to adapt an old saying, take the man out of the kitchen but you cannot take the kitchen out of the man. Peter Kemp wrote an entire book about Wells's appetites, entitled, *H. G. Wells and the Culminating Ape*. People in *The War of the Worlds* are depicted as being part of the food chain. The inhabitants of Woking flee 'as blindly as a flock of sheep' from the Martian fire, as from a cooking pot!

The second instance in which Wells's early experience informs his thinking shines an interesting light on his attitude towards society. Wells the socialist followed a good radical pedigree. Like William Godwin, he regarded humanity as perfectible; like Percy Bysshe Shelley he believed in Free Love. Yet this socialist was never entirely on the side of his fellow men. He had little belief in the immutability of the social order. The artilleryman, an unpleasant character, looks forward to the overturn of society. ' "There won't be any more blessed concerts for a million years or so," ' he says; ' "there won't be any Royal Academy of Arts, and no nice little feeds at restaurants." '

Wells in his youth had experienced a remarkable example of social change which came about peacefully. His mother, Sarah Wells, left his father and went to work as housekeeper at Uppark, 'the big house' in Sussex. Lady Fetherstonehaugh was the owner of Uppark. She had started life as a milkmaid in the grounds, under the rather apt name of Mary Ann Bullock. The lord of the manor had taken a fancy to Mary Bullock; he packed her off to Paris to be educated and refined, and then married her. After his death, Lady Fetherstonehaugh ruled Uppark in solitary splendour. She was a striking instance of the social mobility which Wells himself achieved.

Despite frequent illness, Wells was a high-spirited chap. At the least, he put on high spirits. His letters to his mother and his friends are adorned with comic little sketches – the 'picshuas', as he calls them. But as to the intellectual aspect of the culture, there was much to depress a thinking Victorian. Lord Kelvin had pronounced that the lump of rock on which everyone lived would last for only another twenty million years. The death of the Sun, in the days before nuclear activity was understood, was also thought to be comparatively and depressingly close.

These were matters dramatized in Wells's *The Time Machine*, published in 1895, three years before *The War of the Worlds*.

Patrick Parrinder, a great Wells critic, has resolved the mystery surrounding the year 802,701 prominent in the former book. 'What is missing from *The Time Machine* is the openly prophetic narrative rhetoric exemplified in *The War of the Worlds*, where ... we are given, without benefit of a time machine, an eye witness narrative of events occurring "early in the twentieth century" ...'

It had once been the habit of many English novelists to open their novel with the words, 'It was in the winter of the year 18— . . .', or 'Early in the reign of King William IV . . .', these dates possibly signifying a time when the author was young; things were assumed not greatly to have changed since that date. However, as the nineteenth century progressed, things were greatly changing. Gradually novels crept into the present. Wells, in his impatience, starts his novel in – leaps into – the future.

Could this strange idea of setting novels in future time be a contributory factor for the way in which such novels are ruled out of court by a literary elite? Surely it is not only 'the masses' who think of the future as a proper dwelling-place for the imagination . . . In any case, Wells enjoyed a splendid creativity for the seven years from 1895–1901. The best of his science fiction (though not of his ordinary social fiction) was written then, and most of the stories are of social dissolution, of uncomfortable new worlds opening up, old worlds being bludgeoned down to their knees.

There is an argument which says that much of this mood is attributable to *fin de siècle* angst; I would rather attribute it, as Wells himself did, to a new way of thinking. In his brilliant discourse, 'The Discovery of the Future', delivered to the Royal Institution in 1902, he distinguishes between two divergent mental attitudes. He opens his speech by saying he wishes to 'contrast and separate two divergent types of mind, types which are to be distinguished chiefly by their attitude towards time'.

The predominant type scarcely thinks of the future. A much less abundant but more modern type 'thinks constantly and by preference of things to come, and of present things mainly in relation to the results that must arise from them'. Wells sees this type of person as 'perpetually attacking and altering the established order of things'.

The pungent medicine so artfully infused throughout *The War of the Worlds* is designed to conscript more minds into the futurist category.

An older mistaken point of view was expressed by C. K. Shorter in 1897: 'The imagination is everything, the science is nothing; but the end of the century, which shares Mr Wells's smattering of South Kensington, prefers the two together; and I sympathise with the end of the century.'

Be that as it may, Wells's vivid imagination won the day. His success was assured, his poverty left behind. The destruction of a world that has become so dingy is perhaps Wells's way of living down the ugly world, the sordid scullery, from which he had escaped. He remains troubled nevertheless. His friend Arnold Bennett praises Wells for writing for 'the intelligent masses', in the days when intellectuals were against newspapers, as later they were against the cinema and then television and, in short, anything popular.

Such problems are well aired in John Carey's book, *The Intellectuals and the Masses*. He puts Wells's time and Wells's problems into context by quoting briefly from Wells's *Marriage* (1912), where Trafford speaks of a dyspeptic socialist in these terms:

> It seemed to him that in meeting Dowd he was meeting all that vast new England outside the range of ruling-class dreams, that multitudinous greater England, cheaply treated, rather out of health, angry, energetic, and now becoming intelligent and critical; that England which organised industrialism has created.

Wells's problem was that he liked to consort with the great; yet he could but remain an Outsider, a steppenwolf, forever discontented. Carey well understands Wells's dilemma – as with today's science fiction writers, in general ring-fenced away from 'Literature'.

In 1902, Wells published his book of essays, *Anticipations*. He was listened to increasingly as a prophetic voice. He began to talk about the real world – as he saw it – rather than create more ingenious fantasies. The visionary novel *In the Days of the Comet* was published in 1906, and has never received the attention it deserves. It contains a harsh indictment of the ugliness of the world in which Wells grew up.

Wells, like Charles Dickens before him, became popular and successful in a way no contemporary writer could be, no Salman

Rushdie, no Jeffrey Archer. He flew to Moscow to talk to Lenin and Gorki, he flew to Washington to talk to Roosevelt. Yet he was always an astringent writer, as in the present novel. Nowadays, astringency is out of fashion in popular literature, more's the pity.

How easily the end of *The War of the Worlds* could have been a happy one, full of rejoicing at the defeat of an alien enemy. Instead, the chapter preceding the Epilogue is called 'Wreckage'. London seems to have become a city of tramps. Four weeks have gone by since the first cylinders landed. Mankind's view of a human future has been modified by the Martians: 'To them, and not to us, perhaps, is the future ordained.'

The comment is justified. Humans are not victors but survivors. In comparison with the Martians, humans are a lesser breed. Unpleasant though the Martians are, they are intellectually our superiors. Unlike the Morlocks in *The Time Machine* or the Selenites in *The First Men in the Moon*, both of which groups live subterranean lives, the Martians come from 'above', the realm of the super-ego.

In fact, the novel fizzes with metaphors which signify mankind's low estate. As we see, the very first paragraph of the book shows mankind and their affairs being studied much as a man with a microscope might scrutinize the creatures swarming in a drop of water.

We soon learn that the Martians have 'brightened their intellects, enlarged their powers and hardened their hearts'. In consequence, we who inhabit the Earth 'must be to them at least as alien and lowly as are the monkeys and lemurs to us'.

When it comes to the exodus from London, Wells's fear of the fragility of civilization and his dislike of the masses is again in evidence:

All the railway lines north of the Thames [were choked], and the South-Eastern people at Cannon Street had been warned by midnight on Sunday, and trains were being filled. People were fighting savagely for standing-room in the carriages even at two o'clock. By three, people were being trampled and crushed even in Bishopsgate Street, a couple of hundred yards or more from Liverpool Street station; revolvers were fired, people stabbed, and the policemen who had been sent to direct the traffic, exhausted and infuriated, were breaking the heads of the people they were called out to protect.

Undeniably, Wells had himself brightened his intellect, enlarged his powers and hardened his heart. Yet we know there is another Wells, a playful man who invented brilliant games for boys (I played his 'Little Wars'), who spoke up for women's rights, who led a campaign in 1924 to save the whales. He was generous to other writers, he consorted with many women – who in general remained ever after friendly towards him. He enjoyed good company, good wine. He was a serious man, yet he was fun. The intelligentsia, lacking claret and clarity, have never taken to Wells as a literary force.

I agree with the other members of the H. G. Wells Society in admiring, even loving, Wells. His son Anthony West says of Wells: 'Beyond that close circle of people who knew him, there was the larger army whose hearts were armed by the abundant spirit and courage which emanate from his writings and which make it easy to miss the intensity of his internal struggle with his demon.'

Wells said of himself, 'I fluctuate, I admit, between at the best a cautious and qualified optimism and my persuasion of swiftly advancing, irretrievable disaster.' We find him still so readable because we know in our hearts that the global disaster is still in progress.

If there is a conflict between his temperament as a man and as a writer – a conflict evident in many authors – we can only say that seated at a typewriter (how Wells would have relished the computer!) we know for a certainty that we have, if not the best life, then our very best choice of life for ourselves. And what we pour out, alone in the room, is much like sessions of psychoanalysis, as we produce things that astonish even ourselves.

A similar case is that of Emile Zola, of whom his biographer, F. W. J. Hemmings says that when Zola was writing, 'he passed into a totally different state of being: private terrors, dreams of ecstatic sensual delight, abominable visions of nightmarish intensity, took temporary possession of him.'

It is not difficult to conjecture that the destruction of Woking released similar demons and energies in Wells.

That ghastly optimist, the artilleryman, appears again, to announce that he and his kind will survive. He will live in London's drains and 'degenerate into a sort of big, savage rat'. The passages regarding the artilleryman were inserted by Wells after the serialization of his story. Perhaps he wished to have a mouthpiece who so starkly pronounced on the death of civilization; or, as some critics have suggested, Wells sympathized with this extremism. He also saw the world as too full of people, particularly those, as the artilleryman states, who are 'useless and cumbersome and mischievous'.

Most of those who flee the city meet with no compassion from Wells; they are likened to dodos, sheep, monkeys and rats. People are fighting, being trampled, crushed, shot and stabbed, or ploughed under by railway engines.

The social body has liquefied, like liver under an attack of cancer. Sickness goes with the disorganization. Wells had a lifelong hatred of illness and disorganization. 'Martian sanitary science,' we are told, 'eliminated illness ages ago. A hundred diseases, all the contagions and fevers of human life, consumption, cancers, tumours and such morbidities, never enter the scheme of their life.'

Here one recalls Joseph Conrad's old jibe at Wells: 'You don't care for humanity but think they are to be improved!'

One must admit that there is certainly room for improvement. And we remain grateful to H. G. Wells for pointing the matter out in this brilliant novel, so cogently, so memorably, so unsympathetically.

Brian Aldiss

Further Reading

The most vivid and memorable account of Wells's life and times is his own *Experiment in Autobiography* (2 vols., London: Gollancz and Cresset Press, 1934). It has been reprinted several times. A 'postscript' containing the previously suppressed narrative of his sexual liaisons was published as *H. G. Wells in Love*, edited by his son G. P. Wells (London: Faber & Faber, 1984). His more recent biographers draw on this material, as well as on the large body of letters and personal papers archived at the University of Illinois and elsewhere. The fullest and most scholarly biographies are *The Time Traveller* by Norman and Jeanne Mackenzie (2nd edn, London: Hogarth Press, 1987) and *H. G. Wells: Desperately Mortal* by David C. Smith (New Haven and London: Yale University Press, 1986). Smith has also edited a generous selection of Wells's *Correspondence* (4 vols, London: Pickering & Chatto, 1998). Another highly readable, if controversial and idiosyncratic, biography is *H. G. Wells: Aspects of a Life* (London: Hutchinson, 1984) by Wells's son Anthony West. Michael Foot's *H. G.: The History of Mr Wells* (London and New York: Doubleday, 1995) is enlivened by its author's personal knowledge of Wells and his circle.

Two illuminating general interpretations of Wells and his writings are Michael Draper's *H. G. Wells* (Basingstoke: Macmillan, 1987) and Brian Murray's *H. G. Wells* (New York: Continuum, 1990). Both are introductory in scope, but Draper's approach is critical and philosophical, while Murray packs a remarkable amount of biographical and historical detail into a short space. John Hammond's *An H. G. Wells Com-*

panion (London and Basingstoke: Macmillan, 1979) and *H. G. Wells* (Harlow and London: Longman, 2001) combine criticism with useful contextual material. *H. G. Wells: The Critical Heritage*, edited by Patrick Parrinder (London: Routledge, 1972), is a collection of reviews and essays of Wells published during his lifetime. A number of specialized critical and scholarly studies of Wells concentrate on his scientific romances. These include Bernard Bergonzi's pioneering study of *The Early H. G. Wells* (Manchester: Manchester University Press, 1961); John Huntington, *The Logic of Fantasy: H. G. Wells and Science Fiction* (New York: Columbia University Press, 1982); and Patrick Parrinder, *Shadows of the Future: H. G. Wells, Science Fiction and Prophecy* (Liverpool: Liverpool University Press, 1995). Peter Kemp's *H. G. Wells and the Culminating Ape* (London and Basingstoke: Macmillan, 1982) offers a lively and, at times, lurid tracing of Wells's 'biological themes and imaginative obsessions', while Roslynn D. Haynes's *H. G. Wells: Discoverer of the Future* (London and Basingstoke: Macmillan, 1980) surveys his use of scientific ideas. W. Warren Wagar, *H. G. Wells and the World State* (New Haven: Yale University Press, 1961) and John S. Partington, *Building Cosmopolis* (Aldershot: Ashgate, 2003) are studies of his political thought and his schemes for world government. John S. Partington has also edited *The Wellsian* (The Netherlands: Equilibris, 2003), a selection of essays from the H. G. Wells Society's annual critical journal of the same name. The American branch of the Wells Society maintains a highly informative website at http://hgwellsusa.50megs.com

P. P.

Note on the Text

H. G. Wells started planning *The War of the Worlds* shortly after his move in May 1895 to 'Lynton', Maybury Road, Woking, Surrey, a much humbler address than his narrator's house on nearby Maybury Hill. It was on a visit to Woking that Wells's elder brother Frank first speculated about an invasion from Mars. Soon Wells began cycling around Woking marking out locations for the story. Later, he dedicated the first edition of *The War of the Worlds* 'To my brother Frank Wells, this rendering of his idea'.

In January 1896 he sent an outline of the story to W. M. Coles of the Authors' Syndicate, a literary agency, and by 14 March Coles was able to report an expression of interest by the proprietor of *Pearson's Magazine*, C. A. Pearson. Coles, however, reported Pearson's opinion that 'a great deal depends on the finish of the story'. Wells then drew a pen-and-ink cartoon strip with the caption 'Very nice tale so far but do you mind taking the End out of the inkpot before I decide' – later reproduced in Chapter 8 of *Experiment in Autobiography* (1934) – on Coles's letter.[1] Pearson evidently did like the ending, since *The War of the Worlds* first appeared as an illustrated monthly serial in *Pearson's Magazine* and in the New York *Cosmopolitan* between April and December 1897. The story quickly became notorious. In early 1898, pirated versions appeared in Boston and New York newspapers, with the locations switched so that the Martian invasion was directly aimed at the city concerned.

Book publication was by William Heinemann in London in January 1898, and by Harper in New York in March. The

Harper edition lacks the Epilogue. Wells, however, used the Harper edition (plus the Epilogue) in preparing the slightly revised and corrected text that appeared in Volume III of the Atlantic Edition of the Works of H. G. Wells (London: T. Fisher Unwin, and New York: Scribner's, 1924). Two significant topographical mistakes were corrected in the Essex edition (London: Ernest Benn, 1927), which in most respects is a slightly careless reprint of the Atlantic edition. The Atlantic text fails to distinguish between Cobham (or Street Cobham) and Chobham, two separate locations in Surrey; and in Book II, Chapter 8 the narrator crosses the Thames, in the Atlantic and all earlier editions, from Putney to Lambeth, while the Essex text corrects the latter to 'Fulham'.

The Atlantic text was undoubtedly intended as the definitive version of *The War of the Worlds*, and it is therefore the basis of the current edition, though with a number of modifications. Printed in the United States and published simultaneously in New York and London, the Atlantic edition was meant to follow British spelling conventions but frequently fails to do so. In many instances its spelling, punctuation and hyphenation follow the Harper edition and are the product of US copy-editing on a text that, given the circumstances of transatlantic publishing in the late nineteenth century, Wells himself cannot have seen in proof. In the present text, 'burned' has been changed to 'burnt', 'farther' to 'further', 'gayly' to 'gaily', 'tire' to 'tyre', 'whiskey' to 'whisky', etc. in accordance with Heinemann 1898. The hyphenation of some 60 compound words has been silently modernized (e.g. 'midday' and 'lighthouse' rather than 'mid-day' and 'light-house'), as has the spelling of 'wag(g)on' and 'wag(g)oner'. Words hyphenated in American but not in British English ('shooting-star', 'falling-star') appear as in Heinemann 1898. Changes in punctuation include the addition of commas for the sake of clarity in some 25 instances, occasional deletion of commas and changing semicolons to commas. All other substantive emendations are listed below.

Housestyling of punctuation and spelling has also been implemented to make the text more accessible to the reader:

single quotation marks (for doubles) with doubles inside singles as needed; end punctuation placed outside end quotation marks when appropriate; spaced N-dashes (for the heavier, longer M-dash) and M-dashes (for the double-length 2M-dash); 'ize' spellings (e.g. recognize, not recognise), and acknowledgements and judgement, not acknowledgments and judgment; no full stop after personal titles (Dr, Mr, Mrs) or chapter titles, which may not follow the capitalization of the copy-text.

SOURCES OF SUBSTANTIVE EMENDATIONS

The following abbreviations have been used: E = Essex, H = Heinemann, MS = manuscript.[2]

Page/line	Reading adopted	Atlantic reading rejected
35/20	Even within the five-mile circle (E)	Within the five-mile circle, even
48/22; 56/20; 89/11, 21	Cobham (H, E)	Chobham
71/16	agent, man. (H)	agent.
73/14	the leader-writers (H)	their leader-writer
80/10	ten (MS)	two
145/10	broad (MS)	brown
145/22	waters (MS)	water
163/2	Fulham (E)	Lambeth
169/38– 170/5	intensity. It touched . . . of beauty. (H)	intensity.
170/8	wash (MS)	waves

SIGNIFICANT VARIANT READINGS

The following list shows Wells's principal stylistic revisions for the Atlantic edition. In all but one case, the Harper and Heinemann readings are identical.

Page/line	First edition reading	Atlantic reading
10/24	it quivered a little,	it quivered,
20/chap. head	The Cylinder Unscrews	Cylinder Opens
21/30	It was rounded	The mass that framed them, the head of the thing, was rounded
22/6–7	immense eyes – culminated in an effect akin to nausea.	immense eyes – were at once vital, intense, inhuman, crippled and monstrous.
127/35	a more selfish	a mere selfish
131/5–6	must have seemed a blind of blackness	must have been blank blackness
132/9–11	creatures full of a shifty cunning – who face neither God nor man, who face not even themselves, void of pride . . . souls.	creatures, void of pride . . . souls, full of shifty cunning who face neither God nor man, who face not even themselves.
179/26	[H only] its toils. Should we conquer?	its toils.

In preparing this edition, I have been greatly indebted to the pioneering textual scholarship of David Lake and of David Y. Hughes, editor (with Harry M. Geduld) of *A Critical Edition of 'The War of the Worlds'* (Bloomington and Indianapolis: Indiana University Press, 1993), which includes a transcript of the earliest surviving manuscript fragment of Wells's novel. This, together with an incomplete set of revised proofs of the *Pearson's Magazine* serial version, is in the Wells Collection at the Rare Book and Special Collections Library, University of Illinois at Urbana–Champaign.

P. P.

NOTES

1. H. G. Wells, *Experiment in Autobiography: Discoveries and Conclusions of a Very Ordinary Brain (since 1866)*, 2 vols (London: Gollancz and Cresset Press, 1966), ii, p. 555.
2. The manuscript readings have been identified by David Y. Hughes.

THE WAR OF THE
WORLDS

'But who shall dwell in these Worlds if they be inhabited? . . .
Are we or they Lords of the World? . . . And how are all things
made for man?'

KEPLER (*quoted in* 'The Anatomy of Melancholy.')[1]

Contents

BOOK I

The Coming of the Martians

BOOK II

The Earth under the Martians

BOOK I

THE COMING OF THE MARTIANS

I

THE EVE OF THE WAR

No one would have believed, in the last years of the nineteenth century, that this world was being watched[1] keenly and closely by intelligences greater than man's and yet as mortal as his own; that as men busied themselves about their various concerns they were scrutinized and studied, perhaps almost as narrowly as a man with a microscope might scrutinize the transient creatures that swarm and multiply in a drop of water. With infinite complacency men went to and fro over this globe about their little affairs, serene in their assurance of their empire over matter. It is possible that the infusoria[2] under the microscope do the same. No one gave a thought to the older worlds of space[3] as sources of human danger, or thought of them only to dismiss the idea of life upon them as impossible or improbable. It is curious to recall some of the mental habits of those departed days. At most, terrestrial men fancied there might be other men upon Mars, perhaps inferior to themselves and ready to welcome a missionary enterprise. Yet across the gulf of space, minds that are to our minds as ours are to those of the beasts that perish,[4] intellects vast and cool and unsympathetic, regarded this earth with envious eyes, and slowly and surely drew their plans against us. And early in the twentieth century came the great disillusionment.

The planet Mars,[5] I scarcely need remind the reader,[6] revolves about the sun at a mean distance of 140,000,000 miles, and the light and heat it receives from the sun is barely half of that received by this world. It must be, if the nebular hypothesis[7] has any truth, older than our world; and long before this earth ceased to be molten, life upon its surface must have begun its course. The fact that it is scarcely one-seventh of the volume of the earth must have accelerated its cooling to the temperature at which life could begin. It has air and water and all that is necessary for the support of animated existence.

Yet so vain is man, and so blinded by his vanity, that no writer, up to the very end of the nineteenth century, expressed any idea that intelligent life might have developed there far, or indeed at all, beyond its earthly level. Nor was it generally understood that since Mars is older than our earth, with scarcely a quarter of the superficial area and remoter from the sun, it necessarily follows that it is not only more distant from life's beginning but nearer its end.

The secular cooling that must some day overtake our planet has already gone far indeed with our neighbour. Its physical condition is still largely a mystery, but we know now that even in its equatorial region the midday temperature barely approaches that of our coldest winter. Its air is much more attenuated than ours, its oceans have shrunk until they cover but a third of its surface, and as its slow seasons change huge snow caps gather and melt about either pole and periodically inundate its temperate zones. That last stage of exhaustion, which to us is still incredibly remote, has become a present-day problem for the inhabitants of Mars.[8] The immediate pressure of necessity has brightened their intellects, enlarged their powers, and hardened their hearts. And looking across space with instruments and intelligences such as we have scarcely dreamed of, they see, at its nearest distance only 35,000,000 of miles sunward of them, a morning star of hope, our own warmer planet, green with vegetation and grey with water, with a cloudy atmosphere eloquent of fertility, with glimpses through its drifting cloud-wisps of broad stretches of populous country and narrow, navy-crowded seas.

And we men, the creatures who inhabit this earth, must be to them at least as alien and lowly as are the monkeys and lemurs to us. The intellectual side of man already admits that life is an incessant struggle for existence, and it would seem that this too is the belief of the minds upon Mars. Their world is far gone in its cooling, and this world is still crowded with life, but crowded only with what they regard as inferior animals. To carry warfare sunward is, indeed, their only escape from the destruction that generation after generation creeps upon them.

And before we judge of them too harshly we must remember what ruthless and utter destruction our own species has wrought, not only upon animals, such as the vanished bison and the dodo,[9] but upon its own inferior races. The Tasmanians,[10] in spite of their human likeness, were entirely swept out of existence in a war of extermination waged by European immigrants, in the space of fifty years. Are we such apostles of mercy as to complain if the Martians warred in the same spirit?

The Martians seem to have calculated their descent with amazing subtlety – their mathematical learning is evidently far in excess of ours – and to have carried out their preparations with a well-nigh perfect unanimity. Had our instruments permitted it, we might have seen the gathering trouble far back in the nineteenth century. Men like Schiaparelli[11] watched the red planet – it is odd, by-the-bye, that for countless centuries Mars has been the star of war – but failed to interpret the fluctuating appearances of the markings they mapped so well. All that time the Martians must have been getting ready.

During the opposition of 1894[12] a great light was seen on the illuminated part of the disc, first at the Lick Observatory,[13] then by Perrotin of Nice,[14] and then by other observers. English readers heard of it first in the issue of *Nature* dated August 2nd.[15] I am inclined to think that this blaze may have been the casting of the huge gun, in the vast pit sunk into their planet, from which their shots were fired at us. Peculiar markings, as yet unexplained, were seen near the site of that outbreak during the next two oppositions.

The storm burst upon us six years ago now. As Mars approached opposition, Lavelle of Java set the wires of the astronomical exchange palpitating with the amazing intelligence of a huge outbreak of incandescent gas upon the planet. It had occurred towards midnight of the 12th; and the spectroscope, to which he had at once resorted, indicated a mass of flaming gas, chiefly hydrogen, moving with an enormous velocity towards this earth. This jet of fire had become invisible about a quarter past twelve. He compared it to a colossal puff of flame suddenly and violently squirted out of the planet, 'as flaming gases rushed out of a gun'.

A singularly appropriate phrase it proved. Yet the next day there was nothing of this in the papers except a little note in the *Daily Telegraph*,[16] and the world went in ignorance of one of the gravest dangers that ever threatened the human race. I might not have heard of the eruption at all had I not met Ogilvy, the well-known astronomer, at Ottershaw.[17] He was immensely excited at the news, and in the excess of his feelings invited me up to take a turn with him that night in a scrutiny of the red planet.

In spite of all that has happened since, I still remember that vigil very distinctly: the black and silent observatory, the shadowed lantern throwing a feeble glow upon the floor in the corner, the steady ticking of the clockwork of the telescope, the little slit in the roof – an oblong profundity with the stardust streaked across it. Ogilvy moved about, invisible but audible. Looking through the telescope, one saw a circle of deep blue and the little round planet swimming in the field. It seemed such a little thing, so bright and small and still, faintly marked with transverse stripes, and slightly flattened from the perfect round. But so little it was, so silvery warm – a pin's head of light! It was as if it quivered, but really this was the telescope vibrating with the activity of the clockwork that kept the planet in view.

As I watched, the planet seemed to grow larger and smaller and to advance and recede, but that was simply that my eye was tired. Forty millions of miles it was from us – more than forty millions of miles of void. Few people realize the immensity of vacancy in which the dust of the material universe swims.

Near it in the field, I remember, were three faint points of light, three telescopic stars infinitely remote, and all around it was the unfathomable darkness of empty space. You know how that blackness looks on a frosty starlight night. In a telescope it seems far profounder. And invisible to me, because it was so remote and small, flying swiftly and steadily towards me across that incredible distance, drawing nearer every minute by so many thousands of miles, came the Thing they were sending us, the Thing that was to bring so much struggle and calamity and death to the earth. I never dreamt of it then as I watched; no one on earth dreamt of that unerring missile.

That night, too, there was another jetting out of gas from the distant planet. I saw it. A reddish flash at the edge, the slightest projection of the outline just as the chronometer struck midnight; and at that I told Ogilvy and he took my place. The night was warm and I was thirsty, and I went, stretching my legs clumsily and feeling my way in the darkness, to the little table where the siphon stood, while Ogilvy exclaimed at the streamer of gas that came out towards us.

That night another invisible missile started on its way to the earth from Mars, just a second or so under twenty-four hours after the first one. I remember how I sat on the table there in the blackness, with patches of green and crimson swimming before my eyes. I wished I had a light to smoke by, little suspecting the meaning of the minute gleam I had seen and all that it would presently bring me. Ogilvy watched till one, and then gave it up; and we lit the lantern and walked over to his house. Down below in the darkness were Ottershaw and Chertsey and all their hundreds of people, sleeping in peace.

He was full of speculation that night about the condition of Mars, and scoffed at the vulgar idea of its having inhabitants who were signalling us. His idea was that meteorites might be falling in a heavy shower upon the planet, or that a huge volcanic explosion was in progress. He pointed out to me how unlikely it was that organic evolution had taken the same direction in the two adjacent planets.

'The chances against anything man-like on Mars are a million to one,' he said.

Hundreds of observers saw the flame that night and the night after, about midnight, and again the night after; and so for ten nights, a flame each night. Why the shots ceased after the tenth no one on earth has attempted to explain. It may be the gases of the firing caused the Martians inconvenience. Dense clouds of smoke or dust, visible through a powerful telescope on earth as little grey, fluctuating patches, spread through the clearness of the planet's atmosphere and obscured its more familiar features.

Even the daily papers woke up to the disturbances at last, and popular notes appeared here, there, and everywhere concerning the volcanoes upon Mars. The serio-comic periodical *Punch*,[18] I remember, made a happy use of it in the political cartoon. And, all unsuspected, those missiles the Martians had fired at us drew earthward, rushing now at a pace of many miles a second through the empty gulf of space, hour by hour and day by day, nearer and nearer. It seems to me now almost incredibly wonderful that, with that swift fate hanging over us, men could go about their petty concerns as they did. I remember how jubilant Markham was at securing a new photograph of the planet for the illustrated paper he edited in those days. People in these latter times scarcely realize the abundance and enterprise of our nineteenth-century papers. For my own part, I was much occupied in learning to ride the bicycle,[19] and busy upon a series of papers discussing the probable developments of moral ideas as civilization progressed.

One night (the first missile then could scarcely have been 10,000,000 miles away) I went for a walk with my wife. It was starlight, and I explained the Signs of the Zodiac to her, and pointed out Mars, a bright dot of light creeping zenithward, towards which so many telescopes were pointed. It was a warm night. Coming home, a party of excursionists from Chertsey or Isleworth passed us singing and playing music. There were lights in the upper windows of the houses as the people went to bed. From the railway station in the distance came the sound of shunting trains, ringing and rumbling, softened almost into melody by the distance. My wife pointed out to me the brightness of the red, green, and yellow signal lights hanging in a framework against the sky. It seemed so safe and tranquil.

THE FALLING STAR

Then came the night of the first falling star. It was seen early in the morning rushing over Winchester eastward, a line of flame high in the atmosphere. Hundreds must have seen it, and taken it for an ordinary falling star. Albin described it as leaving a greenish streak behind it that glowed for some seconds. Denning,[1] our greatest authority on meteorites, stated that the height of its first appearance was about ninety or one hundred miles. It seemed to him that it fell to earth about one hundred miles east of him.

I was at home at that hour and writing in my study; and although my French windows face towards Ottershaw and the blind was up (for I loved in those days to look up at the night sky), I saw nothing of it. Yet this strangest of all things that ever came to earth from outer space must have fallen while I was sitting there, visible to me had I only looked up as it passed. Some of those who saw its flight say it travelled with a hissing sound. I myself heard nothing of that. Many people in Berkshire, Surrey, and Middlesex must have seen the fall of it, and, at most, have thought that another meteorite had descended. No one seems to have troubled to look for the fallen mass that night.

But very early in the morning poor Ogilvy, who had seen the shooting star and who was persuaded that a meteorite lay somewhere on the common between Horsell, Ottershaw, and Woking, rose early with the idea of finding it. Find it he did, soon after dawn, and not far from the sand-pits. An enormous hole had been made by the impact of the projectile, and the sand and gravel had been flung violently in every direction over the heath, forming heaps visible a mile and a half away. The heather was on fire eastward, and a thin blue smoke rose against the dawn.

The Thing itself lay almost entirely buried in sand, amidst the scattered splinters of a fir-tree it had shivered to fragments in its descent. The uncovered part had the appearance of a huge cylinder, caked over and its outline softened by a thick scaly dun-coloured incrustation. It had a diameter of about thirty yards. He approached the mass, surprised at the size and more so at the shape, since most meteorites are rounded more or less completely. It was, however, still so hot from its flight through the air as to forbid his near approach. A stirring noise within its cylinder he ascribed to the unequal cooling of its surface; for at that time it had not occurred to him that it might be hollow.

He remained standing at the edge of the pit that the Thing had made for itself, staring at its strange appearance, astonished chiefly at its unusual shape and colour, and dimly perceiving even then some evidence of design in its arrival. The early morning was wonderfully still, and the sun, just clearing the pine-trees towards Weybridge, was already warm. He did not remember hearing any birds that morning, there was certainly no breeze stirring, and the only sounds were the faint movements from within the cindery cylinder. He was all alone on the common.

Then suddenly he noticed with a start that some of the grey clinker, the ashy incrustation that covered the meteorite, was falling off the circular edge of the end. It was dropping off in flakes and raining down upon the sand. A large piece suddenly came off and fell with a sharp noise that brought his heart into his mouth.

For a minute he scarcely realized what this meant, and, although the heat was excessive, he clambered down into the pit close to the bulk to see the Thing more clearly. He fancied even then that the cooling of the body might account for this, but what disturbed that idea was the fact that the ash was falling only from the end of the cylinder.

And then he perceived that, very slowly, the circular top of the cylinder was rotating on its body. It was such a gradual movement that he discovered it only through noticing that a black mark that had been near him five minutes ago was now at the other side of the circumference. Even then he scarcely understood what this indicated, until he heard a muffled grating sound and saw the black mark jerk forward an inch or so. Then the thing came upon him in a flash. The cylinder was artificial – hollow – with an end that screwed out! Something within the cylinder was unscrewing the top!

'Good heavens!' said Ogilvy. 'There's a man in it – men in it! Half roasted to death! Trying to escape!'

At once, with a quick mental leap, he linked the Thing with the flash upon Mars.

The thought of the confined creature was so dreadful to him that he forgot the heat, and went forward to the cylinder to help turn. But luckily the dull radiation arrested him before he could burn his hands on the still glowing metal. At that he stood irresolute for a moment, then turned, scrambled out of the pit, and set off running wildly into Woking. The time then must have been somewhere about six o'clock. He met a wagoner and tried to make him understand, but the tale he told and his appearance were so wild – his hat had fallen off in the pit – that the man simply drove on. He was equally unsuccessful with the potman who was just unlocking the doors of the public-house by Horsell Bridge. The fellow thought he was a lunatic at large, and made an unsuccessful attempt to shut him into the taproom. That sobered him a little; and when he saw Henderson, the London journalist, in his garden, he called over the palings and made himself understood.

'Henderson,' he called, 'you saw that shooting star last night?'

'Well?' said Henderson.

'It's out on Horsell Common now.'

'Good Lord!' said Henderson. 'Fallen meteorite! That's good.'

'But it's something more than a meteorite. It's a cylinder – an artificial cylinder, man! And there's something inside.'

Henderson stood up with his spade in his hand.

'What's that?' he said. He was deaf in one ear.

Ogilvy told him all that he had seen. Henderson was a minute or so taking it in. Then he dropped his spade, snatched up his jacket, and came out into the road. The two men hurried back at once to the common, and found the cylinder still lying in the same position. But now the sounds inside had ceased, and a thin circle of bright metal showed between the top and the body of the cylinder. Air was either entering or escaping at the rim with a thin, sizzling sound.

They listened, rapped on the scaly burnt metal with a stick, and, meeting with no response, they both concluded the man or men inside must be insensible or dead.

Of course the two were quite unable to do anything. They shouted consolation and promises, and went off back to the town again to get help. One can imagine them, covered with sand, excited and disordered, running up the little street in the bright sunlight just as the shop folks were taking down their shutters and people were opening their bedroom windows. Henderson went into the railway station at once, in order to telegraph the news to London. The newspaper articles had prepared men's minds for the reception of the idea.

By eight o'clock a number of boys and unemployed men had already started for the common to see the 'dead men from Mars'. That was the form the story took. I heard of it first from my newspaper boy, about a quarter to nine, when I went out to get my *Daily Chronicle*.[2] I was naturally startled, and lost no time in going out and across the Ottershaw bridge to the sand-pits.

3

ON HORSELL COMMON

I found a little crowd of perhaps twenty people surrounding the huge hole in which the cylinder lay. I have already described the appearance of that colossal bulk, embedded in the ground. The turf and gravel about it seemed charred as if by a sudden explosion. No doubt its impact had caused a flash of fire. Henderson and Ogilvy were not there. I think they perceived that nothing was to be done for the present, and had gone away to breakfast at Henderson's house.

There were four or five boys sitting on the edge of the pit, with their feet dangling, and amusing themselves – until I stopped them – by throwing stones at the giant mass. After I had spoken to them about it, they began playing at 'touch'[1] in and out of the group of bystanders.

Among these were a couple of cyclists, a jobbing gardener I employed sometimes, a girl carrying a baby, Gregg the butcher and his little boy, and two or three loafers and golf caddies who were accustomed to hang about the railway station. There was very little talking. Few of the common people in England had anything but the vaguest astronomical ideas in those days. Most of them were staring quietly at the big table-like end of the cylinder, which was still as Ogilvy and Henderson had left it. I fancy the popular expectation of a heap of charred corpses was disappointed at this inanimate bulk. Some went away while I was there, and other people came. I clambered into the pit and fancied I heard a faint movement under my feet. The top had certainly ceased to rotate.

It was only when I got thus close to it that the strangeness of this object was at all evident to me. At the first glance it was

really no more exciting than an overturned carriage or a tree
blown across the road. Not so much so, indeed. It looked like
a rusty gas-float.[2] It required a certain amount of scientific
education to perceive that the grey scale of the Thing was no
common oxide, that the yellowish-white metal that gleamed in
the crack between the lid and the cylinder had an unfamiliar
hue. 'Extraterrestrial' had no meaning for most of the onlookers.

At that time it was quite clear in my own mind that the Thing
had come from the planet Mars, but I judged it improbable
that it contained any living creature. I thought the unscrewing
might be automatic. In spite of Ogilvy, I still believed that there
were men in Mars. My mind ran fancifully on the possibilities
of its containing manuscript, on the difficulties in translation
that might arise, whether we should find coins and models in
it, and so forth. Yet it was a little too large for assurance on
this idea. I felt an impatience to see it opened. About eleven, as
nothing seemed happening, I walked back, full of such thoughts,
to my home in Maybury. But I found it difficult to get to work
upon my abstract investigations.

In the afternoon the appearance of the common had altered
very much. The early editions of the evening papers had startled
London with enormous headlines:

'A MESSAGE RECEIVED FROM MARS.'
'REMARKABLE STORY FROM WOKING'

and so forth. In addition, Ogilvy's wire to the Astronomical
Exchange had roused every observatory in the three kingdoms.[3]

There were half a dozen flys or more from the Woking station
standing in the road by the sand-pits, a basket-chaise[4] from
Chobham, and a rather lordly carriage. Besides that, there was
quite a heap of bicycles. In addition, a large number of people
must have walked, in spite of the heat of the day, from Woking
and Chertsey, so that there was altogether quite a considerable
crowd – one or two gaily dressed ladies among the others.

It was glaringly hot, not a cloud in the sky nor a breath of
wind, and the only shadow was that of the few scattered pine-

trees. The burning heather had been extinguished, but the level ground towards Ottershaw was blackened as far as one could see, and still giving off vertical streamers of smoke. An enterprising sweet-stuff dealer in the Chobham Road had sent up his son with a barrow-load of green apples and ginger-beer.

Going to the edge of the pit, I found it occupied by a group of about half a dozen men – Henderson, Ogilvy, and a tall, fair-haired man that I afterwards learnt was Stent, the Astronomer Royal,[5] with several workmen wielding spades and pick-axes. Stent was giving directions in a clear, high-pitched voice. He was standing on the cylinder, which was now evidently much cooler; his face was crimson and streaming with perspiration, and something seemed to have irritated him.

A large portion of the cylinder had been uncovered, though its lower end was still embedded. As soon as Ogilvy saw me among the staring crowd on the edge of the pit he called to me to come down, and asked me if I would mind going over to see Lord Hilton, the lord of the manor.

The growing crowd, he said, was becoming a serious impediment to their excavations, especially the boys. They wanted a light railing put up, and help to keep the people back. He told me that a faint stirring was occasionally still audible within the case, but that the workmen had failed to unscrew the top, as it afforded no grip to them. The case appeared to be enormously thick, and it was possible that the faint sounds we heard represented a noisy tumult in the interior.

I was very glad to do as he asked, and so become one of the privileged spectators within the contemplated enclosure. I failed to find Lord Hilton at his house, but I was told he was expected from London by the six o'clock train from Waterloo; and as it was then about a quarter past five, I went home, had some tea, and walked up to the station to waylay him.

4

THE CYLINDER OPENS

When I returned to the common the sun was setting. Scattered groups were hurrying from the direction of Woking, and one or two persons were returning. The crowd about the pit had increased, and stood out black against the lemon-yellow of the sky – a couple of hundred people, perhaps. There were raised voices, and some sort of struggle appeared to be going on about the pit. Strange imaginings passed through my mind. As I drew nearer I heard Stent's voice:

'Keep back! Keep back!'

A boy came running towards me.

'It's a-movin',' he said to me as he passed – 'a-screwin' and a-screwin' out. I don't like it. I'm a-goin' 'ome, I am.'

I went on to the crowd. There were really, I should think, two or three hundred people elbowing and jostling one another, the one or two ladies there being by no means the least active.

'He's fallen in the pit!' cried someone.

'Keep back!' said several.

The crowd swayed a little, and I elbowed my way through. Everyone seemed greatly excited. I heard a peculiar humming sound from the pit.

'I say!' said Ogilvy; 'help keep these idiots back. We don't know what's in the confounded thing, you know!'

I saw a young man, a shop assistant in Woking I believe he was, standing on the cylinder and trying to scramble out of the hole again. The crowd had pushed him in.

The end of the cylinder was being screwed out from within. Nearly two feet of shining screw projected. Somebody blundered against me, and I narrowly missed being pitched on to the top of the screw. I turned, and as I did so the screw must have come out, for the lid of the cylinder fell upon the gravel with a ringing concussion. I stuck my elbow into the person behind me, and turned my head towards the Thing again. For a moment that circular cavity seemed perfectly black. I had the sunset in my eyes.

I think everyone expected to see a man emerge – possibly something a little unlike us terrestrial men, but in all essentials a man. I know I did. But, looking, I presently saw something stirring within the shadow: greyish billowy movements, one above another, and then two luminous discs – like eyes. Then something resembling a little grey snake, about the thickness of a walking-stick, coiled up out of the writhing middle, and wriggled in the air towards me – and then another.

A sudden chill came over me. There was a loud shriek from a woman behind. I half turned, keeping my eyes fixed upon the cylinder still, from which other tentacles were now projecting, and began pushing my way back from the edge of the pit. I saw astonishment giving place to horror on the faces of the people about me. I heard inarticulate exclamations on all sides. There was a general movement backwards. I saw the shopman struggling still on the edge of the pit. I found myself alone, and saw the people on the other side of the pit running off, Stent among them. I looked again at the cylinder, and ungovernable terror gripped me. I stood petrified and staring.

A big greyish rounded bulk,[1] the size, perhaps, of a bear, was rising slowly and painfully out of the cylinder. As it bulged up and caught the light, it glistened like wet leather.

Two large dark-coloured eyes were regarding me steadfastly. The mass that framed them, the head of the thing, was rounded, and had, one might say, a face. There was a mouth under the eyes, the lipless brim of which quivered and panted, and dropped saliva. The whole creature heaved and pulsated convulsively. A lank tentacular appendage gripped the edge of the cylinder, another swayed in the air.

Those who have never seen a living Martian can scarcely imagine the strange horror of its appearance. The peculiar V-shaped mouth with its pointed upper lip, the absence of brow ridges, the absence of a chin beneath the wedge-like lower lip, the incessant quivering of this mouth, the Gorgon[2] groups of tentacles, the tumultuous breathing of the lungs in a strange atmosphere, the evident heaviness and painfulness of movement due to the greater gravitational energy of the earth – above all, the extraordinary intensity of the immense eyes – were at once vital, intense, inhuman, crippled and monstrous. There was something fungoid in the oily brown skin, something in the clumsy deliberation of the tedious movements unspeakably nasty. Even at this first encounter, this first glimpse, I was overcome with disgust and dread.

Suddenly the monster vanished. It had toppled over the brim of the cylinder and fallen into the pit, with a thud like the fall of a great mass of leather. I heard it give a peculiar thick cry, and forthwith another of these creatures appeared darkly in the deep shadow of the aperture.

I turned and, running madly, made for the first group of trees, perhaps a hundred yards away; but I ran slantingly and stumbling, for I could not avert my face from these things.

There, among some young pine-trees and furze-bushes, I stopped, panting, and waited further developments. The common round the sand-pits was dotted with people, standing like myself in a half-fascinated terror, staring at these creatures, or rather at the heaped gravel at the edge of the pit in which they lay. And then, with a renewed horror, I saw a round, black object bobbing up and down on the edge of the pit. It was the head of the shopman who had fallen in, but showing as a little black object against the hot western sky. Now he got his shoulder and knee up, and again he seemed to slip back until only his head was visible. Suddenly he vanished, and I could have fancied a faint shriek had reached me. I had a momentary impulse to go back and help him that my fears overruled.

Everything was then quite invisible, hidden by the deep pit and the heap of sand that the fall of the cylinder had made. Anyone coming along the road from Chobham or Woking would have been amazed at the sight – a dwindling multitude of perhaps a hundred people or more standing in a great irregular circle, in ditches, behind bushes, behind gates and hedges, saying little to one another and that in short, excited shouts, and staring, staring hard at a few heaps of sand. The barrow of ginger-beer stood, a queer derelict, black against the burning sky, and in the sand-pits was a row of deserted vehicles with their horses feeding out of nose-bags or pawing the ground.

5

THE HEAT-RAY[1]

After the glimpse I had had of the Martians emerging from the cylinder in which they had come to the earth from their planet, a kind of fascination paralysed my actions. I remained standing knee-deep in the heather, staring at the mound that hid them. I was a battleground of fear and curiosity.

I did not dare to go back towards the pit, but I felt a passionate longing to peer into it. I began walking, therefore, in a big curve, seeking some point of vantage and continually looking at the sand-heaps that hid these newcomers to our earth. Once a leash of thin black whips, like the arms of an octopus, flashed across the sunset and was immediately withdrawn, and afterwards a thin rod rose up, joint by joint, bearing at its apex a circular disc that spun with a wobbling motion. What could be going on there?

Most of the spectators had gathered in one or two groups – one a little crowd towards Woking, the other a knot of people in the direction of Chobham. Evidently they shared my mental conflict. There were few near me. One man I approached – he was, I perceived, a neighbour of mine, though I did not know his name – and accosted. But it was scarcely a time for articulate conversation.

'What ugly *brutes!*' he said. 'Good God! what ugly brutes!' He repeated this over and over again.

'Did you see a man in the pit?' I said; but he made no answer to that. We became silent, and stood watching for a time side by side, deriving, I fancy, a certain comfort in one another's company. Then I shifted my position to a little knoll that gave me the advantage of a yard or more of elevation, and when

I looked for him presently he was walking towards Woking.

The sunset faded to twilight before anything further happened. The crowd far away on the left, towards Woking, seemed to grow, and I heard now a faint murmur from it. The little knot of people towards Chobham dispersed. There was scarcely an intimation of movement from the pit.

It was this, as much as anything, that gave people courage, and I suppose the new arrivals from Woking also helped to restore confidence. At any rate, as the dusk came on a slow, intermittent movement upon the sand-pits began, a movement that seemed to gather force as the stillness of the evening about the cylinder remained unbroken. Vertical black figures in twos and threes would advance, stop, watch, and advance again, spreading out as they did so in a thin irregular crescent that promised to enclose the pit in its attenuated horns. I, too, on my side began to move towards the pit.

Then I saw some cabmen and others had walked boldly into the sand-pits, and heard the clatter of hoofs and the gride of wheels. I saw a lad trundling off the barrow of apples. And then, within thirty yards of the pit, advancing from the direction of Horsell, I noted a little black knot of men, the foremost of whom was waving a white flag.

This was the Deputation. There had been a hasty consultation, and since the Martians were evidently, in spite of their repulsive forms, intelligent creatures, it had been resolved to show them, by approaching them with signals, that we too were intelligent.

Flutter, flutter, went the flag, first to the right, then to the left. It was too far for me to recognize anyone there, but afterwards I learnt that Ogilvy, Stent, and Henderson were with others in this attempt at communication. This little group had in its advance dragged inward, so to speak, the circumference of the now almost complete circle of people, and a number of dim black figures followed it at discreet distances.

Suddenly there was a flash of light, and a quantity of luminous greenish smoke came out of the pit in three distinct puffs, which drove up, one after the other, straight into the still air.

This smoke (or flame, perhaps, would be the better word for

it) was so bright that the deep blue sky overhead and the hazy stretches of brown common towards Chertsey, set with black pine-trees, seemed to darken abruptly as these puffs arose, and to remain the darker after their dispersal. At the same time a faint hissing sound became audible.

Beyond the pit stood the little wedge of people with the white flag at its apex, arrested by these phenomena, a little knot of small vertical black shapes upon the black ground. As the green smoke rose, their faces flashed out pallid green, and faded again as it vanished. Then slowly the hissing passed into a humming, into a long, loud, droning noise. Slowly a humped shape rose out of the pit, and the ghost of a beam of light seemed to flicker out from it.

Forthwith flashes of actual flame, a bright glare leaping from one to another, sprang from the scattered group of men. It was as if some invisible jet impinged upon them and flashed into white flame. It was as if each man were suddenly and momentarily turned to fire.

Then, by the light of their own destruction, I saw them staggering and falling, and their supporters turning to run.

I stood staring, not as yet realizing that this was death leaping from man to man in that little distant crowd. All I felt was that it was something very strange. An almost noiseless and blinding flash of light, and a man fell headlong and lay still; and as the unseen shaft of heat passed over them, pine-trees burst into fire, and every dry furze-bush became with one dull thud a mass of flames. And far away towards Knaphill I saw the flashes of trees and hedges and wooden buildings suddenly set alight.

It was sweeping round swiftly and steadily, this flaming death, this invisible, inevitable sword of heat. I perceived it coming towards me by the flashing bushes it touched, and was too astounded and stupefied to stir. I heard the crackle of fire in the sand-pits and the sudden squeal of a horse that was as suddenly stilled. Then it was as if an invisible yet intensely heated finger were drawn through the heather between me and the Martians, and all along a curving line beyond the sand-pits the dark ground smoked and crackled. Something fell with a crash far away to the left where the road from Woking station opens out on the common. Forthwith the hissing and humming ceased, and the black, dome-like object sank slowly out of sight into the pit.

All this had happened with such swiftness that I had stood motionless, dumbfounded and dazzled by the flashes of light. Had that death swept through a full circle, it must inevitably have slain me in my surprise. But it passed and spared me, and left the night about me suddenly dark and unfamiliar.

The undulating common seemed now dark almost to blackness, except where its roadways lay grey and pale under the deep-blue sky of the early night. It was dark, and suddenly void of men. Overhead the stars were mustering, and in the west the sky was still a pale, bright, almost greenish blue. The tops of the pine-trees and the roofs of Horsell came out sharp and black against the western afterglow. The Martians and their appliances were altogether invisible, save for that thin mast upon which their restless mirror wobbled. Patches of bush and isolated trees here and there smoked and glowed still, and the houses towards Woking station were sending up spires of flame into the stillness of the evening air.

Nothing was changed save for that and a terrible astonishment. The little group of black specks with the flag of white had been swept out of existence, and the stillness of the evening, so it seemed to me, had scarcely been broken.

It came to me that I was upon this dark common, helpless, unprotected, and alone. Suddenly, like a thing falling upon me from without, came fear.

With an effort I turned and began a stumbling run through the heather.

The fear I felt was no rational fear, but a panic terror not only of the Martians but of the dusk and stillness all about me. Such an extraordinary effect in unmanning me it had that I ran weeping silently as a child might do. Once I had turned, I did not dare to look back.

I remember I felt an extraordinary persuasion that I was being played with, that presently, when I was upon the very verge of safety, this mysterious death – as swift as the passage of light – would leap after me from the pit about the cylinder and strike me down.

6

THE HEAT-RAY IN THE CHOBHAM ROAD

It is still a matter of wonder how the Martians are able to slay men so swiftly and so silently. Many think that in some way they are able to generate an intense heat in a chamber of practically absolute non-conductivity. This intense heat they project in a parallel beam against any object they choose by means of a polished parabolic mirror of unknown composition, much as the parabolic mirror of a lighthouse projects a beam of light. But no one has absolutely proved these details. However it is done, it is certain that a beam of heat is the essence of the matter. Heat, and invisible, instead of visible light. Whatever is combustible flashes into flame at its touch, lead runs like water, it softens iron, cracks and melts glass, and when it falls upon water, incontinently that explodes into steam.

That night nearly forty people lay under the starlight about the pit, charred and distorted beyond recognition, and all night long the common from Horsell to Maybury was deserted and brightly ablaze.

The news of the massacre probably reached Chobham, Woking, and Ottershaw about the same time. In Woking the shops had closed when the tragedy happened, and a number of people, shop-people and so forth, attracted by the stories they had heard, were walking over the Horsell Bridge and along the road between the hedges that runs out at last upon the common. You may imagine the young people brushed up after the labours of the day, and making this novelty, as they would make any novelty, the excuse for walking together and enjoying a trivial flirtation. You may figure to yourself the hum of voices along the road in the gloaming. . .

As yet, of course, few people in Woking even knew that the cylinder had opened, though poor Henderson had sent a messenger on a bicycle to the post-office with a special wire to an evening paper.

As these folks came out by twos and threes upon the open, they found little knots of people talking excitedly and peering at the spinning mirror over the sand-pits, and the newcomers were, no doubt, soon infected by the excitement of the occasion.

By half-past eight, when the Deputation was destroyed, there may have been a crowd of three hundred people or more at this place, besides those who had left the road to approach the Martians nearer. There were three policemen too, one of whom was mounted, doing their best, under instructions from Stent, to keep the people back and deter them from approaching the cylinder. There was some booing from those more thoughtless and excitable souls to whom a crowd is always an occasion for noise and horseplay.

Stent and Ogilvy, anticipating some possibilities of a collision, had telegraphed from Horsell to the barracks as soon as the Martians emerged, for the help of a company of soldiers to protect these strange creatures from violence. After that they returned to lead that ill-fated advance. The description of their death, as it was seen by the crowd, tallies very closely with my own impressions: the three puffs of green smoke, the deep humming note, and the flashes of flame.

But that crowd of people had a far narrower escape than mine. Only the fact that a hummock of heathery sand intercepted the lower part of the Heat-Ray saved them. Had the elevation of the parabolic mirror been a few yards higher, none could have lived to tell the tale. They saw the flashes and the men falling, and an invisible hand, as it were, lit the bushes as it hurried towards them through the twilight. Then, with a whistling note that rose above the droning of the pit, the beam swung close over their heads, lighting the tops of the beech-trees that line the road, and splitting the bricks, smashing the windows, firing the window-frames, and bringing down in crumbling ruin a portion of the gable of the house nearest the corner.

In the sudden thud, hiss, and glare of the igniting trees, the panic-stricken crowd seems to have swayed hesitatingly for some moments. Sparks and burning twigs began to fall into the road, and single leaves like puffs of flame. Hats and dresses caught fire. Then came a crying from the common. There were shrieks and shouts, and suddenly a mounted policeman came galloping through the confusion with his hands clasped over his head, screaming.

'They're coming!' a woman shrieked, and incontinently every-one was turning and pushing at those behind, in order to clear their way to Woking again. They must have bolted as blindly as a flock of sheep. Where the road grows narrow and black between the high banks the crowd jammed, and a desperate struggle occurred. All that crowd did not escape; three persons at least, two women and a little boy, were crushed and trampled there, and left to die amid the terror and the darkness.

7

HOW I REACHED HOME

For my own part, I remember nothing of my flight except the stress of blundering against trees and stumbling through the heather. All about me gathered the invisible terrors of the Martians; that pitiless sword of heat seemed whirling to and fro, flourishing overhead before it descended and smote me out of life. I came into the road between the crossroads and Horsell, and ran along this to the crossroads.

At last I could go no further; I was exhausted with the violence of my emotion and of my flight, and I staggered and fell by the wayside. That was near the bridge that crosses the canal by the gasworks. I fell and lay still.

I must have remained there some time.

I sat up, strangely perplexed. For a moment, perhaps, I could not clearly understand how I came there. My terror had fallen from me like a garment. My hat had gone, and my collar had burst away from its fastener. A few minutes before there had only been three real things before me – the immensity of the night and space and nature, my own feebleness and anguish, and the near approach of death. Now it was as if something turned over, and the point of view altered abruptly. There was no sensible transition from one state of mind to the other. I was immediately the self of every day again – a decent, ordinary citizen. The silent common, the impulse of my flight, the starting flames, were as if they had been in a dream. I asked myself had these latter things indeed happened? I could not credit it.

I rose and walked unsteadily up the steep incline of the bridge. My mind was blank wonder. My muscles and nerves seemed drained of their strength. I dare say I staggered drunkenly. A head rose over the arch, and the figure of a workman carrying a basket appeared. Beside him ran a little boy. He passed me, wishing me good-night. I was minded to speak to him, but did not. I answered his greeting with a meaningless mumble and went on over the bridge.

Over the Maybury arch a train, a billowing tumult of white, firelit smoke, and a long caterpillar of lighted windows, went flying south – clatter, clatter, clap, rap, and it had gone. A dim group of people talked in the gate of one of the houses in the pretty little row of gables that was called Oriental Terrace. It was all so real and so familiar. And that behind me! It was frantic, fantastic! Such things, I told myself, could not be.

Perhaps I am a man of exceptional moods. I do not know how far my experience is common. At times I suffer from the strangest sense of detachment from myself and the world about me; I seem to watch it all from the outside, from somewhere inconceivably remote, out of time, out of space, out of the stress and tragedy of it all. This feeling was very strong upon me that night. Here was another side to my dream.

But the trouble was the blank incongruity of this serenity and the swift death flying yonder, not two miles away. There was a noise of business from the gasworks, and the electric lamps[1] were all alight. I stopped at the group of people.

'What news from the common?' said I.

There were two men and a woman at the gate.

'Eh?' said one of the men, turning.

'What news from the common?' I said.

''Ain't yer just *been* there?' asked the men.

'People seem fair silly about the common,' said the woman over the gate. 'What's it all abart?'

'Haven't you heard of the men from Mars?' said I – 'the creatures from Mars?'

'Quite enough,' said the woman over the gate. 'Thenks'; and all three of them laughed.

I felt foolish and angry. I tried and found I could not tell them what I had seen. They laughed again at my broken sentences.

'You'll hear more yet,' I said, and went on to my home.

I startled my wife at the doorway, so haggard was I. I went

into the dining-room, sat down, drank some wine, and so soon as I could collect myself sufficiently I told her the things I had seen. The dinner, which was a cold one, had already been served, and remained neglected on the table while I told my story.

'There is one thing,' I said, to allay the fears I had aroused – 'they are the most sluggish things I ever saw crawl. They may keep the pit and kill people who come near them, but they cannot get out of it . . . But the horror of them!'

'Don't, dear!' said my wife, knitting her brows and putting her hand on mine.

'Poor Ogilvy!' I said. 'To think he may be lying dead there!'

My wife at least did not find my experience incredible. When I saw how deadly white her face was, I ceased abruptly.

'They may come here,' she said again and again.

I pressed her to take wine, and tried to reassure her.

'They can scarcely move,' I said.

I began to comfort her and myself by repeating all that Ogilvy had told me of the impossibility of the Martians establishing themselves on the earth. In particular I laid stress on the gravitational difficulty. On the surface of the earth the force of gravity is three times what it is on the surface of Mars. A Martian, therefore, would weigh three times more than on Mars, albeit his muscular strength would be the same. His own body would be a cope of lead to him. That, indeed, was the general opinion. Both the *Times*[2] and the *Daily Telegraph*, for instance, insisted on it the next morning, and both overlooked, just as I did, two obvious modifying influences.

The atmosphere of the earth, we now know, contains far more oxygen or far less argon[3] (whichever way one likes to put it) than does Mars. The invigorating influences of this excess of oxygen upon the Martians indisputably did much to counterbalance the increased weight of their bodies. And, in the second place, we all overlooked the fact that such mechanical intelligence as the Martian possessed was quite able to dispense with muscular exertion at a pinch.

But I did not consider these points at the time, and so my reasoning was dead against the chances of the invaders. With wine and food, the confidence of my own table, and the necessity of reassuring my wife, I grew by insensible degrees courageous and secure.

'They have done a foolish thing,' said I, fingering my wineglass. 'They are dangerous because, no doubt, they are mad with terror. Perhaps they expected to find no living things – certainly no intelligent living things.

'A shell in the pit,' said I, 'if the worst comes to the worst, will kill them all.'

The intense excitement of the events had no doubt left my perceptive powers in a state of erethism. I remember that dinner-table with extraordinary vividness even now. My dear wife's sweet, anxious face peering at me from under the pink lampshade, the white cloth with its silver and glass table furniture – for in those days even philosophical writers had many little luxuries – the crimson-purple wine in my glass, are photographically distinct. At the end of it I sat, tempering nuts with a cigarette, regretting Ogilvy's rashness, and denouncing the short-sighted timidity of the Martians.

So some respectable dodo in the Mauritius might have lorded it in his nest, and discussed the arrival of that shipful of pitiless sailors in want of animal food. 'We will peck them to death tomorrow, my dear.'

I did not know it, but that was the last civilized dinner I was to eat for very many strange and terrible days.

8

FRIDAY NIGHT

The most extraordinary thing to my mind, of all the strange and wonderful things that happened upon that Friday, was the dovetailing of the commonplace habits of our social order with the first beginnings of the series of events that was to topple that social order headlong. If on Friday night you had taken a pair of compasses and drawn a circle with a radius of five miles round the Woking sand-pits, I doubt if you would have had one human being outside it, unless it were some relation of Stent or of the three or four cyclists or London people lying dead on the common, whose emotions or habits were at all affected by the newcomers. Many people had heard of the cylinder, of course, and talked about it in their leisure, but it certainly did not make the sensation that an ultimatum to Germany would have done.

In London that night poor Henderson's telegram describing the gradual unscrewing of the shot was judged to be a canard, and his evening paper, after wiring for authentication from him and receiving no reply – the man was killed – decided not to print a special edition.

Even within the five-mile circle the great majority of people were inert. I have already described the behaviour of the men and women to whom I spoke. All over the district people were dining and supping; working-men were gardening after the labours of the day, children were being put to bed, young people were wandering through the lanes love-making, students sat over their books.

Maybe there was a murmur in the village streets, a novel and dominant topic in the public-houses, and here and there a messenger, or even an eye-witness of the later occurrences, caused a whirl of excitement, a shouting, and a running to and fro; but for the most part the daily routine of working, eating, drinking, sleeping, went on as it had done for countless years – as though no planet Mars existed in the sky. Even at Woking station and Horsell and Chobham that was the case.

In Woking junction, until a late hour, trains were stopping and going on, others were shunting on the sidings, passengers were alighting and waiting, and everything was proceeding in the most ordinary way. A boy from the town, trenching on Smith's monopoly,[1] was selling papers with the afternoon's news. The ringing impact of trucks, the sharp whistle of the engines from the junction, mingled with their shouts of 'Men from Mars!' Excited men came into the station about nine o'clock with incredible tidings, and caused no more disturbance than drunkards might have done. People rattling Londonwards peered into the darkness outside the carriage windows and saw only a rare, flickering, vanishing spark dance up from the direction of Horsell, a red glow and a thin veil of smoke driving across the stars, and thought that nothing more serious than a heath fire was happening. It was only round the edge of the common that any disturbance was perceptible. There were half a dozen villas burning on the Woking border. There were lights in all the houses on the common side of the three villages, and the people there kept awake till dawn.

A curious crowd lingered restlessly, people coming and going but the crowd remaining, both on the Chobham and Horsell bridges. One or two adventurous souls, it was afterwards found, went into the darkness and crawled quite near the Martians; but they never returned, for now and again a light-ray, like the beam of a warship's searchlight, swept the common, and the Heat-Ray was ready to follow. Save for such, that big area of common was silent and desolate, and the charred bodies lay about on it all night under the stars, and all the next day. A noise of hammering from the pit was heard by many people.

So you have the state of things on Friday night. In the centre, sticking into the skin of our old planet Earth like a poisoned dart, was this cylinder. But the poison was scarcely working yet. Around it was a patch of silent common, smouldering in places, and with a few dark, dimly seen objects lying in contorted attitudes here and there. Here and there was a burning bush or tree. Beyond was a fringe of excitement, and further than that fringe the inflammation had not crept as yet. In the rest of the world the stream of life still flowed as it had flowed for immemorial years. The fever of war that would presently clog vein and artery, deaden nerve and destroy brain, had still to develop.

All night long the Martians were hammering and stirring, sleepless, indefatigable, at work upon the machines they were making ready, and ever and again a puff of greenish-white smoke whirled up to the starlit sky.

About eleven a company of soldiers came through Horsell, and deployed along the edge of the common to form a cordon. Later a second company marched through Chobham to deploy on the north side of the common. Several officers from the Inkerman barracks had been on the common earlier in the day, and one, Major Eden, was reported to be missing. The colonel of the regiment came to the Chobham bridge and was busy questioning the crowd at midnight. The military authorities were certainly alive to the seriousness of the business. About eleven, the next morning's papers were able to say, a squadron of hussars,[2] two Maxims,[3] and about four hundred men of the Cardigan regiment[4] started from Aldershot.

A few seconds after midnight the crowd in the Chertsey road, Woking, saw a star fall from heaven into the pine-woods to the north-west. It had a greenish colour and caused a silent brightness like summer lightning. This was the second cylinder.

9

THE FIGHTING BEGINS

Saturday lives in my memory as a day of suspense. It was a day of lassitude too, hot and close, with, I am told, a rapidly fluctuating barometer. I had slept but little, though my wife had succeeded in sleeping, and I rose early. I went into my garden before breakfast and stood listening, but towards the common there was nothing stirring but a lark.

The milkman came as usual. I heard the rattle of his chariot, and I went round to the side-gate to ask the latest news. He told me that during the night the Martians had been surrounded by troops, and that guns were expected. Then – a familiar, reassuring note – I heard a train running towards Woking.

'They aren't to be killed,' said the milkman, 'if that can possibly be avoided.'

I saw my neighbour gardening, chatted with him for a time, and then strolled in to breakfast. It was a most unexceptional morning. My neighbour was of opinion that the troops would be able to capture or to destroy the Martians during the day.

'It's a pity they make themselves so unapproachable,' he said. 'It would be curious to know how they live on another planet; we might learn a thing or two.'

He came up to the fence and extended a handful of strawberries, for his gardening was as generous as it was enthusiastic. At the same time he told me of the burning of the pine-woods about the Byfleet Golf Links.

'They say,' said he, 'that there's another of those blessed things fallen there – number two. But one's enough, surely. This lot'll cost the insurance people a pretty penny before everything's settled.' He laughed with an air of the greatest good-humour as he said this. The woods, he said, were still burning, and pointed out a haze of smoke to me. 'They will be hot underfoot for days, on account of the thick soil of pine-needles and turf,' he said, and then grew serious over 'poor Ogilvy'.

After breakfast, instead of working, I decided to walk down towards the common. Under the railway bridge I found a group of soldiers – sappers, I think, men in small round caps, dirty red jackets unbuttoned, and showing their blue shirts, dark trousers, and boots coming to the calf. They told me no one was allowed over the canal, and, looking along the road towards the bridge, I saw one of the Cardigan men standing sentinel there. I talked with these soldiers for a time; I told them of my sight of the Martians on the previous evening. None of them had seen the Martians, and they had but the vaguest ideas of them, so that they plied me with questions. They said that they did not know who had authorized the movements of the troops; their idea was that a dispute had arisen at the Horse Guards.[1] The ordinary sapper is a great deal better educated than the common soldier, and they discussed the peculiar conditions of the possible fight with some acuteness. I described the Heat-Ray to them, and they began to argue among themselves.

'Crawl up under cover and rush 'em, say I,' said one.

'Get aht!' said another. 'What's cover against this 'ere 'eat? Sticks to cook yer! What we got to do is to go as near as the ground'll let us, and then drive a trench.'

'Blow yer trenches! You always want trenches; you ought to ha' been born a rabbit, Snippy.'

''Ain't they got any necks, then?' said a third, abruptly – a little, contemplative, dark man, smoking a pipe.

I repeated my description.

'Octopuses,' said he, 'that's what I calls 'em. Talk about fishers of men[2] – fighters of fish it is this time!'

'It ain't no murder killing beasts like that,' said the first speaker.

'Why not shell the darned things strite off and finish 'em?' said the little dark man. 'You carn tell what they might do.'

'Where's your shells?' said the first speaker. 'There ain't no time. Do it in a rush, that's my tip, and do it at once.'

So they discussed it. After a while I left them, and went on to the railway station to get as many morning papers as I could.

But I will not weary the reader with a description of that long morning and of the longer afternoon. I did not succeed in getting a glimpse of the common, for even Horsell and Chobham church towers were in the hands of the military authorities. The soldiers I addressed didn't know anything; the officers were mysterious as well as busy. I found people in the town quite secure again in the presence of the military, and I heard for the first time from Marshall, the tobacconist, that his son was among the dead on the common. The soldiers had made the people on the outskirts of Horsell lock up and leave their houses.

I got back to lunch about two, very tired, for, as I have said, the day was extremely hot and dull; and in order to refresh myself I took a cold bath in the afternoon. About half-past four I went up to the railway station to get an evening paper, for the morning papers had contained only a very inaccurate description of the killing of Stent, Henderson, Ogilvy, and the others. But there was little I didn't know. The Martians did not show an inch of themselves. They seemed busy in their pit, and there was a sound of hammering and an almost continuous streamer of smoke. Apparently they were busy getting ready for a struggle. 'Fresh attempts have been made to signal, but without success,' was the stereotyped formula of the papers. A sapper told me it was done by a man in a ditch with a flag on a long pole. The Martians took as much notice of such advances as we should of the lowing of a cow.

I must confess the sight of all this armament, all this preparation, greatly excited me. My imagination became belligerent, and defeated the invaders in a dozen striking ways; something of my schoolboy dreams of battle and heroism came back. It hardly seemed a fair fight to me at that time. They seemed very helpless in that pit of theirs.

About three o'clock there began the thud of a gun at measured intervals from Chertsey or Addlestone. I learned that the smouldering pine-wood into which the second cylinder had fallen was being shelled, in the hope of destroying that object before it opened. It was only about five, however, that a field-gun reached Chobham for use against the first body of Martians.

About six in the evening, as I sat at tea with my wife in the summer-house talking vigorously about the battle that was lowering upon us, I heard a muffled detonation from the common, and immediately after a gust of firing. Close on the heels of that came a violent, rattling crash quite close to us, that shook the ground; and, starting out upon the lawn, I saw the tops of the trees about the Oriental College[3] burst into smoky red flame, and the tower of the little church beside it slide down into ruin. The pinnacle of the mosque had vanished, and the roofline of the college itself looked as if a hundred-ton gun had been at work upon it. One of our chimneys cracked as if a shot had hit it, flew, and a piece of it came clattering down the tiles and made a heap of broken red fragments upon the flower-bed by my study window.

I and my wife stood amazed. Then I realized that the crest of Maybury Hill must be within range of the Martians' Heat-Ray now that the college was cleared out of the way.

At that I gripped my wife's arm, and without ceremony ran her out into the road. Then I fetched out the servant, telling her I would go upstairs myself for the box she was clamouring for.

'We can't possibly stay here,' I said; and as I spoke the firing reopened for a moment upon the common.

'But where are we to go?' said my wife in terror.

I thought, perplexed. Then I remembered her cousins[4] at Leatherhead.

'Leatherhead!' I shouted above the sudden noise.

She looked away from me downhill. The people were coming out of their houses astonished.

'How are we to get to Leatherhead?' she said.

Down the hill I saw a bevy of hussars ride under the railway bridge; three galloped through the open gates of the Oriental College; two others dismounted, and began running from house to house. The sun, shining through the smoke that drove up from the tops of the trees, seemed blood-red, and threw an unfamiliar lurid light upon everything.

'Stop here,' said I; 'you are safe here;' and I started off at once for the Spotted Dog,[5] for I knew the landlord had a horse and dogcart.[6] I ran, for I perceived that in a moment everyone upon this side of the hill would be moving. I found him in his bar, quite unaware of what was going on behind his house. A man stood with his back to me, talking to him.

'I must have a pound,' said the landlord, 'and I've no one to drive it.'

'I'll give you two,' said I, over the stranger's shoulder.

'What for?'

'And I'll bring it back by midnight,' I said.

'Lord!' said the landlord; 'what's the hurry? I'm selling my bit of a pig.[7] Two pounds, and you bring it back? What's going on now?'

I explained hastily that I had to leave my home, and so secured the dogcart. At the time it did not seem to me nearly so urgent that the landlord should leave his. I took care to have the cart there and then, drove it off down the road, and, leaving it in charge of my wife and servant, rushed into my house and packed a few valuables, such plate as we had, and so forth. The beech-trees below the house were burning while I did this, and the palings up the road glowed red. While I was occupied in this way, one of the dismounted hussars came running up. He was going from house to house, warning people to leave. He was going on as I came out of my front-door, lugging my treasures, done up in a tablecloth. I shouted after him:

'What news?'

He turned, stared, bawled something about 'crawling out in a thing like a dish cover,' and ran on to the gate of the house at the crest. A sudden whirl of black smoke driving across the road hid him for a moment. I ran to my neighbour's door and rapped to satisfy myself of what I already knew, that his wife had gone to London with him and had locked up their house. I went in again, according to my promise, to get my servant's box, lugged it out, clapped it beside her on the tail of the dogcart, and then caught the reins and jumped up into the driver's seat beside my wife. In another moment we were clear of the smoke and noise, and spanking down the opposite slope of Maybury Hill towards Old Woking.

In front was a quiet, sunny landscape, a wheatfield ahead on either side of the road, and the Maybury Inn with its swinging sign. I saw the doctor's cart ahead of me. At the bottom of the hill I turned my head to look at the hillside I was leaving. Thick streamers of black smoke shot with threads of red fire were driving up into the still air, and throwing dark shadows upon the green tree-tops eastward. The smoke already extended far away to the east and west – to the Byfleet pine-woods eastward, and to Woking on the west. The road was dotted with people running towards us. And very faint now, but very distinct through the hot, quiet air, one heard the whirr of a machine-gun that was presently stilled, and an intermittent cracking of rifles. Apparently the Martians were setting fire to everything within range of their Heat-Ray.

I am not an expert driver, and I had immediately to turn my attention to the horse. When I looked back again the second hill had hidden the black smoke. I slashed the horse with the whip, and gave him a loose rein until Woking and Send lay between us and that quivering tumult. I overtook and passed the doctor between Woking and Send.

10

IN THE STORM

Leatherhead is about twelve miles from Maybury Hill. The scent of hay was in the air through the lush meadows beyond Pyrford, and the hedges on either side were sweet and gay with multitudes of dog-roses. The heavy firing that had broken out while we were driving down Maybury Hill ceased as abruptly as it began, leaving the evening very peaceful and still. We got to Leatherhead without misadventure about nine o'clock, and the horse had an hour's rest while I took supper with my cousins and commended my wife to their care.

My wife was curiously silent throughout the drive, and seemed oppressed with forebodings of evil. I talked to her reassuringly, pointing out that the Martians were tied to the pit by sheer heaviness, and at the utmost could but crawl a little out of it; but she answered only in monosyllables. Had it not been for my promise to the innkeeper, she would, I think, have urged me to stay in Leatherhead that night. Would that I had! Her face, I remember, was very white as we parted.

For my own part, I had been feverishly excited all day. Something very like the war-fever that occasionally runs through a civilized community had got into my blood, and in my heart I was not so very sorry that I had to return to Maybury that night. I was even afraid that that last fusillade I had heard might mean the extermination of our invaders from Mars. I can best express my state of mind by saying that I wanted to be in at the death.

It was nearly eleven when I started to return. The night was unexpectedly dark; to me, walking out of the lighted passage of my cousins' house, it seemed indeed black, and it was as hot and close as the day. Overhead the clouds were driving fast, albeit not a breath stirred the shrubs about us. My cousins' man lit both lamps. Happily, I knew the road intimately. My wife stood in the light of the doorway, and watched me until I jumped up into the dogcart. Then abruptly she turned and went in, leaving my cousins side by side wishing me good hap.

I was a little depressed at first with the contagion of my wife's fears, but very soon my thoughts reverted to the Martians. At that time I was absolutely in the dark as to the course of the evening's fighting. I did not know even the circumstances that had precipitated the conflict. As I came through Ockham (for that was the way I returned, and not through Send and Old Woking) I saw along the western horizon a blood-red glow, which, as I drew nearer, crept slowly up the sky. The driving clouds of the gathering thunderstorm mingled there with masses of black and red smoke.

Ripley Street was deserted, and except for a lighted window or so the village showed not a sign of life; but I narrowly escaped an accident at the corner of the road to Pyrford, where a knot of people stood with their backs to me. They said nothing to me as I passed. I do not know what they knew of the things happening beyond the hill, nor do I know if the silent houses I passed on my way were sleeping securely, or deserted and empty, or harassed and watching against the terror of the night.

From Ripley until I came through Pyrford I was in the valley of the Wey, and the red glare was hidden from me. As I ascended the little hill beyond Pyrford Church the glare came into view again, and the trees about me shivered with the first intimation of the storm that was upon me. Then I heard midnight pealing out from Pyrford Church behind me, and then came the silhouette of Maybury Hill, with its tree-tops and roofs black and sharp against the red.

Even as I beheld this a lurid green glare lit the road about me and showed the distant woods towards Addlestone. I felt a tug at the reins. I saw that the driving clouds had been pierced as it were by a thread of green fire, suddenly lighting their confusion and falling into the field to my left. It was the Third Falling Star!

Close on its apparition, and blindingly violet by contrast, danced out the first lightning of the gathering storm, and the thunder burst like a rocket overhead. The horse took the bit between his teeth and bolted.

A moderate incline runs towards the foot of Maybury Hill, and down this we clattered. Once the lightning had begun, it went on in as rapid a succession of flashes as I have ever seen. The thunderclaps, treading one on the heels of another and with a strange crackling accompaniment, sounded more like the working of a gigantic electric machine than the usual detonating reverberations. The flickering light was blinding and confusing, and a thin hail smote gustily at my face as I drove down the slope.

At first I regarded little but the road before me, and then abruptly my attention was arrested by something that was moving rapidly down the opposite slope of Maybury Hill. At first I took it for the wet roof of a house, but one flash following another showed it to be in swift rolling movement. It was an elusive vision – a moment of bewildering darkness, and then, in a flash like daylight, the red masses of the Orphanage near the crest of the hill, the green tops of the pine-trees, and this problematical object came out clear and sharp and bright.

And this Thing I saw! How can I describe it? A monstrous tripod, higher than many houses, striding over the young pine-trees, and smashing them aside in its career; a walking engine of glittering metal, striding now across the heather; articulate ropes[1] of steel dangling from it, and the clattering tumult of its passage mingling with the riot of the thunder. A flash, and it came out vividly, heeling over one way with two feet in the air, to vanish and reappear almost instantly as it seemed, with the next flash, a hundred yards nearer. Can you imagine a milking-stool tilted and bowled violently along the ground? That was the impression those instant flashes gave. But instead of a milking-stool imagine it a great body of machinery on a tripod stand.

Then suddenly the trees in the pine-wood ahead of me were parted, as brittle reeds are parted by a man thrusting through them; they were snapped off and driven headlong, and a second huge tripod appeared, rushing, as it seemed, headlong towards me. And I was galloping hard to meet it! At the sight of the second monster my nerve went altogether. Not stopping to look again, I wrenched the horse's head hard round to the right, and in another moment the dogcart had heeled over upon the horse; the shafts smashed noisily, and I was flung sideways and fell heavily into a shallow pool of water.

I crawled out almost immediately, and crouched, my feet still in the water, under a clump of furze. The horse lay motionless (his neck was broken, poor brute!) and by the lightning flashes I saw the black bulk of the overturned dogcart and the silhouette of the wheel still spinning slowly. In another moment the colossal mechanism went striding by me, and passed uphill towards Pyrford.

Seen nearer, the Thing was incredibly strange, for it was no mere insensate machine driving on its way. Machine it was, with a ringing metallic pace, and long, flexible, glittering tentacles (one of which gripped a young pine-tree) swinging and rattling about its strange body. It picked its road as it went striding along, and the brazen hood that surmounted it moved to and fro with the inevitable suggestion of a head looking about. Behind the main body was a huge mass of white metal like a gigantic fisherman's basket, and puffs of green smoke squirted out from the joints of the limbs as the monster swept by me. And in an instant it was gone.

So much I saw then, all vaguely for the flickering of the lightning, in blinding high lights and dense black shadows.

As it passed it set up an exultant deafening howl that drowned the thunder – 'Aloo! aloo!' – and in another minute it was with its companion, half a mile away, stooping over something in the field. I have no doubt this Thing in the field was the third of the ten cylinders they had fired at us from Mars.

For some minutes I lay there in the rain and darkness watching, by the intermittent light, these monstrous beings of metal moving about in the distance over the hedge-tops. A thin hail was now beginning, and as it came and went their figures grew misty and then flashed into clearness again. Now and then came a gap in the lightning, and the night swallowed them up.

I was soaked with hail above and puddle-water below. It was sometime before my blank astonishment would let me struggle up the bank to a drier position, or think at all of my imminent peril.

Not far from me was a little one-roomed squatter's hut of wood, surrounded by a patch of potato-garden. I struggled to my feet at last, and, crouching and making use of every chance of cover, I made a run for this. I hammered at the door, but I could not make the people hear (if there were any people inside), and after a time I desisted, and, availing myself of a ditch for the greater part of the way, succeeded in crawling, unobserved by these monstrous machines, into the pine-wood towards Maybury.

Under cover of this I pushed on, wet and shivering now, towards my own house. I walked among the trees trying to find the footpath. It was very dark indeed in the wood, for the lightning was now becoming infrequent, and the hail, which was pouring down in a torrent, fell in columns through the gaps in the heavy foliage.

If I had fully realized the meaning of all the things I had seen I should have immediately worked my way round through Byfleet to Street Cobham, and so gone back to rejoin my wife at Leatherhead. But that night the strangeness of things about me, and my physical wretchedness, prevented me, for I was bruised, weary, wet to the skin, deafened and blinded by the storm.

I had a vague idea of going on to my own house, and that was as much motive as I had. I staggered through the trees, fell into a ditch and bruised my knees against a plank, and finally splashed out into the lane that ran down from the College Arms.[2] I say splashed, for the storm water was sweeping the sand down the hill in a muddy torrent. There in the darkness a man blundered into me and sent me reeling back.

He gave a cry of terror, sprang sideways, and rushed on before I could gather my wits sufficiently to speak to him. So heavy was the stress of the storm just at this place that I had the hardest task to win my way up the hill. I went close up to the fence on the left and worked my way along its palings.

Near the top I stumbled upon something soft, and, by a flash of lightning, saw between my feet a heap of black broadcloth and a pair of boots. Before I could distinguish clearly how the man lay, the flicker of light had passed. I stood over him waiting for the next flash. When it came, I saw that he was a sturdy man, cheaply but not shabbily dressed; his head was bent under his body, and he lay crumpled up close to the fence, as though he had been flung violently against it.

Overcoming the repugnance natural to one who had never before touched a dead body, I stooped and turned him over to feel for his heart. He was quite dead. Apparently his neck had been broken. The lightning flashed for a third time, and his face leapt upon me. I sprang to my feet. It was the landlord of the Spotted Dog, whose conveyance I had taken.

I stepped over him gingerly and pushed on up the hill. I made my way by the police-station and the College Arms towards my own house. Nothing was burning on the hillside, though from the common there still came a red glare and a rolling tumult of ruddy smoke beating up against the drenching hail. So far as I could see by the flashes, the houses about me were mostly uninjured. By the College Arms a dark heap lay in the road.

Down the road towards Maybury Bridge there were voices and the sound of feet, but I had not the courage to shout or to go to them. I let myself in with my latch-key, closed, locked and bolted the door, staggered to the foot of the staircase, and sat down. My imagination was full of those striding metallic monsters, and of the dead body smashed against the fence.

I crouched at the foot of the staircase with my back to the wall, shivering violently.

AT THE WINDOW

I have already said that my storms of emotion have a trick of exhausting themselves. After a time I discovered that I was cold and wet, and with little pools of water about me on the stair-carpet. I got up almost mechanically, went into the dining-room and drank some whisky, and then I was moved to change my clothes.

After I had done that I went upstairs to my study, but why I did so I do not know. The window of my study looks over the trees and the railway towards Horsell Common. In the hurry of our departure this window had been left open. The passage was dark, and, by contrast with the picture the window-frame enclosed, the side of the room seemed impenetrably dark. I stopped short in the doorway.

The thunderstorm had passed. The towers of the Oriental College and the pine-trees about it had gone, and very far away, lit by a vivid red glare, the common about the sand-pits was visible. Across the light, huge black shapes, grotesque and strange, moved busily to and fro.

It seemed indeed as if the whole country in that direction was on fire – a broad hillside set with minute tongues of flame, swaying and writhing with the gusts of the dying storm, and throwing a red reflection upon the cloud-scud above. Every now and then a haze of smoke from some nearer conflagration drove across the window and hid the Martian shapes. I could not see what they were doing, nor the clear form of them, nor recognize the black objects they were busied upon. Neither could I see the nearer fire, though the reflections of it danced on the wall and ceiling of the study. A sharp, resinous tang of burning was in the air.

I closed the door noiselessly and crept towards the window. As I did so, the view opened out until, on the one hand, it reached to the houses about Woking station, and on the other to the charred and blackened pine-woods of Byfleet. There was a light down below the hill, on the railway, near the arch, and several of the houses along the Maybury road and the streets near the station were glowing ruins. The light upon the railway puzzled me at first; there were a black heap and a vivid glare, and to the right of that a row of yellow oblongs. Then I perceived this was a wrecked train, the fore-part smashed and on fire, the hinder carriages still upon the rails.

Between these three main centres of light, the houses, the train, and the burning country towards Chobham, stretched irregular patches of dark country, broken here and there by intervals of dimly glowing and smoking ground. It was the strangest spectacle, that black expanse set with fire. It reminded me, more than anything else, of the Potteries[1] at night. At first I could distinguish no people at all, though I peered intently for them. Later I saw against the light of Woking station a number of black figures hurrying one after the other across the line.

And this was the little world in which I had been living securely for years, this fiery chaos! What had happened in the last seven hours I still did not know; nor did I know, though I was beginning to guess, the relation between these mechanical colossi and the sluggish lumps I had seen disgorged from the cylinder. With a queer feeling of impersonal interest I turned my desk-chair to the window, sat down, and stared at the blackened country, and particularly at the three gigantic black things that were going to and fro in the glare about the sand-pits.

They seemed amazingly busy. I began to ask myself what they could be. Were they intelligent mechanisms? Such a thing I felt was impossible. Or did a Martian sit within each, ruling, directing, using, much as a man's brain sits and rules in his body? I began to compare the things to human machines, to ask myself for the first time in my life how an ironclad[2] or a steam-engine would seem to an intelligent lower animal.

The storm had left the sky clear, and over the smoke of the burning land the little fading pin-point of Mars was dropping into the west, when a soldier came into my garden. I heard a slight scraping at the fence, and rousing myself from the lethargy that had fallen upon me, I looked down and saw him dimly, clambering over the palings. At the sight of another human being my torpor passed, and I leant out of the window eagerly.

'Hist!' said I, in a whisper.

He stopped astride of the fence in doubt. Then he came over and across the lawn to the corner of the house. He bent down and stepped softly.

'Who's there?' he said, also whispering, standing under the window and peering up.

'Where are you going?' I asked.

'God knows.'

'Are you trying to hide?'

'That's it.'

'Come into the house,' I said.

I went down, unfastened the door, and let him in, and locked the door again. I could not see his face. He was hatless, and his coat was unbuttoned.

'My God!' he said, as I drew him in.

'What has happened?' I asked.

'What hasn't?' In the obscurity I could see he made a gesture of despair. 'They wiped us out – simply wiped us out,' he repeated again and again.

He followed me, almost mechanically, into the dining-room.

'Take some whisky,' I said, pouring out a stiff dose.

He drank it. Then abruptly he sat down before the table, put his head on his arms, and began to sob and weep like a little boy, in a perfect passion of emotion, while I, with a curious forgetfulness of my own recent despair, stood beside him, wondering.

It was a long time before he could steady his nerves to answer my questions, and then he answered perplexingly and brokenly.

He was a driver in the artillery, and had only come into action about seven. At that time firing was going on across the common, and it was said the first party of Martians were crawling slowly towards their second cylinder under cover of a metal shield.

Later this shield staggered up on tripod legs and became the first of the fighting-machines I had seen. The gun he drove had been unlimbered near Horsell, in order to command the sand-pits, and its arrival it was that had precipitated the action. As the limber gunners went to the rear, his horse trod in a rabbit-hole and came down, throwing him into a depression of the ground. At the same moment the gun exploded behind him, the ammunition blew up, there was fire all about him, and he found himself lying under a heap of charred dead men and dead horses.

'I lay still,' he said, 'scared out of my wits, with the forequarter of a horse atop of me. We'd been wiped out. And the smell – good God! Like burnt meat! I was hurt across the back by the fall of the horse, and there I had to lie until I felt better. Just like parade it had been a minute before – then stumble, bang, swish!

'Wiped out!' he said.

He had hid under the dead horse for a long time, peeping out furtively across the common. The Cardigan men had tried a rush, in skirmishing order, at the pit, simply to be swept out of existence. Then the monster had risen to its feet, and had begun to walk leisurely to and fro across the common among the few fugitives, with its headlike hood turning about exactly like the head of a cowled human being. A kind of arm carried a complicated metallic case, about which green flashes scintillated, and out of the funnel of this there smote the Heat-Ray.

In a few minutes there was, so far as the soldier could see, not a living thing left upon the common, and every bush and tree upon it that was not already a blackened skeleton was burning. The hussars had been on the road beyond the curvature of the ground, and he saw nothing of them. He heard the Maxims rattle for a time and then become still. The giant saved Woking station and its cluster of houses until the last; then in a moment the Heat-Ray was brought to bear, and the town became a heap of fiery ruins. Then the Thing shut off the Heat-Ray, and, turning its back upon the artilleryman, began to waddle away towards the smouldering pine-woods that sheltered the second cylinder. As it did so a second glittering Titan built itself up out of the pit.

The second monster followed the first, and at that the artilleryman began to crawl very cautiously across the hot heather ash towards Horsell. He managed to get alive into the ditch by the side of the road, and so escaped to Woking. There his story became ejaculatory. The place was impassable. It seems there were a few people alive there, frantic for the most part, and many burnt and scalded. He was turned aside by the fire, and hid among some almost scorching heaps of broken wall as one of the Martian giants returned. He saw this one pursue a man, catch him up in one of its steely tentacles, and knock his head against the trunk of a pine-tree. At last, after nightfall, the artilleryman made a rush for it and got over the railway embankment.

Since then he had been skulking along towards Maybury, in the hope of getting out of danger Londonward. People were hiding in trenches and cellars, and many of the survivors had made off towards Woking village and Send. He had been consumed with thirst until he found one of the water mains near the railway arch smashed, and the water bubbling out like a spring upon the road.

That was the story I got from him, bit by bit. He grew calmer telling me and trying to make me see the things he had seen. He had eaten no food since midday, he told me early in his narrative, and I found some mutton and bread in the pantry and brought it into the room. We lit no lamp for fear of attracting the Martians, and ever and again our hands would touch upon bread or meat. As he talked, things about us came darkly out of the darkness, and the trampled bushes and broken rose-trees outside the window grew distinct. It would seem that a number of men or animals had rushed across the lawn. I began to see his face, blackened and haggard, as no doubt mine was also.

When we had finished eating we went softly upstairs to my study, and I looked again out of the open window. In one night the valley had become a valley of ashes. The fires had dwindled now. Where flames had been there were now streamers of smoke; but the countless ruins of shattered and gutted houses and blasted and blackened trees that the night had hidden stood out now gaunt and terrible in the pitiless light of dawn. Yet here and there some object had had the luck to escape – a white railway signal here, the end of a greenhouse there, white and fresh amid the wreckage. Never before in the history of warfare had destruction been so indiscriminate and so universal. And shining with the growing light of the east, three of the metallic giants stood about the pit, their cowls rotating as though they were surveying the desolation they had made.

It seemed to me that the pit had been enlarged, and ever and again puffs of vivid green vapour streamed up out of it towards the brightening dawn – streamed up, whirled, broke, and vanished.

Beyond were the pillars of fire[3] about Chobham. They became pillars of bloodshot smoke at the first touch of day.

WHAT I SAW OF THE DESTRUCTION OF WEYBRIDGE AND SHEPPERTON

As the dawn grew brighter we withdrew from the window from which we had watched the Martians, and went very quietly downstairs.

The artilleryman agreed with me that the house was no place to stay in. He proposed, he said, to make his way Londonward, and thence rejoin his battery – No. 12, of the Horse Artillery. My plan was to return at once to Leatherhead, and so greatly had the strength of the Martians impressed me that I had determined to take my wife to Newhaven, and go with her out of the country forthwith. For I already perceived clearly that the country about London must inevitably be the scene of a disastrous struggle before such creatures as these could be destroyed.

Between us and Leatherhead, however, lay the Third Cylinder, with its guarding giants. Had I been alone, I think I should have taken my chance and struck across country. But the artilleryman dissuaded me: 'It's no kindness to the right sort of wife,' he said, 'to make her a widow', and in the end I agreed to go with him, under cover of the woods, northward as far as Street Cobham before I parted with him. Thence I would make a big detour by Epsom to reach Leatherhead.

I should have started at once, but my companion had been in active service, and he knew better than that. He made me ransack the house for a flask, which he filled with whisky; and we lined every available pocket with packets of biscuits and slices of meat. Then we crept out of the house, and ran as quickly as we could down the ill-made road by which I had come overnight. The houses seemed deserted. In the road lay a group of three charred bodies close together, struck dead by the Heat-Ray; and here and there were things that people had dropped – a clock, a slipper, a silver spoon, and the like poor valuables. At the corner turning up towards the post-office a little cart, filled with boxes and furniture, and horseless, heeled over on a broken wheel. A cash-box had been hastily smashed open and thrown under the débris.

Except the lodge at the Orphanage, which was still on fire, none of the houses had suffered very greatly here. The Heat-Ray had shaved the chimney-tops and passed. Yet, save ourselves, there did not seem to be a living soul on Maybury Hill. The majority of the inhabitants had escaped, I suppose, by way of the Old Woking road – the road I had taken when I drove to Leatherhead – or they had hidden.

We went down the lane, by the body of the man in black, sodden now from the overnight hail, and broke into the woods at the foot of the hill. We pushed through these towards the railway without meeting a soul. The woods across the line were but the scarred and blackened ruins of woods; for the most part the trees had fallen, but a certain proportion still stood, dismal grey stems, with dark-brown foliage instead of green.

On our side the fire had done no more than scorch the nearer trees; it had failed to secure its footing. In one place the woodmen had been at work on Saturday; trees, felled and freshly trimmed, lay in a clearing, with heaps of sawdust by the sawing-machine and its engine. Hard by was a temporary hut, deserted. There was not a breath of wind this morning, and everything was strangely still. Even the birds were hushed, and as we hurried along I and the artilleryman talked in whispers and looked now and again over our shoulders. Once or twice we stopped to listen.

After a time we drew near the road, and as we did so we heard the clatter of hoofs and saw through the tree-stems three cavalry soldiers riding slowly towards Woking. We hailed them, and they halted while we hurried towards them. It was a lieutenant and a couple of privates of the 8th Hussars, with a stand like a theodolite,[1] which the artilleryman told me was a heliograph.[2]

'You are the first men I've seen coming this way this morning,' said the lieutenant. 'What's brewing?'

His voice and face were eager. The men behind him stared curiously. The artilleryman jumped down the bank into the road and saluted.

'Gun destroyed last night, sir. Have been hiding. Trying to rejoin battery, sir. You'll come in sight of the Martians, I expect, about half a mile along this road.'

'What the dickens are they like?' asked the lieutenant.

'Giants in armour, sir. Hundred feet high. Three legs and a body like 'luminium,[3] with a mighty great head in a hood, sir.'

'Get out!' said the lieutenant. 'What confounded nonsense!'

'You'll see, sir. They carry a kind of box, sir, that shoots fire and strikes you dead.'

'What d'ye mean – a gun?'

'No, sir,' and the artilleryman began a vivid account of the Heat-Ray. Halfway through, the lieutenant interrupted him and looked up at me. I was still standing on the bank by the side of the road.

'Did you see it?' said the lieutenant.

'It's perfectly true,' I said.

'Well,' said the lieutenant, 'I suppose it's my business to see it too. Look here' – to the artilleryman – 'we're detailed here clearing people out of their houses. You'd better go along and report yourself to Brigadier-General Marvin, and tell him all you know. He's at Weybridge. Know the way?'

'I do,' I said; and he turned his horse southward again.

'Half a mile, you say?' said he.

'At most,' I answered, and pointed over the tree-tops south-ward. He thanked me and rode on, and we saw them no more.

Further along we came upon a group of three women and two children in the road, busy clearing out a labourer's cottage. They had got hold of a little hand-truck, and were piling it up with unclean-looking bundles and shabby furniture. They were all too assiduously engaged to talk to us as we passed.

By Byfleet station we emerged from the pine-trees, and found the country calm and peaceful under the morning sunlight. We were far beyond the range of the Heat-Ray there, and had it not been for the silent desertion of some of the houses, the stirring movement of packing in others, and the knot of soldiers standing on the bridge over the railway and staring down the line towards Woking, the day would have seemed very like any other Sunday.

Several farm wagons and carts were moving creakily along the road to Addlestone, and suddenly through the gate of a field we saw, across a stretch of flat meadow, six twelve-pounders, standing neatly at equal distances pointing towards Woking. The gunners stood by the guns waiting, and the ammunition wagons were at a business-like distance. The men stood almost as if under inspection.

'That's good!' said I. 'They will get one fair shot, at any rate.'

The artilleryman hesitated at the gate.

'I shall go on,' he said.

Further on towards Weybridge, just over the bridge, there were a number of men in white fatigue jackets throwing up a long rampart, and more guns behind.

'It's bows and arrows against the lightning, anyhow,' said the artilleryman. 'They 'aven't seen that fire-beam yet.'

The officers who were not actively engaged stood and stared over the tree-tops south-westward, and the men digging would stop every now and again to stare in the same direction.

Byfleet was in a tumult; people packing, and a score of hussars, some of them dismounted, some on horseback, were hunting them about. Three or four black government wagons, with crosses in white circles, and an old omnibus, among other vehicles, were being loaded in the village street. There were scores of people, most of them sufficiently sabbatical[4] to have assumed their best clothes. The soldiers were having the greatest difficulty in making them realize the gravity of their position. We saw one shrivelled old fellow with a huge box and a score or more of flower-pots containing orchids, angrily expostulating with the corporal who would leave them behind. I stopped and gripped his arm.

'Do you know what's over there?' I said, pointing at the pine-tops that hid the Martians.

'Eh?' said he, turning. 'I was explainin' these is vallyble.'

'Death!' I shouted. 'Death is coming! Death!' and leaving him to digest that if he could, I hurried on after the artilleryman. At the corner I looked back. The soldier had left him, and he was still standing by his box, with the pots of orchids on the lid of it, and staring vaguely over the trees.

No one in Weybridge could tell us where the headquarters were established; the whole place was in such confusion as I had never seen in any town before. Carts, carriages everywhere, the most astonishing miscellany of conveyances and horseflesh. The respectable inhabitants of the place, men in golf and boating costumes, wives prettily dressed, were packing, riverside loafers energetically helping, children excited, and, for the most part, highly delighted at this astonishing variation of their Sunday experiences. In the midst of it all the worthy vicar was very pluckily holding an early celebration, and his bell was jangling out above the excitement.

I and the artilleryman, seated on the step of the drinking-fountain, made a very passable meal upon what we had brought with us. Patrols of soldiers – here no longer hussars, but grenadiers in white – were warning people to move now or to take refuge in their cellars as soon as the firing began. We saw as we crossed the railway bridge that a growing crowd of people had assembled in and about the railway station, and the swarming platform was piled with boxes and packages. The ordinary traffic had been stopped, I believe, in order to allow of the passage of troops and guns to Chertsey, and I have heard since that a savage struggle occurred for places in the special trains that were put on at a later hour.

We remained at Weybridge until midday, and at that hour we found ourselves at the place near Shepperton Lock where the Wey and Thames join. Part of the time we spent helping two old women to pack a little cart. The Wey has a treble mouth, and at this point boats are to be hired, and there was a ferry across the river. On the Shepperton side[5] was an inn with a lawn, and beyond that the tower of Shepperton Church – it has been replaced by a spire – rose above the trees.

Here we found an excited and noisy crowd of fugitives. As

yet the flight had not grown to a panic, but there were already far more people than all the boats going to and fro could enable to cross. People came panting along under heavy burdens; one husband and wife were even carrying a small outhouse door between them, with some of their household goods piled thereon. One man told us he meant to try to get away from Shepperton station.

There was a lot of shouting, and one man was even jesting. The idea people seemed to have here was that the Martians were simply formidable human beings, who might attack and sack the town, to be certainly destroyed in the end. Every now and then people would glance nervously across the Wey, at the meadows towards Chertsey, but everything over there was still.

Across the Thames, except just where the boats landed, everything was quiet, in vivid contrast to the Surrey side. The people who landed there from the boats went tramping off down the lane. The big ferry-boat had just made a journey. Three or four soldiers stood on the lawn of the inn, staring and jesting at the fugitives, without offering to help. The inn was closed, as it was now within prohibited hours.

'What's that?' cried a boatman, and 'Shut up, you fool!' said a man near me to a yelping dog. Then the sound came again, this time from the direction of Chertsey, a muffled thud – the sound of a gun.

The fighting was beginning. Almost immediately unseen batteries across the river to our right, unseen because of the trees, took up the chorus, firing heavily one after the other. A woman screamed. Everyone stood arrested by the sudden stir of battle, near us and yet invisible to us. Nothing was to be seen save flat meadows, cows feeding unconcernedly for the most part, and silvery pollard willows motionless in the warm sunlight.

'The sojers'll stop 'em,' said a woman beside me, doubtfully. A haziness rose over the tree-tops.

Then suddenly we saw a rush of smoke far away up the river, a puff of smoke that jerked up into the air and hung; and forthwith the ground heaved underfoot and a heavy explosion shook the air, smashing two or three windows in the houses near, and leaving us astonished.

'Here they are!' shouted a man in a blue jersey. 'Yonder! D'yer see them? Yonder!'

Quickly, one after the other, one, two, three, four of the armoured Martians appeared, far away over the little trees, across the flat meadows that stretch towards Chertsey, and striding hurriedly towards the river. Little cowled figures they seemed at first, going with a rolling motion and as fast as flying birds.

Then, advancing obliquely towards us, came a fifth. Their armoured bodies glittered in the sun as they swept swiftly forward upon the guns, growing rapidly larger as they drew nearer. One on the extreme left, the remotest that is, flourished a huge case high in the air, and the ghostly, terrible Heat-Ray I had already seen on Friday night smote towards Chertsey and struck the town.

At sight of these strange, swift, and terrible creatures the crowd near the water's edge seemed to me to be for a moment horror-struck. There was no screaming or shouting, but a silence. Then a hoarse murmur and a movement of feet – a splashing from the water. A man, too frightened to drop the portmanteau he carried on his shoulder, swung round and sent me staggering with a blow from the corner of his burden. A woman thrust at me with her hand and rushed past me. I turned, with the rush of the people, but I was not too terrified for thought. The terrible Heat-Ray was in my mind. To get under water! That was it!

'Get under water!' I shouted, unheeded.

I faced about again, and rushed towards the approaching Martian, rushed right down the gravelly beach and headlong into the water. Others did the same. A boatload of people putting back came leaping out as I rushed past. The stones under my feet were muddy and slippery, and the river was so low that I ran perhaps twenty feet scarcely waist-deep. Then, as the Martian towered overhead scarcely a couple of hundred yards away, I flung myself forward under the surface. The splashes of the people in the boats leaping into the river sounded like thunderclaps in my ears. People were landing hastily on both sides of the river.

But the Martian machine took no more notice for the moment of the people running this way and that than a man would of the confusion of ants in a nest against which his foot has kicked. When, half suffocated, I raised my head above water, the Martian's hood pointed at the batteries that were still firing across the river, and as it advanced it swung loose what must have been the generator of the Heat-Ray.

In another moment it was on the bank, and in a stride wading halfway across. The knees of its foremost legs bent at the further bank, and in another moment it had raised itself to its full height again, close to the village of Shepperton. Forthwith the six guns which, unknown to anyone on the right bank, had been hidden behind the outskirts of that village, fired simultaneously. The sudden near concussions, the last close upon the first, made my heart jump. The monster was already raising the case generating the Heat-Ray as the first shell burst six yards above the hood.

I gave a cry of astonishment. I saw and thought nothing of the other four Martian monsters; my attention was riveted upon the nearer incident. Simultaneously two other shells burst in the air near the body as the hood twisted round in time to receive, but not in time to dodge, the fourth shell.

The shell burst clean in the face of the Thing. The hood bulged, flashed, was whirled off in a dozen tattered fragments of red flesh and glittering metal.

'Hit!' shouted I, with something between a scream and a cheer.

I heard answering shouts from the people in the water about me. I could have leaped out of the water with that momentary exultation.

The decapitated colossus reeled like a drunken giant; but it did not fall over. It recovered its balance by a miracle, and, no longer heeding its steps and with the camera that fired the Heat-Ray now rigidly upheld, it reeled swiftly upon Shepperton. The living intelligence, the Martian within the hood, was slain and splashed to the four winds of heaven, and the Thing was now but a mere intricate device of metal whirling to destruction. It drove along in a straight line, incapable of guidance. It struck the tower of Shepperton Church, smashing it down as the impact of a battering-ram might have done, swerved aside, blundered on, and collapsed with tremendous force into the river out of my sight.

A violent explosion shook the air, and a spout of water, steam, mud, and shattered metal shot far up into the sky. As the camera of the Heat-Ray hit the water, the latter had immediately flashed into steam. In another moment a huge wave, like a muddy tidal bore but almost scaldingly hot, came sweeping round the bend upstream. I saw people struggling shorewards, and heard their screaming and shouting faintly above the seething and roar of the Martian's collapse.

For the moment I heeded nothing of the heat, forgot the patent need of self-preservation. I splashed through the tumultuous water, pushing aside a man in black to do so, until I could see round the bend. Half a dozen deserted boats pitched aimlessly upon the confusion of the waves. The fallen Martian came into sight downstream, lying across the river, and for the most part submerged.

Thick clouds of steam were pouring off the wreckage, and through the tumultuously whirling wisps I could see, intermittently and vaguely, the gigantic limbs churning the water and flinging a splash and spray of mud and froth into the air. The tentacles swayed and struck like living arms, and, save for the helpless purposelessness of these movements, it was as if some wounded thing were struggling for its life amid the waves. Enormous quantities of a ruddy-brown fluid were spurting up in noisy jets out of the machine.

My attention was diverted from this death flurry by a furious yelling, like that of the thing called a siren in our manufacturing towns. A man, knee-deep near the towing-path, shouted inaudibly to me and pointed. Looking back, I saw the other Martians advancing with gigantic strides down the river-bank from the direction of Chertsey. The Shepperton guns spoke this time unavailingly.

At that I ducked at once under water, and, holding my breath until movement was an agony, blundered painfully ahead under the surface as long as I could. The water was in a tumult about me, and rapidly growing hotter.

When for a moment I raised my head to take breath and throw the hair and water from my eyes, the steam was rising in a whirling white fog that at first hid the Martians altogether. The noise was deafening. Then I saw them dimly, colossal figures of grey, magnified by the mist. They had passed by me, and two were stooping over the frothing, tumultuous ruins of their comrade.

The third and fourth stood beside him in the water, one perhaps two hundred yards from me, the other towards Laleham. The generators of the Heat-Rays waved high, and the hissing beams smote down this way and that.

The air was full of sound, a deafening and confusing conflict of noises – the clangorous din of the Martians, the crash of falling houses, the thud of trees, fences, sheds flashing into flame, and the crackling and roaring of fire. Dense black smoke was leaping up to mingle with the steam from the river, and as the Heat-Ray went to and fro over Weybridge its impact was marked by flashes of incandescent white, that gave place at once to a smoky dance of lurid flames. The nearer houses still stood intact, awaiting their fate, shadowy, faint, and pallid in the steam, with the fire behind them going to and fro.

For a moment perhaps I stood there, breast-high in the almost boiling water, dumbfounded at my position, hopeless of escape. Through the reek I could see the people who had been with me in the river scrambling out of the water through the reeds, like little frogs hurrying through grass from the advance of a man, or running to and fro in utter dismay on the towing-path.

Then suddenly the white flashes of the Heat-Ray came leaping towards me. The houses caved in as they dissolved at its touch, and darted out flames; the trees changed to fire with a roar. The Ray flickered up and down the towing-path, licking off the people who ran this way and that, and came down to the water's edge not fifty yards from where I stood. It swept across the river to Shepperton, and the water in its track rose in a boiling weal crested with steam. I turned shoreward.

In another moment the huge wave, well-nigh at the boiling-point, had rushed upon me. I screamed aloud, and scalded, half blinded, agonized, I staggered through the leaping, hissing water towards the shore. Had my foot stumbled, it would have been the end. I fell helplessly, in full sight of the Martians, upon the broad, bare gravelly spit that runs down to mark the angle of the Wey and Thames. I expected nothing but death.

I have a dim memory of the foot of a Martian coming down within a score of yards of my head, driving straight into the loose gravel, whirling it this way and that, and lifting again; of a long suspense, and then of the four carrying the débris of their comrade between them, now clear and then presently faint through a veil of smoke, receding interminably, as it seemed to me, across a vast space of river and meadow. And then, very slowly, I realized that by a miracle I had escaped.

HOW I FELL IN WITH
THE CURATE

After getting this sudden lesson in the power of terrestrial weapons, the Martians retreated to their original position upon Horsell Common; and in their haste, and encumbered with the débris of their smashed companion, they no doubt overlooked many such a stray and negligible victim as myself. Had they left their comrade and pushed on forthwith, there was nothing at that time between them and London but batteries of twelve-pounder guns, and they would certainly have reached the capital in advance of the tidings of their approach; as sudden, dreadful, and destructive their advent would have been as the earthquake that destroyed Lisbon[1] a century ago.

But they were in no hurry. Cylinder followed cylinder on its interplanetary flight; every twenty-four hours brought them reinforcement. And meanwhile the military and naval authorities, now fully alive to the tremendous power of their antagonists, worked with furious energy. Every minute a fresh gun came into position until, before twilight, every copse, every row of suburban villas on the hilly slopes about Kingston and Richmond, masked an expectant black muzzle. And through the charred and desolated area – perhaps twenty square miles altogether – that encircled the Martian encampment on Horsell Common, through charred and ruined villages among the green trees, through the blackened and smoking arcades that had been but a day ago pine spinneys, crawled the devoted scouts with the heliographs that were presently to warn the gunners of the Martian approach. But the Martians now understood our command of artillery and the danger of human proximity, and not a man ventured within a mile of either cylinder, save at the price of his life.

It would seem that these giants spent the earlier part of the afternoon in going to and fro, transferring everything from the second and third cylinders – the second in Addlestone Golf Links and the third at Pyrford – to their original pit on Horsell Common. Over that, above the blackened heather and ruined buildings that stretched far and wide, stood one as sentinel, while the rest abandoned their vast fighting-machines and descended into the pit. They were hard at work there far into the night, and the towering pillar of dense green smoke that rose therefrom could be seen from the hills about Merrow, and even, it is said, from Banstead and Epsom Downs.

And while the Martians behind me were thus preparing for their next sally, and in front of me Humanity gathered for the battle, I made my way with infinite pains and labour from the fire and smoke of burning Weybridge towards London.

I saw an abandoned boat, very small and remote, drifting downstream; and throwing off the most of my sodden clothes, I went after it, gained it, and so escaped out of that destruction. There were no oars in the boat, but I contrived to paddle, as well as my parboiled hands would allow, down the river towards Halliford and Walton, going very tediously and continually looking behind me, as you may well understand. I followed the river, because I considered that the water gave me my best chance of escape should these giants return.

The hot water from the Martian's overthrow drifted downstream with me, so that for the best part of a mile I could see little of either bank. Once, however, I made out a string of black figures hurrying across the meadows from the direction of Weybridge. Halliford, it seemed, was deserted, and several of the houses facing the river were on fire. It was strange to see the place quite tranquil, quite desolate under the hot, blue sky, with the smoke and little threads of flame going straight up into the heat of the afternoon. Never before had I seen houses burning without the accompaniment of an obstructive crowd. A little further on the dry reeds up the bank were smoking and glowing, and a line of fire inland was marching steadily across a late field of hay.

For a long time I drifted, so painful and weary was I after the violence I had been through, and so intense the heat upon the water. Then my fears got the better of me again, and I resumed my paddling. The sun scorched my bare back. At last, as the bridge at Walton was coming into sight round the bend, my fever and faintness overcame my fears, and I landed on the Middlesex bank and lay down, deadly sick, amid the long grass. I suppose the time was then about four or five o'clock. I got up presently, walked perhaps half a mile without meeting a soul, and then lay down again in the shadow of a hedge. I seem to remember talking, wanderingly, to myself during that last spurt. I was also very thirsty, and bitterly regretful I had drunk no more water. It is a curious thing that I felt angry with my wife; I cannot account for it, but my impotent desire to reach Leatherhead worried me excessively.

I do not clearly remember the arrival of the curate, so that probably I dozed. I became aware of him as a seated figure in soot-smudged shirt-sleeves, and with his upturned, clean-shaven face staring at a faint flickering that danced over the sky. The sky was what is called a mackerel sky – rows and rows of faint down-plumes of cloud, just tinted with the midsummer sunset.

I sat up, and at the rustle of my motion he looked at me quickly.

'Have you any water?' I asked abruptly.

He shook his head.

'You have been asking for water for the last hour,' he said.

For a moment we were silent, taking stock of each other. I dare say he found me a strange enough figure, naked save for my water-soaked trousers and socks, scalded, and my face and shoulders blackened by the smoke. His face was a fair weakness, his chin retreated, and his hair lay in crisp, almost flaxen curls on his low forehead; his eyes were rather large, pale blue, and blankly staring. He spoke abruptly, looking vacantly away from me.

'What does it mean?' he said. 'What do these things mean?'

I stared at him and made no answer.

He extended a thin white hand and spoke in almost a complaining tone.

'Why are these things permitted? What sins have we done? The morning service was over, I was walking through the roads to clear my brain for the afternoon, and then – fire, earthquake, death! As if it were Sodom and Gomorrah![2] All our work undone, all the work – What are these Martians?'

'What are we?' I answered, clearing my throat.

He gripped his knees and turned to look at me again. For half a minute, perhaps, he stared silently.

'I was walking through the roads to clear my brain,' he said. 'And suddenly – fire, earthquake, death!'

He relapsed into silence, with his chin now sunken almost to his knees.

Presently he began waving his hand.

'All the work – all the Sunday-schools – What have we done – what has Weybridge done? Everything gone – everything destroyed. The church! We rebuilt it only three years ago. Gone! – swept out of existence! Why?'

Another pause, and he broke out again like one demented.

'The smoke of her burning goeth up for ever and ever![3]' he shouted.

His eyes flamed, and he pointed a lean finger in the direction of Weybridge.

By this time I was beginning to take his measure. The tremendous tragedy in which he had been involved – it was evident he was a fugitive from Weybridge – had driven him to the very verge of his reason.

'Are we far from Sunbury?' I said, in a matter-of-fact tone.

'What are we to do?' he asked. 'Are these creatures everywhere? Has the earth been given over to them?'

'Are we far from Sunbury?'

'Only this morning I officiated at early celebration—'

'Things have changed,' I said, quietly. 'You must keep your head. There is still hope.'

'Hope!'

'Yes. Plentiful hope – for all this destruction!'

I began to explain my view of our position. He listened at first, but as I went on the dawning interest in his eyes gave place to their former stare, and his regard wandered from me.

'This must be the beginning of the end,' he said, interrupting me. 'The end! The great and terrible day of the Lord! When men shall call upon the mountains and the rocks to fall upon them and hide them – hide them from the face of Him that sitteth upon the throne!'

I began to understand the position. I ceased my laboured reasoning, struggled to my feet, and, standing over him, laid my hand on his shoulder.

'Be a man!' said I. 'You are scared out of your wits! What good is religion if it collapses under calamity? Think of what earthquakes and floods, wars and volcanoes, have done before to men! Did you think God had exempted Weybridge? He is not an insurance agent, man.'

For a time he sat in blank silence.

'But how can we escape?' he asked, suddenly. 'They are invulnerable, they are pitiless.'

'Neither the one nor, perhaps, the other,' I answered. 'And the mightier they are the more sane and wary should we be. One of them was killed yonder not three hours ago.'

'Killed!' he said, staring about him. 'How can God's ministers be killed?'

'I saw it happen.' I proceeded to tell him. 'We have chanced to come in for the thick of it,' said I, 'and that is all.'

'What is that flicker in the sky?' he asked, abruptly.

I told him it was the heliograph signalling – that it was the sign of human help and effort in the sky.

'We are in the midst of it,' I said, 'quiet as it is. That flicker in the sky tells of the gathering storm. Yonder, I take it, are the Martians, and Londonward, where those hills rise about Richmond and Kingston and the trees give cover, earthworks are being thrown up and guns are being placed. Presently the Martians will be coming this way again.'

And even as I spoke he sprang to his feet and stopped me by a gesture.

'Listen!' he said.

From beyond the low hills across the water came the dull resonance of distant guns and a remote, weird crying. Then everything was still. A cockchafer came droning over the hedge and past us. High in the west the crescent moon hung faint and pale above the smoke of Weybridge and Shepperton and the hot, still splendour of the sunset.

'We had better follow this path,' I said, 'northward.'

14

IN LONDON

My younger brother was in London when the Martians fell at Woking. He was a medical student, working for an imminent examination, and he heard nothing of the arrival until Saturday morning. The morning papers on Saturday contained, in addition to lengthy special articles on the planet Mars, on life in the planets, and so forth, a brief and vaguely worded telegram, all the more striking for its brevity.

The Martians, alarmed by the approach of a crowd, had killed a number of people with a quick-firing gun, so the story ran. The telegram concluded with the words: 'Formidable as they seem to be, the Martians have not moved from the pit into which they have fallen, and, indeed, seem incapable of doing so. Probably this is due to the relative strength of the earth's gravitational energy.' On that last text the leader-writers expanded very comfortingly.

Of course, all the students in the crammer's[1] biology class, to which my brother went that day, were intensely interested, but there were no signs of any unusual excitement in the streets. The afternoon papers puffed scraps of news under big headlines. They had nothing to tell beyond the movements of troops about the common, and the burning of the pine-woods between Woking and Weybridge, until eight. Then the *St James's Gazette*,[2] in an extra special edition, announced the bare fact of the interruption of telegraphic communication. This was thought to be due to the falling of burning pine-trees across the line. Nothing more of the fighting was known that night, the night of my drive to Leatherhead and back.

My brother felt no anxiety about us, as he knew from the

description in the papers that the cylinder was a good two miles from my house. He made up his mind to run down that night to me, in order, as he says, to see the Things before they were killed. He despatched a telegram, which never reached me, about four o'clock, and spent the evening at a music-hall.

In London, also, on Saturday night there was a thunderstorm, and my brother reached Waterloo in a cab. On the platform from which the midnight train usually starts he learnt, after some waiting, that an accident prevented trains from reaching Woking that night. The nature of the accident he could not ascertain; indeed, the railway authorities did not clearly know at that time. There was very little excitement in the station, as the officials, failing to realize that anything further than a breakdown between Byfleet and Woking junction had occurred, were running the theatre trains[3] which usually passed through Woking, round by Virginia Water or Guildford. They were busy making the necessary arrangements to alter the route of the Southampton and Portsmouth Sunday League excursions. A nocturnal newspaper reporter, mistaking my brother for the traffic manager, to whom he bears a slight resemblance, waylaid and tried to interview him. Few people, excepting the railway officials, connected the breakdown with the Martians.

I have read, in another account of these events, that on Sunday morning 'all London was electrified by the news from Woking.' As a matter of fact, there was nothing to justify that very extravagant phrase. Plenty of Londoners did not hear of the Martians until the panic of Monday morning. Those who did took some time to realize all that the hastily worded telegrams in the Sunday papers conveyed. The majority of people in London do not read Sunday papers.

The habit of personal security, moreover, is so deeply fixed in the Londoner's mind, and startling intelligence so much a matter of course in the papers, that they could read without any personal tremors: 'About seven o'clock last night the Martians came out of the cylinder, and, moving about under an armour of metallic shields, have completely wrecked Woking station with the adjacent houses, and massacred an entire battalion of the Cardigan Regiment. No details are known. Maxims have been absolutely useless against their armour; the field-guns have been disabled by them. Flying hussars have been galloping into Chertsey. The Martians appear to be moving slowly towards Chertsey or Windsor. Great anxiety prevails in West Surrey, and earthworks are being thrown up to check the advance Londonward.' That was how the Sunday *Sun*[4] put it, and a clever and remarkably prompt 'hand-book' article in the *Referee*[5] compared the affair to a menagerie suddenly let loose in a village.

No one in London knew positively of the nature of the armoured Martians, and there was still a fixed idea that these monsters must be sluggish: 'crawling,' 'creeping painfully' – such expressions occurred in almost all the earlier reports. None of the telegrams could have been written by an eye-witness of their advance. The Sunday papers printed separate editions as further news came to hand, some even in default of it. But there was practically nothing more to tell people until late in the afternoon, when the authorities gave the press agencies the news in their possession. It was stated that the people of Walton and Weybridge, and all that district, were pouring along the roads Londonward, and that was all.

My brother went to church at the Foundling Hospital[6] in the morning, still in ignorance of what had happened on the previous night. There he heard allusions made to the invasion, and a special prayer for peace. Coming out, he bought a *Referee*. He became alarmed at the news in this, and went again to Waterloo station to find out if communication were restored. The omnibuses, carriages, cyclists, and innumerable people walking in their best clothes seemed scarcely affected by the strange intelligence that the newsvendors were disseminating. People were interested, or, if alarmed, alarmed only on account of the local residents. At the station he heard for the first time that the Windsor and Chertsey lines were now interrupted. The porters told him that several remarkable telegrams had been received in the morning from Byfleet and Chertsey stations, but that these had abruptly ceased. My brother could get very little precise detail out of them. 'There's fighting going on about Weybridge' was the extent of their information.

The train service was now very much disorganized. Quite a number of people who had been expecting friends from places on the South-Western network were standing about the station. One grey-headed old gentleman came and abused the South-Western Company bitterly to my brother. 'It wants showing up,' he said.

One or two trains came in from Richmond, Putney, and Kingston, containing people who had gone out for a day's boating and found the locks closed and a feeling of panic in the air. A man in a blue-and-white blazer addressed my brother, full of strange tidings.

'There's hosts of people driving into Kingston in traps and carts and things, with boxes of valuables and all that,' he said. 'They come from Molesey and Weybridge and Walton, and they say there's been guns heard at Chertsey, heavy firing, and that mounted soldiers have told them to get off at once because the Martians are coming. *We* heard guns firing at Hampton Court station, but we thought it was thunder. What the dickens does it all mean? The Martians can't get out of their pit, can they?'

My brother could not tell him.

Afterwards he found that the vague feeling of alarm had spread to the clients of the underground railway, and that the Sunday excursionists began to return from all over the South-Western 'lungs'[7] – Barnes, Wimbledon, Richmond Park, Kew, and so forth – at unnaturally early hours; but not a soul had anything more than vague hearsay to tell of. Everyone connected with the terminus seemed ill-tempered.

About five o'clock the gathering crowd in the station was immensely excited by the opening of the line of communication, which is almost invariably closed, between the South-Eastern and the South-Western stations, and the passage of carriage-trucks bearing huge guns and carriages crammed with soldiers. These were the guns that were brought up from Woolwich and Chatham to cover Kingston. There was an exchange of pleasantries: 'You'll get eaten!' 'We're the beast-tamers!' and so forth. A little while after that a squad of police came into the station and began to clear the public off the platforms, and my brother went out into the street again.

The church bells were ringing for evensong, and a squad of Salvation Army lasses came singing down Waterloo Road. On the bridge a number of loafers were watching a curious brown scum that came drifting down the stream in patches. The sun was just setting, and the Clock Tower and the Houses of Parliament rose against one of the most peaceful skies it is possible to imagine, a sky of gold, barred with long transverse stripes of reddish-purple cloud. There was talk of a floating body. One of the men there, a reservist he said he was, told my brother he had seen the heliograph flickering in the west.

In Wellington Street my brother met a couple of sturdy roughs who had just rushed out of Fleet Street with still wet newspapers and staring placards. 'Dreadful catastrophe!' they bawled one to the other down Wellington Street. 'Fighting at Weybridge! Full description! Repulse of the Martians! London in Danger!' He had to give threepence for a copy of that paper.

Then it was, and then only, that he realized something of the full power and terror of these monsters. He learnt that they were not merely a handful of small sluggish creatures, but that they were minds swaying vast mechanical bodies; and that they could move swiftly and smite with such power that even the mightiest guns could not stand against them.

They were described as 'vast spider-like machines, nearly a hundred feet high, capable of the speed of an express train, and able to shoot out a beam of intense heat.' Masked batteries, chiefly of field-guns, had been planted in the country about Horsell Common, and especially between the Woking district and London. Five of the machines had been seen moving towards the Thames, and one, by a happy chance, had been destroyed. In the other cases the shells had missed, and the batteries had been at once annihilated by the Heat-Rays. Heavy losses of soldiers were mentioned, but the tone of the despatch was optimistic.

The Martians had been repulsed; they were not invulnerable. They had retreated to their triangle of cylinders again, in the circle about Woking. Signallers with heliographs were pushing forward upon them from all sides. Guns were in rapid transit from Windsor, Portsmouth, Aldershot, Woolwich – even from the north; among others, long wire-guns of ninety-five tons from Woolwich. Altogether one hundred and sixteen were in position or being hastily placed, chiefly covering London. Never before in England had there been such a vast or rapid concentration of military material.

Any further cylinders that fell, it was hoped, could be destroyed at once by high explosives, which were being rapidly manufactured and distributed. No doubt, ran the report, the situation was of the strangest and gravest description, but the public was exhorted to avoid and discourage panic. No doubt the Martians were strange and terrible in the extreme, but at the outside there could not be more than twenty of them against our millions.

The authorities had reason to suppose, from the size of the cylinders, that at the outside there could not be more than five in each cylinder – fifteen altogether. And one at least was disposed of – perhaps more. The public would be fairly warned of the approach of danger, and elaborate measures were being taken for the protection of the people in the threatened south-western suburbs. And so, with reiterated assurances of the safety of London and the ability of the authorities to cope with the difficulty, this quasi-proclamation closed.

This was printed in enormous type on paper so fresh that it was still wet, and there had been no time to add a word of comment. It was curious, my brother said, to see how ruthlessly the usual contents of the paper had been hacked and taken out to give this place.

All down Wellington Street people could be seen fluttering out the pink sheets and reading, and the Strand was suddenly noisy with the voices of an army of hawkers following these pioneers. Men came scrambling off buses to secure copies. Certainly this news excited people intensely, whatever their previous apathy. The shutters of a map-shop in the Strand were being taken down, my brother said, and a man in his Sunday raiment, lemon-yellow gloves even, was visible inside the window hastily fastening maps of Surrey to the glass.

Going on along the Strand to Trafalgar Square, the paper in his hand, my brother saw some of the fugitives from West

Surrey. There was a man with his wife and two boys and some articles of furniture in a cart such as greengrocers use. He was driving from the direction of Westminster Bridge; and close behind him came a hay-wagon with five or six respectable-looking people in it, and some boxes and bundles. The faces of these people were haggard, and their entire appearance contrasted conspicuously with the Sabbath-best appearance of the people on the omnibuses.[8] People in fashionable clothing peeped at them out of cabs. They stopped at the Square as if undecided which way to take, and finally turned eastward along the Strand. Some way behind these came a man in work-day clothes, riding one of those old-fashioned tricycles with a small front-wheel. He was dirty and white in the face.

My brother turned down towards Victoria, and met a number of such people. He had a vague idea that he might see something of me. He noticed an unusual number of police regulating the traffic. Some of the refugees were exchanging news with the people on the omnibuses. One was professing to have seen the Martians. 'Boilers on stilts, I tell you, striding along like men.' Most of them were excited and animated by their strange experience.

Beyond Victoria the public-houses were doing a lively trade with these arrivals. At all the street corners groups of people were reading papers, talking excitedly, or staring at these unusual Sunday visitors. They seemed to increase as night drew on, until at last the roads, my brother said, were like Epsom High Street on a Derby Day.[9] My brother addressed several of these fugitives and got unsatisfactory answers from most.

None of them could tell him any news of Woking except one man, who assured him that Woking had been entirely destroyed on the previous night.

'I come from Byfleet,' he said; 'a man on a bicycle came through the place in the early morning, and ran from door to door warning us to come away. Then came soldiers. We went out to look, and there were clouds of smoke to the south – nothing but smoke, and not a soul coming that way. Then we heard the guns at Chertsey, and folks coming from Weybridge. So I've locked up my house and come on.'

At that time there was a strong feeling in the streets that the authorities were to blame for their incapacity to dispose of the invaders without all this inconvenience.

About eight o'clock a noise of heavy firing was distinctly audible all over the south of London. My brother could not hear it for the traffic in the main thoroughfares, but by striking through the quiet back-streets to the river he was able to distinguish it quite plainly.

He walked from Westminster to his apartments near Regent's Park, about ten. He was now very anxious on my account, and disturbed at the evident magnitude of the trouble. His mind was inclined to run, even as mine had run on Saturday, on military details. He thought of all those silent, expectant guns, of the suddenly nomadic countryside; he tried to imagine 'boilers on stilts' a hundred feet high.

There were one or two cart-loads of refugees passing along Oxford Street, and several in the Marylebone Road, but so slowly was the news spreading that Regent Street and Portland Place were full of their usual Sunday-night promenaders, albeit they talked in groups, and along the edge of Regent's Park there were as many silent couples 'walking out' together under the scattered gas-lamps as ever there had been. The night was warm and still, and a little oppressive; the sound of guns continued intermittently, and after midnight there seemed to be sheet lightning in the south.

He read and reread the paper, fearing the worst had happened to me. He was restless, and after supper prowled out again aimlessly. He returned and tried in vain to divert his attention to his examination notes. He went to bed a little after midnight, and was awakened from lurid dreams in the small hours of Monday by the sound of door-knockers, feet running in the street, distant drumming, and a clamour of bells. Red reflections danced on the ceiling. For a moment he lay astonished, wondering whether day had come or the world gone mad. Then he jumped out of bed and ran to the window.

His room was an attic; and as he thrust his head out, up and down the street there were a dozen echoes to the noise of his window-sash, and heads in every kind of night disarray appeared. Inquiries were being shouted. 'They are coming!' bawled a policeman, hammering at the door; 'the Martians are coming!' and hurried to the next door.

The sound of drumming and trumpeting came from the Albany Street Barracks, and every church within earshot was hard at work killing sleep with a vehement disorderly tocsin. There was a noise of doors opening, and window after window in the houses opposite flashed from darkness into yellow illumination.

Up the street came galloping a closed carriage, bursting abruptly into noise at the corner, rising to a clattering climax under the window, and dying away slowly in the distance. Close on the rear of this came a couple of cabs, the forerunners of a long procession of flying vehicles, going for the most part to Chalk Farm station, where the North-Western special trains were loading up, instead of coming down the gradient into Euston.

For a long time my brother stared out of the window in blank astonishment, watching the policemen hammering at door after door, and delivering their incomprehensible message. Then the door behind him opened, and the man who lodged across the landing came in, dressed only in shirt, trousers, and slippers, his braces loose about his waist, his hair disordered from his pillow.

'What the devil is it?' he asked. 'A fire? What a devil of a row!'

They both craned their heads out of the window, straining to hear what the policemen were shouting. People were coming out of the side-streets, and standing in groups at the corners talking.

'What the devil is it all about?' said my brother's fellow-lodger.

My brother answered him vaguely and began to dress, running with each garment to the window in order to miss nothing of the growing excitement. And presently men selling unnaturally early newspapers came bawling into the street:

'London in danger of suffocation! The Kingston and Richmond defences forced! Fearful massacres in the Thames Valley!'

And all about him – in the rooms below, in the houses on each side and across the road, and behind in the Park Terraces and in the hundred other streets of that part of Marylebone, and the Westbourne Park district and St Pancras, and westward and northward in Kilburn and St John's Wood and Hampstead, and eastward in Shoreditch and Highbury and Haggerston and Hoxton, and, indeed, through all the vastness of London from Ealing to East Ham – people were rubbing their eyes, and opening windows to stare out and ask aimless questions, and dressing hastily as the first breath of the coming storm of Fear blew through the streets. It was the dawn of the great panic. London, which had gone to bed on Sunday night oblivious and inert, was awakened in the small hours of Monday morning to a vivid sense of danger.

Unable from his window to learn what was happening, my brother went down and out into the street, just as the sky between the parapets of the houses grew pink with the early dawn. The flying people on foot and in vehicles grew more numerous every moment. 'Black Smoke!' he heard people crying, and again 'Black Smoke!' The contagion of such a unanimous fear was inevitable. As my brother hesitated on the doorstep, he saw another newsvendor approaching him, and got a paper forthwith. The man was running away with the rest, and selling his papers for a shilling each as he ran – a grotesque mingling of profit and panic.

And from this paper my brother read that catastrophic despatch of the Commander-in-Chief:

'The Martians are able to discharge enormous clouds of a black and poisonous vapour by means of rockets. They have smothered our batteries, destroyed Richmond, Kingston, and Wimbledon, and are advancing slowly towards London, destroying everything on the way. It is impossible to stop them. There is no safety from the Black Smoke but in instant flight.'

That was all, but it was enough. The whole population of the great six-million city was stirring, slipping, running; presently it would be pouring *en masse* northward.

'Black Smoke!' the voices cried. 'Fire!'

The bells of the neighbouring church made a jangling tumult, a cart carelessly driven smashed, amid shrieks and curses, against the water-trough up the street. Sickly yellow light went to and fro in the houses, and some of the passing cabs flaunted unextinguished lamps. And overhead the dawn was growing brighter, clear and steady and calm.

He heard footsteps running to and fro in the rooms, and up and down stairs behind him. His landlady came to the door, loosely wrapped in dressing-gown and shawl; her husband followed ejaculating.

As my brother began to realize the import of all these things, he turned hastily to his own room, put all his available money – some ten pounds altogether – into his pockets, and went out again into the streets.

WHAT HAD HAPPENED
IN SURREY

It was while the curate had sat and talked so wildly to me under the hedge in the flat meadows near Halliford, and while my brother was watching the fugitives stream over Westminster Bridge, that the Martians had resumed the offensive. So far as one can ascertain from the conflicting accounts that have been put forth, the majority of them remained busied with preparations in the Horsell pit until nine that night, hurrying on some operation that disengaged huge volumes of green smoke.

But three certainly came out about eight o'clock, and, advancing slowly and cautiously, made their way through Byfleet and Pyrford towards Ripley and Weybridge, and so came in sight of the expectant batteries against the setting sun. These Martians did not advance in a body, but in a line, each perhaps a mile and a half from his nearest fellow. They communicated with one another by means of siren-like howls, running up and down the scale from one note to another.

It was this howling and the firing of the guns at Ripley and St George's Hill[1] that we had heard at Upper Halliford. The Ripley gunners, unseasoned artillery volunteers who ought never to have been placed in such a position, fired one wild, premature, ineffectual volley, and bolted on horse and foot through the deserted village, while the Martian without using his Heat-Ray, walked serenely over their guns, stepped gingerly among them, passed in front of them, and so came unexpectedly upon the guns in Painshill Park, which he destroyed.

The St George's Hill men, however, were better led or of a better mettle. Hidden by a pine-wood as they were, they seem to have been quite unsuspected by the Martian nearest to them. They laid their guns as deliberately as if they had been on parade, and fired at about a thousand yards' range.

The shells flashed all round him, and he was seen to advance a few paces, stagger, and go down. Everybody yelled together, and the guns were reloaded in frantic haste. The overthrown Martian set up a prolonged ululation, and immediately a second glittering giant, answering him, appeared over the trees to the south. It would seem that a leg of the tripod had been smashed by one of the shells. The whole of the second volley flew wide of the Martian on the ground, and, simultaneously, both his companions brought their Heat-Rays to bear on the battery. The ammunition blew up, the pine-trees all about the guns flashed into fire, and only one or two of the men who were already running over the crest of the hill escaped.

After this it would seem that the three took counsel together and halted, and the scouts who were watching them report that they remained absolutely stationary for the next half-hour. The Martian who had been overthrown crawled tediously out of his hood, a small brown figure, oddly suggestive from that distance of a speck of blight, and apparently engaged in the repair of his support. About nine he had finished, for his cowl was then seen above the trees again.

It was a few minutes past nine that night when these three sentinels were joined by four other Martians, each carrying a thick black tube. A similar tube was handed to each of the three, and the seven proceeded to distribute themselves at equal distances along a curved line between St George's Hill, Weybridge, and the village of Send, south-west of Ripley.

A dozen rockets sprang out of the hills before them so soon as they began to move, and warned the waiting batteries about Ditton and Esher. At the same time four of their fighting-machines, similarly armed with tubes, crossed the river, and two of them, black against the western sky, came into sight of myself and the curate as we hurried wearily and painfully along the road that runs northward out of Halliford. They moved, as it seemed to us, upon a cloud, for a milky mist covered the fields and rose to a third of their height.

At this sight the curate cried faintly in his throat, and began running; but I knew it was no good running from a Martian, and I turned aside and crawled through dewy nettles and brambles into the broad ditch by the side of the road. He looked back, saw what I was doing, and turned to join me.

The two halted, the nearer to us standing and facing Sunbury, the remoter being a grey indistinctness towards the evening star,[2] away towards Staines.

The occasional howling of the Martians had ceased; they took up their positions in the huge crescent about their cylinders in absolute silence. It was a crescent with twelve miles between its horns. Never since the devising of gunpowder was the beginning of a battle so still. To us and to an observer about Ripley it would have had precisely the same effect – the Martians seemed in solitary possession of the darkling night, lit only as it was by the slender moon, the stars, the after-glow of the daylight, and the ruddy glare from St George's Hill and the woods of Painshill.

But facing that crescent everywhere – at Staines, Hounslow, Ditton, Esher, Ockham, behind hills and woods south of the river, and across the flat grass meadows to the north of it, wherever a cluster of trees or village houses gave sufficient cover – the guns were waiting. The signal rockets burst and rained their sparks through the night and vanished, and the spirit of all those watching batteries rose to a tense expectation. The Martians had but to advance into the line of fire, and instantly those motionless black forms of men, those guns glittering so darkly in the early night, would explode into a thunderous fury of battle.

No doubt the thought that was uppermost in a thousand of those vigilant minds, even as it was uppermost in mine, was the riddle – how much they understood of us. Did they grasp that we in our millions were organized, disciplined, working together? Or did they interpret our spurts of fire, the sudden stinging of our shells, our steady investment of their encampment, as we should the furious unanimity of onslaught in a disturbed hive of bees? Did they dream they might extermimate us? (At that time no one knew what food they needed.) A hundred such questions struggled together in my mind as I watched that vast sentinel shape. And in the back of my mind was the sense of all the huge unknown and hidden forces Londonward. Had they prepared pitfalls? Were the powder-mills at Hounslow ready as a snare? Would the Londoners have the heart and courage to make a greater Moscow[3] of their mighty province of houses?

Then, after an interminable time, as it seemed to us, crouching and peering through the hedge, came a sound like the distant concussion of a gun. Another nearer, and then another. And then the Martian beside us raised his tube on high and discharged it, gunwise, with a heavy report that made the ground heave. The one towards Staines answered him. There was no flash, no smoke, simply that loaded detonation.

I was so excited by these heavy minute-guns following one another that I so far forgot my personal safety and my scalded hands as to clamber up into the hedge and stare towards Sunbury. As I did so a second report followed, and a big projectile hurtled overhead towards Hounslow. I expected at least to see smoke or fire, or some such evidence of its work. But all I saw was the deep-blue sky above, with one solitary star, and the white mist spreading wide and low beneath. And there had been no crash, no answering explosion. The silence was restored; the minute lengthened to three.

'What has happened?' said the curate, standing up beside me.

'Heaven knows!' said I.

A bat flickered by and vanished. A distant tumult of shouting began and ceased. I looked again at the Martian, and saw he was now moving eastward along the river-bank, with a swift, rolling motion.

Every moment I expected the fire of some hidden battery to spring upon him; but the evening calm was unbroken. The figure of the Martian grew smaller as he receded, and presently the mist and the gathering night had swallowed him up. By a common impulse we clambered higher. Towards Sunbury was a dark appearance, as though a conical hill had suddenly come into being there, hiding our view of the further country; and then, remoter across the river, over Walton, we saw another such summit. These hill-like forms grew lower and broader even as we stared.

Moved by a sudden thought, I looked northward, and there I perceived a third of these cloudy black kopjes[4] had arisen.

Everything had suddenly become very still. Far away to the south-east, marking the quiet, we heard the Martians hooting to one another, and then the air quivered again with the distant thud of their guns. But the earthly artillery made no reply.

Now at the time we could not understand these things, but later I was to learn the meaning of these ominous kopjes that gathered in the twilight. Each of the Martians, standing in the great crescent I have described, had discharged, by means of the gun-like tube he carried, a huge canister over whatever hill, copse, cluster of houses, or other possible cover for guns, chanced to be in front of him. Some fired only one of these, some two – as in the case of the one we had seen; the one at Ripley is said to have discharged no fewer than five at that time. These canisters smashed on striking the ground – they did not explode – and incontinently disengaged an enormous volume of heavy, inky vapour, coiling and pouring upward in a huge and ebony cumulus cloud, a gaseous hill that sank and spread itself slowly over the surrounding country. And the touch of that vapour, the inhaling of its pungent wisps, was death to all that breathes.

It was heavy, this vapour, heavier than the densest smoke, so that, after the first tumultuous uprush and outflow of its impact, it sank down through the air and poured over the ground in a manner rather liquid than gaseous, abandoning the hills, and streaming into the valleys and ditches and water-courses even as I have heard the carbonic acid gas[5] that pours from volcanic clefts is wont to do. And where it came upon water some chemical action occurred, and the surface would be instantly covered with a powdery scum that sank slowly and made way for more. The scum was absolutely insoluble, and it is a strange thing, seeing the instant effect of the gas, that one could drink without hurt the water from which it had been strained. The vapour did not diffuse as a true gas would do. It hung together in banks, flowing sluggishly down the slope of the land and driving reluctantly before the wind, and very slowly it combined with the mist and moisture of the air, and sank to the earth in the form of dust. Save that an unknown element giving a group of four lines in the blue of the spectrum[6] is concerned, we are still entirely ignorant of the nature of this substance.

Once the tumultuous upheaval of its dispersion was over, the black smoke clung so closely to the ground, even before its precipitation, that fifty feet up in the air, on the roofs and upper stories of high houses and on great trees, there was a chance of escaping its poison altogether, as was proved even that night at Street Cobham and Ditton.

The man who escaped at the former place tells a wonderful story of the strangeness of its coiling flow, and how he looked down from the church spire and saw the houses of the village rising like ghosts out of its inky nothingness. For a day and a half he remained there, weary, starving and sun-scorched, the earth under the blue sky and against the prospect of the distant hills a velvet-black expanse, with red roofs, green trees, and, later, black-veiled shrubs and gates, barns, outhouses, and walls, rising here and there into the sunlight.

But that was at Street Cobham, where the black vapour was allowed to remain until it sank of its own accord into the ground. As a rule the Martians, when it had served its purpose, cleared the air of it again by wading into it and directing a jet of steam upon it.

This they did with the vapour-banks near us, as we saw in the starlight from the window of a deserted house at Upper Halliford, whither we had returned. From there we could see the searchlights on Richmond Hill and Kingston Hill going to and fro, and about eleven the windows rattled, and we heard the sound of the huge siege guns that had been put in position there. These continued intermittently for the space of a quarter of an hour, sending chance shots at the invisible Martians at Hampton and Ditton, and then the pale beams of the electric light vanished, and were replaced by a bright red glow.

Then the fourth cylinder fell – a brilliant green meteor – as I learnt afterwards, in Bushey Park. Before the guns on the Richmond and Kingston line of hills began, there was a fitful cannonade far away in the south-west, due, I believe, to guns being fired haphazard before the black vapour could overwhelm the gunners.

So, setting about it as methodically as men might smoke out a wasps' nest, the Martians spread this strange stifling vapour over the Londonward country. The horns of the crescent slowly moved apart, until at last they formed a line from Hanwell to Coombe and Malden. All night through their destructive tubes advanced. Never once, after the Martian at St George's Hill was brought down, did they give the artillery the ghost of a chance against them. Wherever there was a possibility of guns being laid for them unseen, a fresh canister of the black vapour was discharged, and where the guns were openly displayed the Heat-Ray was brought to bear.

By midnight the blazing trees along the slopes of Richmond Park and the glare of Kingston Hill threw their light upon a network of black smoke, blotting out the whole Valley of the Thames and extending as far as the eye could reach. And through this two Martians slowly waded, and turned their hissing steam-jets this way and that.

They were sparing of the Heat-Ray that night, either because they had but a limited supply of material for its production or because they did not wish to destroy the country but only to crush and overawe the opposition they had aroused. In the latter aim they certainly succeeded. Sunday night was the end of the organized opposition to their movements. After that no body of men would stand against them, so hopeless was the enterprise. Even the crews of the torpedo boats and destroyers that had brought their quick-firers up the Thames refused to stop, mutinied, and went down again. The only offensive oper-ation men ventured upon after that night was the preparation of mines and pitfalls, and even in that their energies were frantic and spasmodic.

One has to imagine, as well as one may, the fate of those batteries towards Esher, waiting so tensely in the twilight. Sur-vivors there were none. One may picture the orderly expec-tation, the officers alert and watchful, the gunners ready, the ammunition piled to hand, the limber gunners with their horses and wagons, the groups of civilian spectators standing as near as they were permitted, the evening stillness, the ambulances and hospital tents with the burnt and wounded from Weybridge; then the dull resonance of the shots the Martians fired, and the clumsy projectile whirling over the trees and houses and smashing amid the neighbouring fields.

One may picture, too, the sudden shifting of the attention, the swiftly spreading coils and bellyings of that blackness advancing headlong, towering heavenward, turning the twilight to a palpable darkness, a strange and horrible antagonist of vapour striding upon its victims, men and horses near it seen dimly, running, shrieking, falling headlong, shouts of dismay, the guns suddenly abandoned, men choking and writhing on the ground, and the swift broadening-out of the opaque cone of smoke. And then night and extinction – nothing but a silent mass of impenetrable vapour hiding its dead.

Before dawn the black vapour was pouring through the streets of Richmond, and the disintegrating organism of government was, with a last expiring effort, rousing the population of London to the necessity of flight.

THE EXODUS
FROM LONDON

So you understand the roaring wave of fear that swept through the greatest city in the world just as Monday was dawning – the stream of flight rising swiftly to a torrent, lashing in a foaming tumult round the railway stations, banked up into a horrible struggle about the shipping in the Thames, and hurrying by every available channel northward and eastward. By ten o'clock the police organization, and by midday even the railway organizations, were losing coherency, losing shape and efficiency, guttering, softening, running at last in that swift liquefaction of the social body.

All the railway lines north of the Thames and the South-Eastern people at Cannon Street had been warned by midnight on Sunday, and trains were being filled. People were fighting savagely for standing-room in the carriages even at two o'clock. By three, people were being trampled and crushed even in Bishopsgate Street, a couple of hundred yards or more from Liverpool Street station; revolvers were fired, people stabbed, and the policemen who had been sent to direct the traffic, exhausted and infuriated, were breaking the heads of the people they were called out to protect.

And as the day advanced and the engine-drivers and stokers refused to return to London, the pressure of the flight drove the people in an ever-thickening multitude away from the stations and along the northward-running roads. By midday a Martian had been seen at Barnes, and a cloud of slowly sinking black vapour drove along the Thames and across the flats of Lambeth, cutting off all escape over the bridges in its sluggish advance. Another bank drove over Ealing, and surrounded a little island of survivors on Castle Hill, alive, but unable to escape.

After a fruitless struggle to get aboard a North-Western train at Chalk Farm – the engines of the trains that had loaded in the goods yard there *ploughed* through shrieking people, and a dozen stalwart men fought to keep the crowd from crushing the driver against his furnace – my brother emerged upon the Chalk Farm road, dodged across through a hurrying swarm of vehicles, and had the luck to be foremost in the sack of a cycle shop. The front tyre of the machine he got was punctured in dragging it through the window, but he got up and off, notwithstanding, with no further injury than a cut wrist. The steep foot of Haverstock Hill was impassable owing to several overturned horses, and my brother struck into Belsize Road.

So he got out of the fury of the panic, and, skirting the Edgware Road, reached Edgware about seven, fasting and wearied, but well ahead of the crowd. Along the road people were standing in the roadway, curious, wondering. He was passed by a number of cyclists, some horsemen, and two motor-cars. A mile from Edgware the rim of the wheel broke, and the machine became unrideable. He left it by the roadside and trudged through the village. There were shops half opened in the main street of the place, and people crowded on the pavement and in the doorways and windows, staring astonished at this extraordinary procession of fugitives that was beginning. He succeeded in getting some food at an inn.

For a time he remained in Edgware not knowing what next to do. The flying people increased in number. Many of them, like my brother, seemed inclined to loiter in the place. There was no fresh news of the invaders from Mars.

At that time the road was crowded, but as yet far from congested. Most of the fugitives at that hour were mounted on cycles, but there were soon motor-cars, hansom cabs, and carriages hurrying along, and the dust hung in heavy clouds along the road to St Albans.

It was perhaps a vague idea of making his way to Chelmsford, where some friends of his lived, that at last induced my brother to strike into a quiet lane running eastward. Presently he came upon a stile, and, crossing it, followed a footpath north-eastward. He passed near several farmhouses and some little places whose names he did not learn. He saw few fugitives until, in a grass lane towards High Barnet, he happened upon the two ladies who became his fellow-travellers. He came upon them just in time to save them.

He heard their screams, and, hurrying round the corner, saw a couple of men struggling to drag them out of the little pony-chaise[1] in which they had been driving, while a third with difficulty held the frightened pony's head. One of the ladies, a short woman dressed in white, was simply screaming; the other, a dark, slender figure, slashed at the man who gripped her arm with a whip she held in her disengaged hand.

My brother immediately grasped the situation, shouted, and hurried towards the struggle. One of the men desisted and turned towards him, and my brother, realizing from his antagonist's face that a fight was unavoidable, and being an expert boxer, went into him forthwith and sent him down against the wheel of the chaise.

It was no time for pugilistic chivalry, and my brother laid him quiet with a kick, and gripped the collar of the man who pulled at the slender lady's arm. He heard the clatter of hoofs, the whip stung across his face, a third antagonist struck him between the eyes, and the man he held wrenched himself free and made off down the lane in the direction from which he had come.

Partly stunned, he found himself facing the man who had held the horse's head, and became aware of the chaise receding from him down the lane, swaying from side to side, and with the women in it looking back. The man before him, a burly rough, tried to close, and he stopped him with a blow in the face. Then, realizing that he was deserted, he dodged round and made off down the lane after the chaise, with the sturdy man close behind him, and the fugitive, who had turned now, following remotely.

Suddenly he stumbled and fell; his immediate pursuer went headlong, and he rose to his feet to find himself with a couple of antagonists again. He would have had little chance against them had not the slender lady very pluckily pulled up and returned to his help. It seems she had had a revolver all this time, but it had been under the seat when she and her companion were attacked. She fired at six yards' distance, narrowly missing my brother. The less courageous of the robbers made off, and his companion followed him, cursing his cowardice. They both stopped in sight down the lane where the third man lay insensible.

'Take this!' said the slender lady, and she gave my brother her revolver.

'Go back to the chaise,' said my brother, wiping the blood from his split lip.

She turned without a word – they were both panting – and they went back to where the lady in white struggled to hold back the frightened pony.

The robbers had evidently had enough of it. When my brother looked again they were retreating.

'I'll sit here,' said my brother, 'if I may'; and he got upon the empty front seat. The lady looked over her shoulder.

'Give me the reins,' she said, and laid the whip along the pony's side. In another moment a bend in the road hid the three men from my brother's eyes.

So, quite unexpectedly, my brother found himself, panting, with a cut mouth, a bruised jaw, and bloodstained knuckles, driving along an unknown lane with these two women.

He learned they were the wife and the younger sister of a surgeon living at Stanmore, who had come in the small hours from a dangerous case at Pinner, and heard at some railway station on his way of the Martian advance. He had hurried home, roused the women – their servant had left them two days before – packed some provisions, put his revolver under the seat – luckily for my brother – and told them to drive on to Edgware, with the idea of getting a train there. He stopped behind to tell the neighbours. He would overtake them, he said, at about half-past four in the morning, and now it was nearly nine and they had seen nothing of him. They could not stop in Edgware because of the growing traffic through the place, and so they had come into this side lane.

That was the story they told my brother in fragments when presently they stopped again, nearer to New Barnet. He promised to stay with them, at least until they could determine what to do, or until the missing man arrived, and professed to be an expert shot with the revolver – a weapon strange to him – in order to give them confidence.

They made a sort of encampment by the wayside, and the pony became happy in the hedge. He told them of his own escape out of London, and all that he knew of these Martians and their ways. The sun crept higher in the sky, and after a time their talk died out and gave place to an uneasy state of anticipation. Several wayfarers came along the lane, and of these my brother gathered such news as he could. Every broken answer he had deepened his impression of the great disaster that had come on humanity, deepened his persuasion of the immediate necessity for prosecuting this flight. He urged the matter upon them.

'We have money,' said the slender woman, and hesitated.

Her eyes met my brother's, and her hesitation ended.

'So have I,' said my brother.

She explained that they had as much as thirty pounds in gold,[2] besides a five-pound note, and suggested that with that they might get upon a train at St Albans or New Barnet. My brother thought that was hopeless, seeing the fury of the Londoners to crowd upon the trains, and broached his own idea of striking across Essex towards Harwich and thence escaping from the country altogether.

Mrs Elphinstone – that was the name of the woman in white – would listen to no reasoning, and kept calling upon 'George'; but her sister-in-law was astonishingly quiet and deliberate, and at last agreed to my brother's suggestion. So, designing to cross the Great North Road, they went on towards Barnet, my brother leading the pony to save it as much as possible.

As the sun crept up the sky the day became excessively hot, and under foot a thick, whitish sand grew burning and blinding, so that they travelled only very slowly. The hedges were grey with dust. And as they advanced towards Barnet a tumultuous murmuring grew stronger.

They began to meet more people. For the most part these were staring before them, murmuring indistinct questions, jaded, haggard, unclean. One man in evening dress passed them on foot, his eyes on the ground. They heard his voice, and, looking back at him, saw one hand clutched in his hair and the other beating invisible things. His paroxysm of rage over, he went on his way without once looking back.

As my brother's party went on towards the crossroads to the south of Barnet they saw a woman approaching the road across some fields on their left, carrying a child and with two other children; and then passed a man in dirty black, with a thick stick in one hand and a small portmanteau in the other. Then round the corner of the lane, from between the villas that guarded it at its confluence with the highroad, came a little cart drawn by a sweating black pony and driven by a sallow youth in a bowler hat grey with dust. There were three girls, East End[3] factory girls, and a couple of little children crowded in the cart.

'This'll tike us rahnd Edgware?' asked the driver, wild-eyed, white-faced; and when my brother told him it would if he turned to the left, he whipped up at once without the formality of thanks.

My brother noticed a pale grey smoke or haze rising among the houses in front of them, and veiling the white façade of a terrace beyond the road that appeared between the backs of the villas. Mrs Elphinstone suddenly cried out at a number of tongues of smoky red flame leaping up above the houses in front of them against the hot, blue sky. The tumultuous noise resolved itself now into the disorderly mingling of many voices, the gride of many wheels, the creaking of wagons, and the staccato of hoofs. The lane came round sharply, not fifty yards from the crossroads.

'Good heavens!' cried Mrs Elphinstone. 'What is this you are driving us into?'

My brother stopped.

For the main road was a boiling stream of people, a torrent of human beings rushing northward, one pressing on another. A great bank of dust, white and luminous in the blaze of the sun, made everything within twenty feet of the ground grey and indistinct, and was perpetually renewed by the hurrying feet of a dense crowd of horses and of men and women on foot, and by the wheels of vehicles of every description.

'Way!' my brother heard voices crying. 'Make way!'

It was like riding into the smoke of a fire to approach the meeting-point of the lane and road; the crowd roared like a fire, and the dust was hot and pungent. And, indeed, a little way up the road a villa was burning and sending rolling masses of black smoke across the road to add to the confusion.

Two men came past them. Then a dirty woman, carrying a heavy bundle and weeping. A lost retriever dog, with hanging tongue, circled dubiously round them, scared and wretched, and fled at my brother's threat.

So much as they could see of the road Londonward between the houses to the right was a tumultuous stream of dirty, hurrying people, pent in between the villas on either side; the black heads, the crowded forms, grew into distinctness as they rushed towards the corner, hurried past, and merged their individuality again in a receding multitude that was swallowed up at last in a cloud of dust.

'Go on! Go on!' cried the voices. 'Way! Way!'

One man's hands pressed on the back of another. My brother stood at the pony's head. Irresistibly attracted, he advanced slowly, pace by pace, down the lane.

Edgware had been a scene of confusion, Chalk Farm a riotous tumult, but this was a whole population in movement. It is hard to imagine that host. It had no character of its own. The figures poured out past the corner, and receded with their backs to the group in the lane. Along the margin came those who were on foot, threatened by the wheels, stumbling in the ditches, blundering into one another.

The carts and carriages crowded close upon one another, making little way for those swifter and more impatient vehicles that darted forward every now and then when an opportunity showed itself of doing so, sending the people scattering against the fences and gates of the villas.

'Push on!' was the cry. 'Push on! They are coming!'

In one cart stood a blind man in the uniform of the Salvation Army, gesticulating with his crooked fingers and bawling, 'Eternity! eternity!' His voice was hoarse and very loud, so that my brother could hear him long after he was lost to sight in the dust. Some of the people who crowded in the carts whipped stupidly at their horses and quarrelled with other drivers; some sat motionless, staring at nothing with miserable eyes; some gnawed their hands with thirst, or lay prostrate in the bottoms of their conveyances. The horses' bits were covered with foam, their eyes bloodshot.

There were cabs, carriages, shop-carts, wagons, beyond counting; a mail-cart, a road-cleaner's cart marked 'Vestry[4] of St Pancras', a huge timber-wagon crowded with roughs. A brewer's dray rumbled by with its two near wheels splashed with fresh blood.

'Clear the way!' cried the voices. 'Clear the way!'

'Eter-nity! eter-nity!' came echoing down the road.

There were sad, haggard women tramping by, well dressed, with children that cried and stumbled, their dainty clothes smothered in dust, their weary faces smeared with tears. With many of these came men, sometimes helpful, sometimes lowering and savage. Fighting side by side with them pushed some weary street outcast in faded black rags, wide-eyed, loud-voiced, and foul-mouthed. There were sturdy workmen thrusting their way along, wretched, unkempt men clothed like clerks or shopmen, struggling spasmodically; a wounded soldier my brother noticed, men dressed in the clothes of railway porters, one wretched creature in a nightshirt with a coat thrown over it.

But varied as its composition was, certain things all that host had in common. There were fear and pain on their faces, and fear behind them. A tumult up the road, a quarrel for a place in a wagon, sent the whole host of them quickening their pace; even a man so scared and broken that his knees bent under him was galvanized for a moment into renewed activity. The heat and dust had already been at work upon this multitude. Their skins were dry, their lips black and cracked. They were all thirsty, weary, and footsore. And amid the various cries one heard disputes, reproaches, groans of weariness and fatigue; the voices of most of them were hoarse and weak. Through it all ran a refrain:

'Way! way! The Martians are coming!'

Few stopped and came aside from that flood. The lane opened slantingly into the main road with a narrow opening, and had a delusive appearance of coming from the direction of London. Yet a kind of eddy of people drove into its mouth; weaklings elbowed out of the stream, who for the most part rested but a moment before plunging into it again. A little way down the lane, with two friends bending over him, lay a man with a bare leg, wrapped about with bloody rags. He was a lucky man to have friends.

A little old man, with a grey military moustache and a filthy black frock-coat, limped out and sat down beside the trap, removed his boot – his sock was bloodstained – shook out a pebble, and hobbled on again; and then a little girl of eight or nine, all alone, threw herself under the hedge close by my brother, weeping.

'I can't go on! I can't go on!'

My brother woke from his torpor of astonishment and lifted her up, speaking gently to her, and carried her to Miss Elphinstone. So soon as my brother touched her she became quite still, as if frightened.

'Ellen!' shrieked a woman in the crowd, with tears in her voice – 'Ellen!' And the child suddenly darted away from my brother, crying 'Mother!'

'They are coming,' said a man on horseback, riding past along the lane.

'Out of the way, there!' bawled a coachman, towering high; and my brother saw a closed carriage turning into the lane.

The people crushed back on one another to avoid the horse. My brother pushed the pony and chaise back into the hedge, and the man drove by and stopped at the turn of the way. It was a carriage, with a pole for a pair of horses, but only one was in the traces. My brother saw dimly through the dust that two men lifted out something on a white stretcher and put it gently on the grass beneath the privet hedge.

One of the men came running to my brother.

'Where is there any water?' he said. 'He is dying fast, and very thirsty. It is Lord Garrick.'

'Lord Garrick!' said my brother – 'the Chief Justice?'[5]

'The water?' he said.

'There may be a tap,' said my brother, 'in some of the houses. We have no water. I dare not leave my people.'

The man pushed against the crowd towards the gate of the corner house.

'Go on!' said the people, thrusting at him. 'They are coming! Go on!'

Then my brother's attention was distracted by a bearded, eagle-faced man lugging a small handbag, which split even as my brother's eyes rested on it and disgorged a mass of sovereigns that seemed to break up into separate coins as it struck the ground. They rolled hither and thither among the struggling feet of men and horses. The man stopped and looked stupidly at the heap, and the shaft of a cab struck his shoulder and sent him reeling. He gave a shriek and dodged back, and a cart-wheel shaved him narrowly.

'Way!' cried the men all about him. 'Make way!'

So soon as the cab had passed, he flung himself, with both hands open, upon the heap of coins, and began thrusting handfuls in his pocket. A horse rose close upon him, and in another moment half rising, he had been borne down under the horse's hoofs.

'Stop!' screamed my brother, and pushing a woman out of his way, tried to clutch the bit of the horse.

Before he could get to it, he heard a scream under the wheels, and saw through the dust the rim passing over the poor wretch's back. The driver of the cart slashed his whip at my brother, who ran round behind the cart. The multitudinous shouting confused his ears. The man was writhing in the dust among his scattered money, unable to rise, for the wheel had broken his back, and his lower limbs lay limp and dead. My brother stood up and yelled at the next driver, and a man on a black horse came to his assistance.

'Get him out of the road,' said he; and, clutching the man's collar with his free hand, my brother lugged him sideways. But he still clutched after his money, and regarded my brother fiercely, hammering at his arm with a handful of gold. 'Go on! Go on!' shouted angry voices behind. 'Way! Way!'

There was a smash as the pole of a carriage crashed into the cart that the man on horseback stopped. My brother looked up, and the man with the gold twisted his head round and bit the wrist that held his collar. There was a concussion, and the black horse came staggering sideways, and the cart-horse pushed beside it. A hoof missed my brother's foot by a hair's breadth. He released his grip on the fallen man and jumped back. He saw anger change to terror on the face of the poor wretch on the ground, and in a moment he was hidden and my brother was borne backward and carried past the entrance of the lane, and had to fight hard in the torrent to recover it.

He saw Miss Elphinstone covering her eyes, and a little child, with all a child's want of sympathetic imagination, staring with dilated eyes at a dusty something that lay black and still, ground and crushed under the rolling wheels. 'Let us go back!' he shouted, and began turning the pony round. 'We cannot cross this – hell,' he said; and they went back a hundred yards the way they had come, until the fighting crowd was hidden. As they passed the bend in the lane my brother saw the face of the dying man in the ditch under the privet, deadly white and drawn, and shining with perspiration. The two women sat silent, crouching in their seats and shivering.

Then beyond the bend my brother stopped again. Miss Elphinstone was white and pale, and her sister-in-law sat weeping, too wretched even to call upon 'George'. My brother was horrified and perplexed. So soon as they had retreated he realized how urgent and unavoidable it was to attempt this crossing. He turned to Miss Elphinstone, suddenly resolute.

'We must go that way,' he said, and led the pony round again.

For the second time that day this girl proved her quality. To force their way into the torrent of people, my brother plunged into the traffic and held back a cab-horse, while she drove the pony across its head. A wagon locked wheels for a moment and ripped a long splinter from the chaise. In another moment they were caught and swept forward by the stream. My brother, with the cabman's whip-marks red across his face and hands, scrambled into the chaise and took the reins from her.

'Point the revolver at the man behind,' he said, giving it to her, 'if he presses us too hard. No! – point it at his horse.'

Then he began to look out for a chance of edging to the right across the road. But once in the stream he seemed to lose volition, to become a part of that dusty rout. They swept through Chipping Barnet with the torrent; they were nearly a mile beyond the centre of the town before they had fought across to the opposite side of the way. It was din and confusion indescribable; but in and beyond the town the road forks repeatedly, and this to some extent relieved the stress.

They struck eastward through Hadley, and there on either side of the road, and at another place further on they came upon a great multitude of people drinking at the stream, some fighting to come at the water. And further on, from a hill near East Barnet, they saw two trains running slowly one after the other without signal or order – trains swarming with people, with men even among the coals behind the engines – going northward along the Great Northern Railway. My brother supposes they must have filled outside London, for at that time the furious terror of the people had rendered the central termini impossible.

Near this place they halted for the rest of the afternoon, for the violence of the day had already utterly exhausted all three of them. They began to suffer the beginnings of hunger; the night was cold, and none of them dared to sleep. And in the evening many people came hurrying along the road near by their stopping-place, fleeing from unknown dangers before them, and going in the direction from which my brother had come.

THE 'THUNDER CHILD'

Had the Martians aimed only at destruction, they might on Monday have annihilated the entire population of London, as it spread itself slowly through the home counties.[1] Not only along the road through Barnet, but also through Edgware and Waltham Abbey, and along the roads eastward to Southend and Shoeburyness, and south of the Thames to Deal and Broadstairs, poured the same frantic rout. If one could have hung that June morning in a balloon in the blazing blue above London, every northward and eastward road running out of the tangled maze of streets would have seemed stippled black with the streaming fugitives, each dot a human agony of terror and physical distress. I have set forth at length in the last chapter my brother's account of the road through Chipping Barnet, in order that my readers may realize how that swarming of black dots appeared to one of those concerned. Never before in the history of the world had such a mass of human beings moved and suffered together. The legendary hosts of Goths and Huns,[2] the hugest armies Asia has ever seen, would have been but a drop in that current. And this was no disciplined march; it was a stampede – a stampede gigantic and terrible – without order and without a goal, six million people, unarmed and unprovisioned, driving headlong. It was the beginning of the rout of civilization, of the massacre of mankind.

Directly below him the balloonist would have seen the network of streets far and wide, houses, churches, squares, crescents, gardens – already derelict – spread out like a huge map, and in the southward *blotted*. Over Ealing, Richmond, Wimbledon, it would have seemed as if some monstrous pen had flung ink upon the chart. Steadily, incessantly, each black splash grew and spread, shooting out ramifications this way and that, now banking itself against rising ground, now pouring swiftly over a crest into a new-found valley, exactly as a gout of ink would spread itself upon blotting-paper.

And beyond, over the blue hills that rise southward of the river, the glittering Martians went to and fro, calmly and methodically spreading their poison-cloud over this patch of country and then over that, laying it again with their steam-jets when it had served its purpose, and taking possession of the conquered country. They do not seem to have aimed at extermination so much as at complete demoralization and the destruction of any opposition. They exploded any stores of powder they came upon, cut every telegraph, and wrecked the railways here and there. They were hamstringing mankind. They seemed in no hurry to extend the field of their operations, and did not come beyond the central part of London all that day. It is possible that a very considerable number of people in London stuck to their houses through Monday morning. Certain it is that many died at home, suffocated by the Black Smoke.

Until about midday the Pool of London[3] was an astonishing scene. Steamboats and shipping of all sorts lay there, tempted by the enormous sums of money offered by fugitives, and it is said that many who swam out to these vessels were thrust off with boat-hooks and drowned. About one o'clock in the afternoon the thinning remnant of a cloud of the black vapour appeared between the arches of Blackfriars Bridge. At that the Pool became a scene of mad confusion, fighting, and collision, and for some time a multitude of boats and barges jammed in the northern arch of the Tower Bridge, and the sailors and lightermen[4] had to fight savagely against the people who swarmed upon them from the river front. People were actually clambering down the piers of the bridge from above.

When, an hour later, a Martian appeared beyond the Clock Tower and waded down the river, nothing but wreckage floated above Limehouse.

Of the falling of the fifth cylinder I have presently to tell. The sixth star fell at Wimbledon. My brother, keeping watch beside the women in the chaise in a meadow, saw the green flash of it far beyond the hills. On Tuesday the little party, still set upon getting across the sea, made its way through the swarming country towards Colchester. The news that the Martians were now in possession of the whole of London was confirmed. They had been seen at Highgate, and even, it was said, at Neasden. But they did not come into my brother's view until the morrow.

That day the scattered multitudes began to realize the urgent need of provisions. As they grew hungry the rights of property ceased to be regarded. Farmers were out to defend their cattle-sheds, granaries, and ripening root crops with arms in their hands. A number of people now, like my brother, had their faces eastward, and there were some desperate souls even going back towards London to get food. These were chiefly people from the northern suburbs, whose knowledge of the Black Smoke came by hearsay. He heard that about half the members of the government had gathered at Birmingham, and that enormous quantities of high explosives were being prepared to be used in automatic mines across the Midland counties.

He was also told that the Midland Railway Company had replaced the desertions of the first day's panic, had resumed traffic, and was running northward trains from St Albans to relieve the congestion of the home counties. There was also a placard in Chipping Ongar announcing that large stores of flour were available in the northern towns, and that within twenty-four hours bread would be distributed among the starving people in the neighbourhood. But this intelligence did not deter him from the plan of escape he had formed, and the three pressed eastward all day, and heard no more of the bread distribution than this promise. Nor, as a matter of fact, did anyone else hear more of it. That night fell the seventh star, falling upon Primrose Hill. It fell while Miss Elphinstone was watching, for she took that duty alternately with my brother. She saw it.

On Wednesday the three fugitives – they had passed the night in a field of unripe wheat – reached Chelmsford, and there a body of the inhabitants, calling itself the Committee of Public Supply,[5] seized the pony as provisions, and would give nothing in exchange for it but the promise of a share in it the next day. Here there were rumours of Martians at Epping, and news of the destruction of Waltham Abbey Powder Mills[6] in a vain attempt to blow up one of the invaders.

People were watching for Martians here from the church towers. My brother, very luckily for him as it chanced, preferred to push on at once to the coast rather than wait for food, although all three of them were very hungry. By midday they passed through Tillingham, which, strangely enough, seemed to be quite silent and deserted, save for a few furtive plunderers hunting for food. Near Tillingham they suddenly came in sight of the sea, and the most amazing crowd of shipping of all sorts that it is possible to imagine.

For after the sailors could no longer come up the Thames, they came on to the Essex coast, to Harwich and Walton and Clacton, and afterwards to Foulness and Shoebury, to bring off the people. They lay in a huge sickle-shaped curve that vanished into mist at last towards the Naze. Close inshore was a multitude of fishing-smacks – English, Scotch, French, Dutch, and Swedish; steam-launches from the Thames, yachts, electric boats;[7] and beyond were ships of large burden, a multitude of filthy colliers, trim merchantmen, cattle-ships, passenger-boats, petroleum-tanks, ocean tramps, an old white transport even, neat white and grey liners from Southampton and Hamburg; and along the blue coast across the Blackwater my brother could make out dimly a dense swarm of boats chaffering with the people on the beach, a swarm which also extended up the Blackwater almost to Maldon.

About a couple of miles out lay an ironclad, very low in the water, almost, to my brother's perception, like a waterlogged ship. This was the ram *Thunder Child*. It was the only warship in sight, but far away to the right over the smooth surface of the sea – for that day there was a dead calm – lay a serpent of black smoke to mark the next ironclads of the Channel Fleet, which hovered in an extended line, steam up and ready for action, across the Thames estuary during the course of the Martian conquest, vigilant and yet powerless to prevent it.

At the sight of the sea, Mrs Elphinstone, in spite of the

assurances of her sister-in-law, gave way to panic. She had
never been out of England before, she would rather die than
trust herself friendless in a foreign country, and so forth. She
seemed, poor woman, to imagine that the French and the
Martians might prove very similar. She had been growing increasingly hysterical, fearful, and depressed during the two
days' journeyings. Her great idea was to return to Stanmore.
Things had been always well and safe at Stanmore. They would
find George at Stanmore.

It was with the greatest difficulty they could get her down to
the beach, where presently my brother succeeded in attracting
the attention of some men on a paddle-steamer from the
Thames. They sent a boat and drove a bargain for thirty-six
pounds for the three. The steamer was going, these men said,
to Ostend.

It was about two o'clock when my brother, having paid their
fares at the gangway, found himself safely aboard the steamboat
with his charges. There was food aboard, albeit at exorbitant
prices, and the three of them contrived to eat a meal on one of
the seats forward.

There were already a couple of score of passengers aboard,
some of whom had expended their last money in securing a
passage, but the captain lay off the Blackwater until five in the
afternoon, picking up passengers until the seated decks were
even dangerously crowded. He would probably have remained
longer had it not been for the sound of guns that began about
that hour in the south. As if in answer, the ironclad seaward
fired a small gun and hoisted a string of flags. A jet of smoke
sprang out of her funnels.

Some of the passengers were of opinion that this firing came
from Shoeburyness, until it was noticed that it was growing
louder. At the same time, far away in the south-east, the masts
and upper-works of three ironclads rose one after the other out
of the sea, beneath clouds of black smoke. But my brother's
attention speedily reverted to the distant firing in the south.
He fancied he saw a column of smoke rising out of the distant
grey haze.

The little steamer was already flapping her way eastward of

the big crescent of shipping, and the low Essex coast was growing blue and hazy, when a Martian appeared, small and faint
in the remote distance, advancing along the muddy coast from
the direction of Foulness. At that the captain on the bridge
swore at the top of his voice with fear and anger at his own
delay, and the paddles seemed infected with his terror. Every
soul aboard stood at the bulwarks or on the seats of the steamer
and stared at that distant shape, higher than the trees or church
towers inland, and advancing with a leisurely parody of a
human stride.

It was the first Martian my brother had seen, and he stood,
more amazed than terrified, watching this Titan advancing
deliberately towards the shipping, wading further and further
into the water as the coast fell away. Then, far away beyond
the Crouch, came another, striding over some stunted trees,
and then yet another, still further off, wading deeply through a
shiny mud-flat that seemed to hang halfway up between sea
and sky. They were all stalking seaward, as if to intercept the
escape of the multitudinous vessels that were crowded between
Foulness and the Naze. In spite of the throbbing exertions of
the engines of the little paddle-boat, and the pouring foam
that her wheels flung behind her, she receded with terrifying
slowness from this ominous advance.

Glancing north-westward, my brother saw the large crescent
of shipping already writhing with the approaching terror; one
ship passing behind another, another coming round from
broadside to end on, steamships whistling and giving off volumes of steam, sails being let out, launches rushing hither and
thither. He was so fascinated by this and by the creeping danger
away to the left that he had no eyes for anything seaward. And
then a swift movement of the steamboat (she had suddenly
come round to avoid being run down) flung him headlong from
the seat upon which he was standing. There was a shouting all
about him, a trampling of feet, and a cheer that seemed to be
answered faintly. The steamboat lurched and rolled him over
upon his hands.

He sprang to his feet and saw to starboard, and not a hundred
yards from their heeling, pitching boat, a vast iron bulk like the

blade of a plough tearing through the water, tossing it on either side in huge waves of foam that leapt towards the steamer, flinging her paddles helplessly in the air, and then sucking her deck down almost to the waterline.

A douche of spray blinded my brother for a moment. When his eyes were clear again he saw the monster had passed and was rushing landward. Big iron upper-works rose out of this headlong structure, and from that twin funnels projected and spat a smoking blast shot with fire. It was the torpedo-ram, *Thunder Child*, steaming headlong, coming to the rescue of the threatened shipping.

Keeping his footing on the heaving deck by clutching the bulwarks, my brother looked past this charging leviathan at the Martians again, and he saw the three of them now close together, and standing so far out to sea that their tripod supports were almost entirely submerged. Thus sunken, and seen in remote perspective, they appeared far less formidable than the huge iron bulk in whose wake the steamer was pitching so helplessly. It would seem they were regarding this new antagonist with astonishment. To their intelligence, it may be, the giant was even such another as themselves. The *Thunder Child* fired no gun, but simply drove full speed towards them. It was probably her not firing that enabled her to get so near the enemy as she did. They did not know what to make of her. One shell, and they would have sent her to the bottom forthwith with the Heat-Ray.

She was steaming at such a pace that in a minute she seemed halfway between the steamboat and the Martians – a diminishing black bulk against the receding horizontal expanse of the Essex coast.

Suddenly the foremost Martian lowered his tube and discharged a canister of the black gas at the ironclad. It hit her larboard side and glanced off in an inky jet that rolled away to seaward, an unfolding torrent of Black Smoke, from which the ironclad drove clear. To the watchers from the steamer, low in the water and with the sun in their eyes, it seemed as though she were already among the Martians.

They saw the gaunt figures separating and rising out of the

water as they retreated shoreward, and one of them raised the camera-like generator of the Heat-Ray. He held it pointing obliquely downward, and a bank of steam sprang from the water at its touch. It must have driven through the iron of the ship's side like a white-hot iron rod through paper.

A flicker of flame went up through the rising steam, and then the Martian reeled and staggered. In another moment he was cut down, and a great body of water and steam shot high in the air. The guns of the *Thunder Child* sounded through the reek, going off one after the other, and one shot splashed the water high close by the steamer, ricocheted towards the other flying ships to the north, and smashed a smack to matchwood.

But no one heeded that very much. At the sight of the Martian's collapse the captain on the bridge yelled inarticulately, and all the crowding passengers on the steamer's stern shouted together. And then they yelled again. For, surging out beyond the white tumult drove something long and black, the flames streaming from its middle parts, its ventilators and funnels spouting fire.

She was alive still; the steering gear, it seems, was intact and her engines working. She headed straight for a second Martian, and was within a hundred yards of him when the Heat-Ray came to bear. Then with a violent thud, a blinding flash, her decks, her funnels, leaped upward. The Martian staggered with the violence of her explosion, and in another moment the flaming wreckage, still driving forward with the impetus of its pace, had struck him and crumpled him up like a thing of cardboard. My brother shouted involuntarily. A boiling tumult of steam hid everything again.

'Two!' yelled the captain.

Everyone was shouting. The whole steamer from end to end rang with frantic cheering that was taken up first by one and then by all in the crowding multitude of ships and boats that was driving out to sea.

The steam hung upon the water for many minutes, hiding the third Martian and the coast altogether. And all this time the boat was paddling steadily out to sea and away from the fight; and when at last the confusion cleared, the drifting bank of black vapour intervened, and nothing of the *Thunder Child* could be made out, nor could the third Martian be seen. But the ironclads to seaward were now quite close and standing in towards shore past the steamboat.

The little vessel continued to beat its way seaward, and the ironclads receded slowly towards the coast, which was hidden still by a marbled bank of vapour, part steam, part black gas, eddying and combining in the strangest ways. The fleet of refugees was scattering to the north-east; several smacks were sailing between the ironclads and the steamboat. After a time, and before they reached the sinking cloud-bank, the warships turned northward, and then abruptly went about and passed into the thickening haze of evening southward. The coast grew faint, and at last indistinguishable amid the low banks of clouds that were gathering about the sinking sun.

Then suddenly out of the golden haze of the sunset came the vibration of guns, and a form of black shadows moving. Everyone struggled to the rail of the steamer and peered into the blinding furnace of the west, but nothing was to be distinguished clearly. A mass of smoke rose slantingly and barred the face of the sun. The steamboat throbbed on its way through an interminable suspense.

The sun sank into grey clouds, the sky flushed and darkened, the evening star trembled into sight. It was deep twilight when the captain cried out and pointed. My brother strained his eyes. Something rushed up into the sky out of the greyness – rushed slantingly upward and very swiftly into the luminous clearness above the clouds in the western sky; something flat and broad and very large, that swept round in a vast curve, grew smaller, sank slowly, and vanished again into the grey mystery of the night. And as it flew it rained down darkness upon the land.[8]

BOOK II

THE EARTH UNDER
THE MARTIANS

I

UNDER FOOT

In the first book I have wandered so much from my own adventures to tell of the experiences of my brother, that all through the last two chapters I and the curate have been lurking in the empty house at Halliford, whither we fled to escape the Black Smoke. There I will resume. We stopped there all Sunday night and all the next day – the day of the panic – in a little island of daylight, cut off by the Black Smoke from the rest of the world. We could do nothing but wait in an aching inactivity during those two weary days.

My mind was occupied by anxiety for my wife. I figured her at Leatherhead, terrified, in danger, mourning me already as a dead man. I paced the rooms and cried aloud when I thought of how I was cut off from her, of all that might happen to her in my absence. My cousin I knew was brave enough for any emergency, but he was not the sort of man to realize danger quickly, to rise promptly. What was needed now was not bravery, but circumspection. My only consolation was to believe that the Martians were moving Londonward and away from her. Such vague anxieties keep the mind sensitive and painful. I grew very weary and irritable with the curate's perpetual ejaculations, I tired of the sight of his selfish despair. After some ineffectual remonstrance I kept away from him, staying in a room – evidently a children's schoolroom – containing globes, forms, and copy-books. When he followed me thither, I went to a box-room at the top of the house and, in order to be alone with my aching miseries, locked myself in.

We were hopelessly hemmed in by the Black Smoke all that day and the morning of the next. There were signs of people in the next house on Sunday evening – a face at a window and moving lights, and later the slamming of a door. But I do not know who these people were, nor what became of them. We saw nothing of them next day. The Black Smoke drifted slowly riverward all through Monday morning, creeping nearer and nearer to us, driving at last along the roadway outside the house that hid us.

A Martian came across the fields about midday, laying the stuff with a jet of superheated steam that hissed against the walls, smashed all the windows it touched, and scalded the curate's hand as he fled out of the front room. When at last we crept across the sodden rooms and looked out again, the country northward was as though a black snowstorm had passed over it. Looking towards the river, we were astonished to see an unaccountable redness mingling with the black of the scorched meadows.

For a time we did not see how this change affected our position, save that we were relieved of our fear of the Black Smoke. But later I perceived that we were no longer hemmed in, that now we might get away. So soon as I realized that the way of escape was open, my dream of action returned. But the curate was lethargic, unreasonable.

'We are safe here,' he repeated; 'safe here.'

I resolved to leave him – would that I had! Wiser now for the artilleryman's teaching, I sought out food and drink. I had found oil and rags for my burns, and I also took a hat and a flannel shirt that I found in one of the bedrooms. When it was clear to him that I meant to go alone – had reconciled myself to going alone – he suddenly roused himself to come. And, all being quiet throughout the afternoon, we started about five o'clock, as I should judge, along the blackened road to Sunbury.

In Sunbury, and at intervals along the road, were dead bodies lying in contorted attitudes, horses as well as men, overturned carts and luggage, all covered thickly with black dust. That pall of cindery powder made me think of what I had read of the destruction of Pompeii.[1] We got to Hampton Court without misadventure, our minds full of strange and unfamiliar appearances, and at Hampton Court our eyes were relieved to find a patch of green that had escaped the suffocating drift. We went through Bushey Park, with its deer going to and fro under the chestnuts, and some men and women hurrying in the distance towards Hampton, and so we came to Twickenham. These were the first people we saw.

Away across the road the woods beyond Ham and Petersham were still afire. Twickenham was uninjured by either Heat-Ray or Black Smoke, and there were more people about here, though none could give us news. For the most part they were like ourselves, taking advantage of a lull to shift their quarters. I have an impression that many of the houses here were still occupied by scared inhabitants, too frightened even for flight. Here, too, the evidence of a hasty rout was abundant along the road. I remember most vividly three smashed bicycles in a heap, pounded into the road by the wheels of subsequent carts. We crossed Richmond Bridge about half-past eight. We hurried across the exposed bridge, of course, but I noticed floating down the stream a number of red masses, some many feet across. I did not know what these were – there was no time for scrutiny – and I put a more horrible interpretation on them than they deserved. Here again on the Surrey side were black dust that had once been smoke, and dead bodies – a heap near the approach to the station; but we had no glimpse of the Martians until we were some way towards Barnes.

We saw in the blackened distance a group of three people running down a side street towards the river, but otherwise it seemed deserted. Up the hill Richmond town was burning briskly; outside the town of Richmond there was no trace of the Black Smoke.

Then, suddenly, as we approached Kew, came a number of people running, and the upper-works of a Martian fighting-machine loomed in sight over the housetops, not a hundred yards away from us. We stood aghast at our danger, and had the Martian looked down we must immediately have perished. We were so terrified that we dared not go on, but turned aside and hid in a shed in a garden. There the curate crouched, weeping silently, and refusing to stir again.

But my fixed idea of reaching Leatherhead would not let me

rest, and in the twilight I ventured out again. I went through a shrubbery, and along a passage beside a big house standing in its own grounds, and so emerged upon the road towards Kew. The curate I left in the shed, but he came hurrying after me.

That second start was the most foolhardy thing I ever did. For it was manifest the Martians were about us. No sooner had the curate overtaken me than we saw either the fighting-machine we had seen before or another, far away across the meadows in the direction of Kew Lodge. Four or five little black figures hurried before it across the green-grey of the field, and in a moment it was evident this Martian pursued them. In three strides he was among them, and they ran radiating from his feet in all directions. He used no Heat-Ray to destroy them, but picked them up one by one. Apparently he tossed them into the great metallic carrier which projected behind him, much as a workman's basket hangs over his shoulder.

It was the first time I realized that the Martians might have any other purpose than destruction with defeated humanity. We stood for a moment petrified, then turned and fled through a gate behind us into a walled garden, fell into, rather than found, a fortunate ditch, and lay there, scarce daring to whisper to each other until the stars were out.

I suppose it was nearly eleven o'clock before we gathered courage to start again, no longer venturing into the road, but sneaking along hedgerows and through plantations, and watching keenly through the darkness, he on the right and I on the left, for the Martians, who seemed to be all about us. In one place we blundered upon a scorched and blackened area, now cooling and ashen, and a number of scattered dead bodies of men, burnt horribly about the heads and trunks, but with their legs and boots mostly intact; and of dead horses, fifty feet, perhaps, behind a line of four ripped guns and smashed gun-carriages.

Sheen, it seemed, had escaped destruction, but the place was silent and deserted. Here we happened on no dead, though the night was too dark for us to see into the side-roads of the place. In Sheen my companion suddenly complained of faintness and thirst, and we decided to try one of the houses.

The first house we entered, after a little difficulty with the window, was a small semi-detached villa,[2] and I found nothing eatable left in the place but some mouldy cheese. There was, however, water to drink, and I took a hatchet, which promised to be useful in our next house-breaking.

We then crossed to a place where the road turns towards Mortlake. Here there stood a white house within a walled garden, and in the pantry of this domicile we found a store of food – two loaves of bread in a pan, an uncooked steak, and the half of a ham. I give this catalogue so precisely because, as it happened, we were destined to subsist upon this store for the next fortnight. Bottled beer stood under a shelf, and there were two bags of haricot beans and some limp lettuces. This pantry opened into a kind of wash-up kitchen, and in this was fire-wood; there was also a cupboard, in which we found nearly a dozen of burgundy, tinned soups and salmon, and two tins of biscuits.

We sat in the adjacent kitchen in the dark – for we dared not strike a light – and ate bread and ham, and drank beer out of the same bottle. The curate, who was still timorous and restless, was now, oddly enough, for pushing on, and I was urging him to keep up his strength by eating, when the thing happened that was to imprison us.

'It can't be midnight yet,' I said, and then came a blinding glare of vivid green light. Everything in the kitchen leapt out, clearly visible in green and black, and vanished again. And then followed such a concussion as I have never heard before or since. So close on the heels of this as to seem instantaneous came a thud behind me, a clash of glass, a crash and rattle of falling masonry all about us, and the plaster of the ceiling came down upon us, smashing into a multitude of fragments upon our heads. I was knocked headlong across the floor against the oven handle and stunned. I was insensible for a long time, the curate told me, and when I came to we were in darkness again, and he, with a face wet, as I found afterwards, with blood from a cut forehead, was dabbing water over me.

For some time I could not recollect what had happened. Then things came to me slowly. A bruise on my temple asserted itself.

'Are you better?' asked the curate, in a whisper.

At last I answered him. I sat up.

'Don't move,' he said. 'The floor is covered with smashed crockery from the dresser. You can't possibly move without making a noise, and I fancy *they* are outside.'

We both sat quite silent, so that we could scarcely hear each other breathing. Everything seemed deadly still, but once something near us, some plaster or broken brickwork, slid down with a rumbling sound. Outside and very near was an intermittent, metallic rattle.

'That!' said the curate, when presently it happened again.

'Yes,' I said. 'But what is it?'

'A Martian!' said the curate.

I listened again.

'It was not like the Heat-Ray,' I said, and for a time I was inclined to think one of the great fighting-machines had stumbled against the house, as I had seen one stumble against the tower of Shepperton Church.

Our situation was so strange and incomprehensible that for three or four hours, until the dawn came, we scarcely moved. And then the light filtered in, not through the window, which remained black, but through a triangular aperture between a beam and a heap of broken bricks in the wall behind us. The interior of the kitchen we now saw greyly for the first time.

The window had been burst in by a mass of garden mould, which flowed over the table upon which we had been sitting and lay about our feet. Outside, the soil was banked high against the house. At the top of the window-frame we could see an uprooted drainpipe. The floor was littered with smashed hardware; the end of the kitchen towards the house was broken into, and since the daylight shone in there, it was evident the greater part of the house had collapsed. Contrasting vividly with this ruin was the neat dresser, stained in the fashion, pale green, and with a number of copper and tin vessels below it, the wallpaper imitating blue and white tiles, and a couple of coloured supplements[3] fluttering from the walls above the kitchen range.

As the dawn grew clearer, we saw through the gap in the

wall the body of a Martian, standing sentinel, I suppose, over the still glowing cylinder. At the sight of that we crawled as circumspectly as possible out of the twilight of the kitchen into the darkness of the scullery.

Abruptly the right interpretation dawned upon my mind.

'The fifth cylinder,' I whispered, 'the fifth shot from Mars, has struck this house and buried us under the ruins!'

For a time the curate was silent, and then he whispered:

'God have mercy upon us!'

I heard him presently whimpering to himself.

Save for that sound we lay quite still in the scullery; I for my part scarce dared breathe, and sat with my eyes fixed on the faint light of the kitchen door. I could just see the curate's face, a dim, oval shape, and his collar and cuffs. Outside there began a metallic hammering, then a violent hooting, and then again, after a quiet interval, a hissing like the hissing of an engine. These noises, for the most part problematical, continued intermittently, and seemed if anything to increase in number as time wore on. Presently a measured thudding, and a vibration that made everything about us quiver and the vessels in the pantry ring and shift, began and continued. Once the light was eclipsed, and the ghostly kitchen doorway became absolutely dark. For many hours we must have crouched there, silent and shivering, until our tired attention failed . . .

At last I found myself awake and very hungry. I am inclined to believe we must have spent the greater portion of a day before that awakening. My hunger was at a stride so insistent that it moved me to action. I told the curate I was going to seek food, and felt my way towards the pantry. He made me no answer, but so soon as I began eating the faint noise I made stirred him up and I heard him crawling after me.

2

WHAT WE SAW FROM THE RUINED HOUSE

After eating we crept back to the scullery, and there I must have dozed again, for when presently I looked round I was alone. The thudding vibration continued with wearisome persistence. I whispered for the curate several times, and at last felt my way to the door of the kitchen. It was still daylight, and I perceived him across the room, lying against the triangular hole that looked out upon the Martians. His shoulders were hunched, so that his head was hidden from me.

I could hear a number of noises almost like those in an engine-shed, and the place rocked with that beating thud. Through the aperture in the wall I could see the top of a tree touched with gold, and the warm blue of a tranquil evening sky. For a minute or so I remained watching the curate, and then I advanced, crouching and stepping with extreme care amid the broken crockery that littered the floor.

I touched the curate's leg, and he started so violently that a mass of plaster went sliding down outside and fell with a loud impact. I gripped his arm, fearing he might cry out, and for a long time we crouched motionless. Then I turned to see how much of our rampart remained. The detachment of the plaster had left a vertical slit open in the débris, and by raising myself cautiously across a beam I was able to see out of this gap into what had been overnight a quiet suburban roadway. Vast, indeed, was the change that we beheld.

The fifth cylinder must have fallen right into the midst of the house we had first visited. The building had vanished, completely smashed, pulverized, and dispersed by the blow. The cylinder lay now far beneath the original foundations – deep in a hole, already vastly larger than the pit I had looked into at Woking. The earth all round it had splashed under that tremendous impact – 'splashed' is the only word – and lay in heaped piles that hid the masses of the adjacent houses. It had behaved exactly like mud under the violent blow of a hammer. Our house had collapsed backward; the front portion, even on the ground floor, had been destroyed completely; by a chance the kitchen and scullery had escaped, and stood buried now under soil and ruins, closed in by tons of earth on every side save towards the cylinder. Over that aspect we hung now on the very edge of the great circular pit the Martians were engaged in making. The heavy beating sound was evidently just behind us, and ever and again a bright green vapour drove up like a veil across our peephole.

The cylinder was already opened in the centre of the pit, and on the further edge of the pit, amid the smashed and gravel-heaped shrubbery, one of the great fighting-machines, deserted by its occupant, stood stiff and tall against the evening sky. At first I scarcely noticed the pit and the cylinder, although it has been convenient to describe them first, on account of the extraordinary glittering mechanism I saw busy in the excavation, and on account of the strange creatures that were crawling slowly and painfully across the heaped mould near it.

The mechanism it certainly was that held my attention first. It was one of those complicated fabrics that have since been called handling-machines, and the study of which has already given such an enormous impetus to terrestrial invention. As it dawned upon me first it presented a sort of metallic spider with five jointed, agile legs, and with an extraordinary number of jointed levers, bars, and reaching and clutching tentacles about its body. Most of its arms were retracted, but with three long tentacles it was fishing out a number of rods, plates, and bars which lined the covering, and apparently strengthened the walls, of the cylinder. These, as it extracted them, were lifted out and deposited upon a level surface of earth behind it.

Its motion was so swift, complex, and perfect that at first I did not see it as a machine, in spite of its metallic glitter. The fighting-machines were co-ordinated and animated to an extraordinary pitch, but nothing to compare with this. People who have never seen these structures, and have only the ill-imagined efforts of artists or the imperfect descriptions of such eye-witnesses as myself to go upon, scarcely realize that living quality.

I recall particularly the illustration of one of the first pamphlets[1] to give a consecutive account of the war. The artist had evidently made a hasty study of one of the fighting-machines, and there his knowledge ended. He presented them as tilted, stiff tripods, without either flexibility or subtlety, and with an altogether misleading monotony of effect. The pamphlet containing these renderings had a considerable vogue, and I mention them here simply to warn the reader against the impression they may have created. They were no more like the Martians I saw in action than a Dutch doll is like a human being. To my mind, the pamphlet would have been much better without them.

At first, I say, the handling-machine did not impress me as a machine, but as a crab-like creature with a glittering integument, the controlling Martian whose delicate tentacles actuated its movements seeming to be simply the equivalent of the crab's cerebral portion. But then I perceived the resemblance of its grey-brown, shiny, leathery integument to that of the other sprawling bodies beyond, and the true nature of this dexterous workman dawned upon me. With that realization my interest shifted to those other creatures, the real Martians. Already I had had a transient impression of these, and the first nausea no longer obscured my observation. Moreover, I was concealed and motionless, and under no urgency of action.

They were, I now saw, the most unearthly creatures it is possible to conceive. They were huge round bodies – or, rather, heads – about four feet in diameter, each body having in front of it a face. This face had no nostrils – indeed, the Martians do not seem to have had any sense of smell – but it had a pair of very large, dark-coloured eyes, and just beneath this a kind of fleshy beak. In the back of this head or body – I scarcely know how to speak of it – was the single tight tympanic surface, since known to be anatomically an ear, though it must have been almost useless in our denser air. In a group round the mouth were sixteen slender, almost whip-like tentacles, arranged in two bunches of eight each. These bunches have since been named rather aptly, by that distinguished anatomist, Professor Howes,[2] the *hands*. Even as I saw these Martians for the first time they seemed to be endeavouring to raise themselves on these hands, but of course, with the increased weight of terrestrial conditions, this was impossible. There is reason to suppose that on Mars they may have progressed upon them with some facility.

The internal anatomy, I may remark here, as dissection has since shown, was almost equally simple. The greater part of the structure was the brain, sending enormous nerves to the eyes, ear, and tactile tentacles. Besides this were the bulky lungs, into which the mouth opened, and the heart and its vessels. The pulmonary distress caused by the denser atmosphere and greater gravitational attraction was only too evident in the convulsive movements of the outer skin.

And this was the sum of the Martian organs. Strange as it may seem to a human being, all the complex apparatus of digestion, which makes up the bulk of our bodies, did not exist in the Martians. They were heads – merely heads. Entrails they had none. They did not eat, much less digest. Instead, they took the fresh, living blood of other creatures, and *injected* it into their own veins. I have myself seen this being done, as I shall mention in its place. But, squeamish as I may seem, I cannot bring myself to describe what I could not endure even to continue watching. Let it suffice to say, blood obtained from a still living animal, in most cases from a human being, was run directly by means of a little pipette into the recipient canal . . .

The bare idea of this is no doubt horribly repulsive to us, but at the same time I think that we should remember how repulsive our carnivorous habits would seem to an intelligent rabbit.

The physiological advantages of the practice of injection are undeniable, if one thinks of the tremendous waste of human time and energy occasioned by eating and the digestive process. Our bodies are half made up of glands and tubes and organs, occupied in turning heterogeneous food into blood. The digestive processes and their reaction upon the nervous system sap our strength and colour our minds. Men go happy or miserable as they have healthy or unhealthy livers, or sound gastric glands. But the Martians were lifted above all these organic fluctuations of mood and emotion.

Their undeniable preference for men as their source of nourishment is partly explained by the nature of the remains of the victims they had brought with them as provisions from Mars. These creatures, to judge from the shrivelled remains that have fallen into human hands, were bipeds with flimsy, silicious skeletons (almost like those of the silicious sponges) and feeble musculature, standing about six feet high and having round, erect heads, and large eyes in flinty sockets. Two or three of these seem to have been brought in each cylinder, and all were killed before earth was reached. It was just as well for them, for the mere attempt to stand upright upon our planet would have broken every bone in their bodies.

And while I am engaged in this description, I may add in this place certain further details which, although they were not all evident to us at the time, will enable the reader who is unacquainted with them to form a clearer picture of these offensive creatures.

In three other points their physiology differed strangely from ours. Their organisms did not sleep, any more than the heart of man sleeps. Since they had no extensive muscular mechanism to recuperate, that periodical extinction was unknown to them. They had little or no sense of fatigue, it would seem. On earth they could never have moved without effort, yet even to the last they kept in action. In twenty-four hours they did twenty-four hours of work, as even on earth is perhaps the case with the ants.

In the next place, wonderful as it seems in a sexual world, the Martians were absolutely without sex, and therefore without any of the tumultuous emotions that arise from that difference among men. A young Martian, there can now be no dispute, was really born upon earth during the war, and it was found attached to its parent, partially *budded* off, just as young lily-bulbs bud off, or like the young animals in the fresh-water polyp.[3]

In man, in all the higher terrestrial animals, such a method of increase has disappeared; but even on this earth it was certainly the primitive method. Among the lower animals, up even to those first cousins of the vertebrated animals, the Tunicates,[4] the two processes occur side by side, but finally the sexual method superseded its competitor altogether. On Mars, however, just the reverse has apparently been the case.

It is worthy of remark that a certain speculative writer[5] of quasi-scientific repute, writing long before the Martian invasion, did forecast for man a final structure not unlike the actual Martian condition. His prophecy, I remember, appeared in November or December, 1893, in a long-defunct publication, the *Pall Mall Budget*, and I recall a caricature of it in a pre-Martian periodical called *Punch*. He pointed out – writing in a foolish, facetious tone – that the perfection of mechanical appliances must ultimately supersede limbs; the perfection of chemical devices, digestion; that such organs as hair, external nose, teeth, ears, and chin were no longer essential parts of the human being, and that the tendency of natural selection would lie in the direction of their steady diminution through the coming ages. The brain alone remained a cardinal necessity. Only one other part of the body had a strong case for survival, and that was the hand, 'teacher and agent of the brain'.[6] While the rest of the body dwindled, the hands would grow larger.

There is many a true word written in jest, and here in the Martians we have beyond dispute the actual accomplishment of such a suppression of the animal side of the organism by the intelligence. To me it is quite credible that the Martians may be descended from beings not unlike ourselves, by a gradual development of brain and hands (the latter giving rise to the two bunches of delicate tentacles at last) at the expense of the rest of the body. Without the body the brain would, of course, become a mere selfish intelligence, without any of the emotional substratum of the human being.

The last salient point in which the systems of these creatures differed from ours was in what one might have thought a very trivial particular. Micro-organisms, which cause so much disease and pain on earth, have either never appeared upon Mars, or Martian sanitary science eliminated them ages ago. A hundred diseases, all the fevers and contagions of human life, consumption, cancers, tumours and such morbidities, never enter the scheme of their life. And speaking of the differences between the life on Mars and terrestrial life, I may allude here to the curious suggestions of the red weed.

Apparently the vegetable kingdom in Mars, instead of having green for a dominant colour, is of a vivid blood-red tint. At any rate, the seeds which the Martians (intentionally or accidentally) brought with them gave rise in all cases to red-coloured growths. Only that known popularly as the red weed,[7] however, gained any footing in competition with terrestrial forms. The red creeper was quite a transitory growth, and few people have seen it growing. For a time, however, the red weed grew with astonishing vigour and luxuriance. It spread up the sides of the pit by the third or fourth day of our imprisonment, and its cactus-like branches formed a carmine fringe to the edges of our triangular window. And afterwards I found it broadcast throughout the country, and especially wherever there was a stream of water.

The Martians had what appears to have been an auditory organ, a single round drum at the back of the head-body, and eyes with a visual range not very different from ours except that, according to Philips,[8] blue and violet were as black to them. It is commonly supposed that they communicated by sounds and tentacular gesticulations; this is asserted, for instance, in the able but hastily compiled pamphlet[9] (written evidently by someone not an eye-witness of Martian actions) to which I have already alluded, and which, so far, has been the chief source of information concerning them. Now no surviving human being saw so much of the Martians in action as I did. I take no credit to myself for an accident, but the fact is so. And I assert that I watched them closely time after time, and that I have seen four, five, and (once) six of them sluggishly performing the most elaborately complicated operations together without either sound or gesture. Their peculiar hooting invariably preceded feeding; it had no modulation, and was, I believe, in no sense a signal, but merely the expiration of air preparatory to the suctional operation. I have a certain claim to at least an elementary knowledge of psychology, and in this matter I am convinced – as firmly as I am convinced of anything – that the Martians interchanged thoughts without any physical intermediation. And I have been convinced of this in spite of strong preconceptions. Before the Martian invasion, as an occasional reader here or there may remember, I had written with some little vehemence against the telepathic theory.[10]

The Martians wore no clothing. Their conceptions of ornament and decorum were necessarily different from ours; and not only were they evidently much less sensible of changes of temperature than we are, but changes of pressure do not seem to have affected their health at all seriously. Yet though they wore no clothing, it was in the other artificial additions to their bodily resources that their great superiority over man lay. We men, with our bicycles and road-skates,[11] our Lilienthal[12] soaring-machines, our guns and sticks[13] and so forth, are just in the beginning of the evolution that the Martians have worked out. They have become practically mere brains, wearing different bodies according to their needs just as men wear suits of clothes and take a bicycle in a hurry or an umbrella in the wet. And of their appliances, perhaps nothing is more wonderful to a man than the curious fact that what is the dominant feature of almost all human devices in mechanism is absent – the *wheel* is absent;[14] among all the things they brought to earth there is no trace or suggestion of their use of wheels. One would have at least expected it in locomotion. And in this connection it is curious to remark that even on this earth Nature has never hit upon the wheel, or has preferred other expedients to its development. And not only did the Martians either not know of (which is incredible), or abstain from, the wheel, but in their apparatus singularly little use is made of the fixed pivot, or relatively fixed pivot, with circular motions thereabout confined to one plane. Almost all the joints of the machinery present a complicated system of sliding parts moving over small but beautifully curved friction bearings.[15] And while upon this matter of detail, it is remarkable that the long leverages of their machines are in most cases actuated by a sort of sham musculature of discs in an elastic sheath; these discs become polarized and drawn closely and powerfully together when traversed by a current of electricity. In this way the curious parallelism to animal motions, which was so striking and disturbing to the human beholder, was attained. Such quasi-muscles abounded in the crab-like handling-machine which, on my first peeping out of the slit, I watched unpacking the cylinder. It seemed infinitely more alive than the actual Martians lying beyond it in the sunset light, panting, stirring ineffectual tentacles, and moving feebly after their vast journey across space.

While I was still watching their sluggish motions in the sunlight, and noting each strange detail of their form, the curate reminded me of his presence by pulling violently at my arm. I turned to a scowling face, and silent, eloquent lips. He wanted the slit, which permitted only one of us to peep through; and so I had to forgo watching them for a time while he enjoyed that privilege.

When I looked again, the busy handling-machine had already put together several of the pieces of apparatus it had taken out of the cylinder into a shape having an unmistakable likeness to its own; and down on the left a busy little digging mechanism had come into view, emitting jets of green vapour and working its way round the pit, excavating and embanking in a methodical and discriminating manner. This it was which had caused the regular beating noise, and the rhythmic shocks that had kept our ruinous refuge quivering. It piped and whistled as it worked. So far as I could see, the thing was without a directing Martian at all.

3
THE DAYS OF IMPRISONMENT

The arrival of a second fighting-machine drove us from our peephole into the scullery, for we feared that from his elevation the Martian might see down upon us behind our barrier. At a later date we began to feel less in danger of their eyes, for to an eye in the dazzle of the sunlight outside our refuge must have been blank blackness, but at first the slightest suggestion of approach drove us into the scullery in heart-throbbing retreat. Yet terrible as was the danger we incurred, the attraction of peeping was for both of us irresistible. And I recall now with a sort of wonder that, in spite of the infinite danger in which we were between starvation and a still more terrible death, we could yet struggle bitterly for that horrible privilege of sight. We would race across the kitchen in a grotesque way between eagerness and the dread of making a noise, and strike each other, and thrust and kick, within a few inches of exposure.

The fact is that we had absolutely incompatible dispositions and habits of thought and action, and our danger and isolation only accentuated the incompatibility. At Halliford I had already come to hate the curate's trick of helpless exclamation, his stupid rigidity of mind. His endless muttering monologue vitiated every effort I made to think out a line of action, and drove me at times, thus pent up and intensified, almost to the verge of craziness. He was as lacking in restraint as a silly woman. He would weep for hours together, and I verily believe that to the very end this spoilt child of life thought his weak tears in some way efficacious. And I would sit in the darkness unable to keep my mind off him by reason of his importunities. He ate more than I did, and it was in vain I pointed out that our only chance of life was to stop in the house until the Martians had done with their pit, that in that long patience a time might presently come when we should need food. He ate and drank impulsively in heavy meals at long intervals. He slept little.

As the days wore on, his utter carelessness of any consideration so intensified our distress and danger that I had, much as I loathed doing it, to resort to threats, and at last to blows. That brought him to reason for a time. But he was one of those weak creatures, void of pride, timorous, anæmic, hateful souls, full of shifty cunning, who face neither God nor man, who face not even themselves.

It is disagreeable for me to recall and write these things, but I set them down that my story may lack nothing. Those who have escaped the dark and terrible aspects of life will find my brutality, my flash of rage in our final tragedy, easy enough to blame; for they know what is wrong as well as any, but not what is possible to tortured men. But those who have been under the shadow, who have gone down at last to elemental things, will have a wider charity.

And while within we fought out our dark, dim contest of whispers, snatched food and drink and gripping hands and blows, without, in the pitiless sunlight of that terrible June, was the strange wonder, the unfamiliar routine of the Martians in the pit. Let me return to those first new experiences of mine. After a long time I ventured back to the peephole, to find that the newcomers had been reinforced by the occupants of no fewer than three of the fighting-machines. These last had brought with them certain fresh appliances that stood in an orderly manner about the cylinder. The second handling-machine was now completed, and was busied in serving one of the novel contrivances the big machine had brought. This was a body resembling a milk-can in its general form, above which oscillated a pear-shaped receptacle, and from which a stream of white powder flowed into a circular basin below.

The oscillatory motion was imparted to this by one tentacle of the handling-machine. With two spatulate hands the handling-machine was digging out and flinging masses of clay into the pear-shaped receptacle above, while with another arm it periodically opened a door and removed rusty and blackened clinkers from the middle part of the machine. Another steely tentacle directed the powder from the basin along a ribbed channel towards some receiver that was hidden from me by the mound of bluish dust. From this unseen receiver a little thread of green smoke rose vertically into the quiet air. As I looked, the handling-machine, with a faint and musical clinking, extended, telescopic fashion, a tentacle that had been a moment before a mere blunt projection, until its end was hidden behind the mound of clay. In another second it had lifted a bar of white aluminium into sight, untarnished as yet and shining dazzlingly, and deposited it in a growing stack of bars that stood at the side of the pit. Between sunset and starlight this dexterous machine must have made more than a hundred such bars out of the crude clay, and the mound of bluish dust rose steadily until it topped the side of the pit.

The contrast between the swift and complex movements of these contrivances and the inert, panting clumsiness of their masters was acute, and for days I had to tell myself repeatedly that these latter were indeed the living of the two things.

The curate had possession of the slit when the first men were brought to the pit. I was sitting below, huddled up, listening with all my ears. He made a sudden movement backward, and I, fearful that we were observed, crouched in a spasm of terror. He came sliding down the rubbish and crept beside me in the darkness, inarticulate, gesticulating, and for a moment I shared his panic. His gesture suggested a resignation of the slit, and after a little while my curiosity gave me courage, and I rose up, stepped across him, and clambered up to it. At first I could see no reason for his frantic behaviour. The twilight had now come, the stars were little and faint, but the pit was illuminated by the flickering green fire that came from the aluminium-making. The whole picture was a flickering scheme of green gleams and shifting rusty black shadows, strangely trying to the eyes. Over and through it all went the bats, heeding it not at all. The sprawling Martians were no longer to be seen, the mound of blue-green powder had risen to cover them from sight, and a fighting-machine, with its legs contracted, crumpled, and abbreviated, stood across the corner of the pit. And then, amid the clangour of the machinery, came a drifting suspicion of human voices, that I entertained at first only to dismiss.

I crouched, watching this fighting-machine closely, satisfying myself now for the first time that the hood did indeed contain a Martian. As the green flames lifted I could see the oily gleam of his integument and the brightness of his eyes. And suddenly I heard a yell, and saw a long tentacle reaching over the shoulder of the machine to the little cage that hunched upon its back. Then something – something struggling violently – was lifted high against the sky, a black, vague enigma against the starlight; and as this black object came down again, I saw by the green brightness that it was a man. For an instant he was clearly visible. He was a stout, ruddy, middle-aged man, well dressed; three days before he must have been walking the world, a man of considerable consequence. I could see his staring eyes and gleams of light on his studs and watch-chain. He vanished behind the mound, and for a moment there was silence. And then began a shrieking and a sustained and cheerful hooting from the Martians.

I slid down the rubbish, struggled to my feet, clapped my hands over my ears, and bolted into the scullery. The curate, who had been crouching silently with his arms over his head, looked up as I passed, cried out quite loudly at my desertion of him, and came running after me.

That night, as we lurked in the scullery balanced between our horror and the terrible fascination this peeping had, although I felt an urgent need of action I tried in vain to conceive some plan of escape; but afterwards, during the second day, I was able to consider our position with great clearness. The curate, I found, was quite incapable of discussion; this new and culmin-ating atrocity had robbed him of all vestiges of reason or fore-thought. Practically he had already sunk to the level of an animal. But, as the saying goes, I gripped myself with both hands. It grew upon my mind, once I could face the facts, that, terrible as our position was, there was as yet no justification for absolute despair. Our chief chance lay in the possibility of the Martians making the pit nothing more than a temporary encampment. Or even if they kept it permanently, they might not consider it necessary to guard it, and a chance of escape might be afforded us. I also weighed very carefully the possibility of our digging a way out in a direction away from the pit, but the chances of our emerging within sight of some sentinel fighting-machine seemed at first too great. And I should have had to do all the digging myself. The curate would certainly have failed me.

It was on the third day, if my memory serves me right, that I saw the lad killed. It was the only occasion on which I actually saw the Martians feed. After that experience I avoided the hole in the wall for the better part of a day. I went into the scullery, removed the door, and spent some hours digging with my hatchet as silently as possible; but when I had made a hole about a couple of feet deep the loose earth collapsed noisily, and I did not dare continue. I lost heart, and lay down on the scullery floor for a long time, having no spirit even to move. And after that I abandoned altogether the idea of escaping by excavation.

It says much for the impression the Martians had made upon me that at first I entertained little or no hope of our escape being brought about by their overthrow through any human effort. But on the fourth or fifth night I heard a sound like heavy guns.

It was very late in the night, and the moon was shining brightly. The Martians had taken away the excavating-machine, and, save for a fighting-machine that stood on the remoter bank of the pit and a handling-machine that was busied out of my sight in a corner of the pit immediately beneath my peephole, the place was deserted by them. Except for the pale glow from the handling-machine and the bars and patches of white moonlight, the pit was in darkness, and, except for the clinking of the handling-machine, quite still. That night was a beautiful serenity; save for one planet, the moon seemed to have the sky to herself. I heard a dog howling, and that familiar sound it was that made me listen. Then I heard quite distinctly a booming exactly like the sound of great guns. Six distinct reports I counted, and after a long interval six again. And that was all.

4

THE DEATH OF
THE CURATE

It was on the sixth day of our imprisonment that I peeped for the last time, and presently found myself alone. Instead of keeping close to me and trying to oust me from the slit, the curate had gone back into the scullery. I was struck by a sudden thought. I went back quickly and quietly into the scullery. In the darkness I heard the curate drinking. I snatched in the darkness, and my fingers caught a bottle of burgundy.

For a few minutes there was a tussle. The bottle struck the floor and broke, and I desisted and rose. We stood panting, threatening each other. In the end I planted myself between him and the food, and told him of my determination to begin a discipline. I divided the food in the pantry into rations to last us ten days. I would not let him eat any more that day. In the afternoon he made a feeble effort to get at the food. I had been dozing, but in an instant I was awake. All day and all night we sat face to face, I weary but resolute, and he weeping and complaining of his immediate hunger. It was, I know, a night and a day, but to me it seemed – it seems now – an interminable length of time.

And so our widened incompatibility ended at last in open conflict. For two vast days we struggled in undertones and wrestling contests. There were times when I beat and kicked him madly, times when I cajoled and persuaded him, and once I tried to bribe him with the last bottle of burgundy, for there was a rain-water pump from which I could get water. But neither force nor kindness availed; he was indeed beyond reason. He would neither desist from his attacks on the food nor from his noisy babbling to himself. The rudimentary precautions to keep our imprisonment endurable he would not observe. Slowly I began to realize the complete overthrow of his intelligence, to perceive that my sole companion in this close and sickly darkness was a man insane.

From certain vague memories I am inclined to think my own mind wandered at times. I had strange and hideous dreams whenever I slept. It sounds paradoxical, but I am inclined to think that the weakness and insanity of the curate warned me, braced me, and kept me a sane man.

On the eighth day he began to talk aloud instead of whispering, and nothing I could do would moderate his speech.

'It is just, O God!' he would say, over and over again. 'It is just. On me and mine be the punishment laid. We have sinned, we have fallen short. There was poverty, sorrow; the poor were trodden in the dust, and I held my peace. I preached acceptable folly – my God, what folly! – when I should have stood up, though I died for it, and called upon them to repent – repent! ... Oppressors of the poor and needy! ... The wine-press of God!'[1]

Then he would suddenly revert to the matter of the food I withheld from him, praying, begging, weeping, at last threatening. He began to raise his voice – I prayed him not to. He perceived a hold on me – he threatened he would shout and bring the Martians upon us. For a time that scared me; but any concession would have shortened our chance of escape beyond estimating. I defied him, although I felt no assurance that he might not do this thing. But that day, at any rate, he did not. He talked, with his voice rising slowly, through the greater part of the eighth and ninth days – threats, entreaties, mingled with a torrent of half-sane and always frothy repentance for his vacant sham of God's service, such as made me pity him. Then he slept awhile, and began again with renewed strength, so loudly that I must needs make him desist.

'Be still!' I implored.

He rose to his knees, for he had been sitting in the darkness near the copper.

'I have been still too long,' he said, in a tone that must have reached the pit, 'and now I must bear my witness. Woe unto

this unfaithful city!² Woe! woe! Woe! woe! woe! to the inhabitants of the earth by reason of the other voices of the trumpet—'

'Shut up!' I said, rising to my feet, and in a terror lest the
Martians should hear us. 'For God's sake—'

'Nay!' shouted the curate, at the top of his voice, standing
likewise and extending his arms. 'Speak! The word of the Lord
is upon me!'

In three strides he was at the door leading into the kitchen.

'I must bear my witness! I go! It has already been too long
delayed.'

I put out my hand and felt the meat-chopper hanging to the
wall. In a flash I was after him. I was fierce with fear. Before he
was halfway across the kitchen I had overtaken him. With one
last touch of humanity I turned the blade back and struck him
with the butt. He went headlong forward and lay stretched on
the ground. I stumbled over him and stood panting. He lay still.

Suddenly I heard a noise without, the run and smash of
slipping plaster, and the triangular aperture in the wall was
darkened. I looked up and saw the lower surface of a handling-
machine coming slowly across the hole. One of its gripping
limbs curled amid the débris; another limb appeared, feeling its
way over the fallen beams. I stood petrified, staring. Then I saw
through a sort of glass plate near the edge of the body the face,
as we may call it, and the large dark eyes of a Martian, peering,
and then a long metallic snake of tentacle came feeling slowly
through the hole.

I turned by an effort, stumbled over the curate, and stopped
at the scullery door. The tentacle was now some way, two yards
or more, in the room, and twisting and turning, with queer
sudden movements, this way and that. For a while I stood
fascinated by that slow, fitful advance. Then, with a faint,
hoarse cry, I forced myself across the scullery. I trembled violently; I could scarcely stand upright. I opened the door of the
coal-cellar, and stood there in the darkness staring at the faintly
lit doorway into the kitchen, and listening. Had the Martian
seen me? What was it doing now?

Something was moving to and fro there, very quietly; every
now and then it tapped against the wall, or started on its

movements with a faint metallic ringing, like the movement of keys on a split-ring.[3] Then a heavy body – I knew too well what – was dragged across the floor of the kitchen towards the opening. Irresistibly attracted, I crept to the door and peeped into the kitchen. In the triangle of bright outer sunlight I saw the Martian, in its Briareus[4] of a handling-machine, scrutinizing the curate's head. I thought at once that it would infer my presence from the mark of the blow I had given him.

I crept back to the coal-cellar, shut the door, and began to cover myself up as much as I could, and as noiselessly as possible in the darkness, among the firewood and coal therein. Every now and then I paused, rigid, to hear if the Martian had thrust its tentacle through the opening again.

Then the faint metallic jingle returned. I traced it slowly feeling over the kitchen. Presently I heard it nearer – in the scullery, as I judged. I thought that its length might be insufficient to reach me. I prayed copiously. It passed, scraping faintly across the cellar door. An age of almost intolerable suspense intervened; then I heard it fumbling at the latch. It had found the door! The Martians understood doors!

It worried at the catch for a minute, perhaps, and then the door opened.

In the darkness I could just see the thing – like an elephant's trunk more than anything else – waving towards me and touching and examining the wall, coals, wood, and ceiling. It was like a black worm swaying its blind head to and fro.

Once, even, it touched the heel of my boot. I was on the verge of screaming; I bit my hand. For a time the tentacle was silent. I could have fancied it had been withdrawn. Presently, with an abrupt click, it gripped something – I thought it had me! – and seemed to go out of the cellar again. For a minute I was not sure. Apparently it had taken a lump of coal to examine.

I seized the opportunity of slightly shifting my position, which had become cramped, and then listened. I whispered passionate prayers for safety.

Then I heard the slow, deliberate sound creeping towards me again. Slowly, slowly it drew near, scratching against the walls and tapping the furniture.

While I was still doubtful, it rapped smartly against the cellar door and closed it. I heard it go into the pantry, and the biscuit-tins rattled and a bottle smashed, and then came a heavy bump against the cellar door. Then silence, that passed into an infinity of suspense.

Had it gone?

At last I decided that it had.

It came into the scullery no more; but I lay all the tenth day in the close darkness, buried among coals and firewood, not daring even to crawl out for the drink for which I craved. It was the eleventh day before I ventured so far from my security.

5
THE STILLNESS

My first act before I went into the pantry was to fasten the door between the kitchen and the scullery. But the pantry was empty; every scrap of food had gone. Apparently, the Martian had taken it all on the previous day. At that discovery I despaired for the first time. I took no food, or no drink either, on the eleventh or the twelfth day.

At first my mouth and throat were parched, and my strength ebbed sensibly. I sat about in the darkness of the scullery, in a state of despondent wretchedness. My mind ran on eating. I thought I had become deaf, for the noises of movement I had been accustomed to hear from the pit had ceased absolutely. I did not feel strong enough to crawl noiselessly to the peephole, or I would have gone there.

On the twelfth day my throat was so painful that, taking the chance of alarming the Martians, I attacked the creaking rain-water pump that stood by the sink, and got a couple of glassfuls of blackened and tainted rain-water. I was greatly refreshed by this, and emboldened by the fact that no inquiring tentacle followed the noise of my pumping.

During these days, in a rambling, inconclusive way, I thought much of the curate and of the manner of his death.

On the thirteenth day I drank some more water, and dozed and thought disjointedly of eating and of vague impossible plans of escape. Whenever I dozed I dreamt of horrible phantasms, of the death of the curate, or of sumptuous dinners; but, asleep or awake, I felt a keen pain that urged me to drink again and again. The light that came into the scullery was no longer grey, but red. To my disordered imagination it seemed the colour of blood.

On the fourteenth day I went into the kitchen, and I was surprised to find that the fronds of the red weed had grown right across the hole in the wall, turning the half-light of the place into a crimson-coloured obscurity.

It was early on the fifteenth day that I heard a curious, familiar sequence of sounds in the kitchen, and, listening, identified it as the snuffing and scratching of a dog. Going into the kitchen, I saw a dog's nose peering in through a break among the ruddy fronds. This greatly surprised me. At the scent of me he barked shortly.

I thought if I could induce him to come into the place quietly I should be able, perhaps, to kill and eat him; and, in any case, it would be advisable to kill him, lest his actions attracted the attention of the Martians.

I crept forward, saying 'Good dog!' very softly; but he suddenly withdrew his head and disappeared.

I listened – I was not deaf – but certainly the pit was still. I heard a sound like the flutter of a bird's wings, and a hoarse croaking, but that was all.

For a long while I lay close to the peephole, but not daring to move aside the red plants that obscured it. Once or twice I heard a faint pitter-patter like the feet of the dog going hither and thither on the sand far below me, and there were more birdlike sounds, but that was all. At length, encouraged by the silence, I looked out.

Except in the corner, where a multitude of crows hopped and fought over the skeletons of the dead the Martians had consumed, there was not a living thing in the pit.

I stared about me, scarcely believing my eyes. All the machinery had gone. Save for the big mound of greyish-blue powder in one corner, certain bars of aluminium in another, the black birds, and the skeletons of the killed, the place was merely an empty circular pit in the sand.

Slowly I thrust myself out through the red weed, and stood upon the mound of rubble. I could see in any direction save behind me, to the north, and neither Martians nor sign of

Martians were to be seen. The pit dropped sheerly from my feet, but a little way along the rubbish afforded a practicable slope to the summit of the ruins. My chance of escape had come. I began to tremble.

I hesitated for some time, and then, in a gust of desperate resolution, and with a heart that throbbed violently, I scrambled to the top of the mound in which I had been buried so long.

I looked about again. To the northward, too, no Martian was visible.

When I had last seen this part of Sheen in the daylight it had been a straggling street of comfortable white and red houses, interspersed with abundant shady trees. Now I stood on a mound of smashed brickwork, clay, and gravel, over which spread a multitude of red cactus-shaped plants, knee-high, without a solitary terrestrial growth to dispute their footing. The trees near me were dead and brown, but further a network of red threads scaled the still living stems.

The neighbouring houses had all been wrecked, but none had been burned; their walls stood, sometimes to the second story, with smashed windows and shattered doors. The red weed grew tumultuously in their roofless rooms. Below me was the great pit, with the crows struggling for its refuse. A number of other birds hopped about among the ruins. Far away I saw a gaunt cat slink crouchingly along a wall, but traces of men there were none.

The day seemed, by contrast with my recent confinement, dazzlingly bright, the sky a glowing blue. A gentle breeze kept the red weed that covered every scrap of unoccupied ground gently swaying. And oh! the sweetness of the air!

6

THE WORK OF
FIFTEEN DAYS

For some time I stood tottering on the mound regardless of my safety. Within that noisome den from which I had emerged, I had thought with a narrow intensity only of our immediate security. I had not realized what had been happening to the world, had not anticipated this startling vision of unfamiliar things. I had expected to see Sheen in ruins – I found about me the landscape, weird and lurid, of another planet.

For that moment I touched an emotion beyond the common range of men, yet one that the poor brutes we dominate know only too well. I felt as a rabbit might feel returning to his burrow, and suddenly confronted by the work of a dozen busy navvies digging the foundations of a house. I felt the first inkling of a thing that presently grew quite clear in my mind, that oppressed me for many days, a sense of dethronement, a persuasion that I was no longer a master, but an animal among the animals, under the Martian heel. With us it would be as with them, to lurk and watch, to run and hide; the fear and empire of man had passed away.

But so soon as this strangeness had been realized it passed, and my dominant motive became the hunger of my long and dismal fast. In the direction away from the pit I saw, beyond a red-covered wall, a patch of garden ground unburied. This gave me a hint, and I went knee-deep, and sometimes neck-deep, in the red weed. The density of the weed gave me a reassuring sense of hiding. The wall was some six feet high, and when I attempted to clamber it I found I could not lift my feet to the crest. So I went along by the side of it, and came to a corner and a rockwork that enabled me to get to the top and tumble into the garden I coveted. Here I found some young onions, a couple of gladiolus bulbs, and a quantity of immature carrots, all of which I secured, and, scrambling over a ruined wall, went on my way through scarlet and crimson trees towards Kew – it was like walking through an avenue of gigantic blood-drops – possessed with two ideas: to get more food, and to limp, as soon and as far as my strength permitted, out of this accursed unearthly region of the pit.

Some way further, in a grassy place, was a group of mushrooms which also I devoured, and then I came upon a broad sheet of flowing shallow water, where meadows used to be. These fragments of nourishment served only to whet my hunger. At first I was surprised at this flood in a hot, dry summer, but afterwards I discovered that it was caused by the tropical exuberance of the red weed. Directly this extraordinary growth encountered water, it straightway became gigantic and of unparalleled fecundity. Its seeds were simply poured down into the water of the Wey and Thames, and its swiftly growing and Titanic water-fronds speedily choked both those rivers.

At Putney,[1] as I afterwards saw, the bridge was almost lost in a tangle of this weed, and at Richmond, too, the Thames waters poured in a broad and shallow stream across the meadows of Hampton and Twickenham. As the waters spread the weed followed them, until the ruined villas of the Thames Valley were for a time lost in this red swamp, whose margin I explored, and much of the desolation the Martians had caused was concealed.

In the end the red weed succumbed almost as quickly as it had spread. A cankering[2] disease, due, it is believed, to the action of certain bacteria, presently seized upon it. Now, by the action of natural selection, all terrestrial plants have acquired a resisting power against bacterial diseases – they never succumb without a severe struggle, but the red weed rotted like a thing already dead. The fronds became bleached, and then shrivelled and brittle. They broke off at the least touch, and the waters that had stimulated their early growth carried their last vestiges out to sea.

My first act on coming to this water was, of course, to slake my thirst. I drank a great deal of it, and, moved by an impulse, gnawed some fronds of red weed; but they were watery, and had a sickly, metallic taste. I found the water was sufficiently shallow for me to wade securely, although the red weed impeded my feet a little; but the flood evidently got deeper towards the river, and I turned back to Mortlake. I managed to make out the road by means of occasional ruins of its villas and fences and lamps, and so presently I got out of this spate and made my way to the hill going up towards Roehampton and came out on Putney Common.

Here the scenery changed from the strange and unfamiliar to the wreckage of the familiar: patches of ground exhibited the devastation of a cyclone, and in a few score yards I would come upon perfectly undisturbed spaces, houses with their blinds trimly drawn and doors closed, as if they had been left for a day by the owners, or as if their inhabitants slept within. The red weed was less abundant; the tall trees along the lane were free from the red creeper. I hunted for food among the trees, finding nothing, and I also raided a couple of silent houses, but they had already been broken into and ransacked. I rested for the remainder of the daylight in a shrubbery, being, in my enfeebled condition, too fatigued to push on.

All this time I saw no human beings, and no signs of the Martians. I encountered a couple of hungry-looking dogs, but both hurried circuitously away from the advances I made them. Near Roehampton I had seen two human skeletons – not bodies, but skeletons, picked clean – and in the wood by me I found the crushed and scattered bones of several cats and rabbits and the skull of a sheep. But though I gnawed parts of these in my mouth, there was nothing to be got from them.

After sunset I struggled on along the road towards Putney, where I think the Heat-Ray must have been used for some reason. And in a garden beyond Roehampton I got a quantity of immature potatoes, sufficient to stay my hunger. From this garden one looked down upon Putney and the river. The aspect of the place in the dusk was singularly desolate: blackened trees, blackened, desolate ruins, and down the hill the sheets of the flooded river, red-tinged with the weed. And over all – silence.

It filled me with indescribable terror to think how swiftly that desolating change had come.

For a time I believed that mankind had been swept out of existence, and that I stood there alone, the last man left alive. Hard by the top of Putney Hill I came upon another skeleton, with the arms dislocated and removed several yards from the rest of the body. As I proceeded I became more and more convinced that the extermination of mankind was, save for such stragglers as myself, already accomplished in this part of the world. The Martians, I thought, had gone on and left the country desolated, seeking food elsewhere. Perhaps even now they were destroying Berlin or Paris, or it might be they had gone northward.

7

THE MAN ON PUTNEY HILL

I spent that night in the inn that stands at the top of Putney Hill, sleeping in a made bed for the first time since my flight to Leatherhead. I will not tell the needless trouble I had breaking into that house – afterwards I found the front door was on the latch – nor how I ransacked every room for food, until, just on the verge of despair, in what seemed to me to be a servant's bedroom, I found a rat-gnawed crust and two tins of pineapple. The place had been already searched and emptied. In the bar I afterwards found some biscuits and sandwiches that had been overlooked. The latter I could not eat, they were too rotten, but the former not only stayed my hunger, but filled my pockets. I lit no lamps, fearing some Martian might come beating that part of London for food in the night. Before I went to bed I had an interval of restlessness, and prowled from window to window, peering out for some sign of these monsters. I slept little. As I lay in bed I found myself thinking consecutively – a thing I do not remember to have done since my last argument with the curate. During all the intervening time my mental condition had been a hurrying succession of vague emotional states or a sort of stupid receptivity. But in the night my brain, reinforced, I suppose, by the food I had eaten, grew clear again, and I thought.

Three things struggled for possession of my mind: the killing of the curate, the whereabouts of the Martians, and the possible fate of my wife. The former gave me no sensation of horror or remorse to recall; I saw it simply as a thing done, a memory infinitely disagreeable but quite without the quality of remorse. I saw myself then as I see myself now, driven step by step towards that hasty blow, the creature of a sequence of accidents leading inevitably to that. I felt no condemnation; yet the memory, static, unprogressive, haunted me. In the silence of the night, with that sense of the nearness of God that sometimes comes into the stillness and the darkness, I stood my trial, my only trial, for that moment of wrath and fear. I retraced every step of our conversation from the moment when I had found him crouching beside me, heedless of my thirst, and pointing to the fire and smoke that streamed up from the ruins of Weybridge. We had been incapable of co-operation – grim chance had taken no heed of that. Had I foreseen, I should have left him at Halliford. But I did not foresee; and crime is to foresee and do. And I set this down as I have set all this story down, as it was. There were no witnesses – all these things I might have concealed. But I set it down, and the reader must form his judgement as he will.

And when, by an effort, I had set aside that picture of a prostrate body, I faced the problem of the Martians and the fate of my wife. For the former I had no data; I could imagine a hundred things, and so, unhappily, I could for the latter. And suddenly that night became terrible. I found myself sitting up in bed, staring at the dark. I found myself praying that the Heat-Ray might have suddenly and painlessly struck her out of being. Since the night of my return from Leatherhead I had not prayed. I had uttered prayers, fetish prayers, had prayed as heathens mutter charms when I was in extremity; but now I prayed indeed, pleading steadfastly and sanely, face to face with the darkness of God. Strange night! strangest in this, that so soon as dawn had come, I, who had talked with God, crept out of the house like a rat leaving its hiding-place – a creature scarcely larger, an inferior animal, a thing that for any passing whim of our masters might be hunted and killed. Perhaps they also prayed confidently to God. Surely, if we have learnt nothing else, this war has taught us pity – pity for those witless souls that suffer our dominion.

The morning was bright and fine, and the eastern sky glowed pink, and was fretted with little golden clouds. In the road that runs from the top of Putney Hill to Wimbledon was a number of poor vestiges of the panic torrent that must have poured Londonward on the Sunday night after the fighting began. There was a little two-wheeled cart inscribed with the name of Thomas Lobb, Greengrocer, New Malden, with a smashed wheel and an abandoned tin trunk; there was a straw hat trampled into the now hardened mud, and at the top of West Hill a lot of bloodstained glass about the overturned water-trough. My movements were languid, my plans of the vaguest. I had an idea of going to Leatherhead, though I knew that there I had the poorest chance of finding my wife. Certainly, unless death had overtaken them suddenly, my cousins and she would have fled thence; but it seemed to me I might find or learn there whither the Surrey people had fled. I knew I wanted to find my wife, that my heart ached for her and the world of men, but I had no clear idea how the finding might be done. I was also sharply aware now of my intense loneliness. From the corner I went, under cover of a thicket of trees and bushes, to the edge of Wimbledon Common, stretching wide and far.

That dark expanse was lit in patches by yellow gorse and broom; there was no red weed to be seen, and as I prowled, hesitating, on the verge of the open, the sun rose, flooding it all with light and vitality. I came upon a busy swarm of little frogs in a swampy place among the trees. I stopped to look at them, drawing a lesson from their stout resolve to live. And presently, turning suddenly, with an odd feeling of being watched, I beheld something crouching amid a clump of bushes. I stood regarding this. I made a step towards it, and it rose up and became a man armed with a cutlass. I approached him slowly. He stood silent and motionless, regarding me.

As I drew nearer I perceived he was dressed in clothes as dusty and filthy as my own; he looked, indeed, as though he had been dragged through a culvert. Nearer, I distinguished the green slime of ditches mixing with the pale drab of dried clay and shiny, coaly patches. His black hair fell over his eyes, and his face was dark and dirty and sunken, so that at first I did not recognize him. There was a red cut across the lower part of his face.

'Stop!' he cried, when I was within ten yards of him, and I

stopped. His voice was hoarse. 'Where do you come from?' he said.

I thought, surveying him.

'I come from Mortlake,' I said. 'I was buried near the pit the Martians made about their cylinder. I have worked my way out and escaped.'

'There is no food about here,' he said. 'This is my country. All this hill down to the river, and back to Clapham, and up to the edge of the common. There is only food for one. Which way are you going?'

I answered slowly.

'I don't know,' I said. 'I have been buried in the ruins of a house thirteen or fourteen days. I don't know what has happened.'

He looked at me doubtfully, then started, and looked with a changed expression.

'I've no wish to stop about here,' said I. 'I think I shall go to Leatherhead, for my wife was there.'

He shot out a pointing finger.

'It is you,' said he – 'the man from Woking. And you weren't killed at Weybridge?'

I recognized him at the same moment.

'You are the artilleryman who came into my garden.'

'Good luck!' he said. 'We are lucky ones! Fancy *you!*' He put out a hand, and I took it. 'I crawled up a drain,' he said. 'But they didn't kill everyone. And after they went away I got off towards Walton across the fields. But – It's not sixteen days altogether – and your hair is grey.' He looked over his shoulder suddenly. 'Only a rook,' he said. 'One gets to know that birds have shadows these days. This *is* a bit open. Let us crawl under those bushes and talk.'

'Have you seen any Martians?' I said. 'Since I crawled out—'

'They've gone away across London,' he said. 'I guess they've got a bigger camp there. Of a night, all over there, Hampstead way, the sky is alive with their lights. It's like a great city, and in the glare you can just see them moving. By daylight you can't. But nearer – I haven't seen them –' (he counted on his fingers) 'five days. Then I saw a couple across Hammersmith way carrying something big. And the night before last' – he stopped and spoke impressively – 'it was just a matter of lights, but it was something up in the air. I believe they've built a flying-machine, and are learning to fly.'

I stopped, on hands and knees, for we had come to the bushes.

'Fly!'

'Yes,' he said, 'fly.'

I went on into a little bower, and sat down.

'It is all over with humanity,' I said. 'If they can do that they will simply go round the world.'

He nodded.

'They will. But – It will relieve things over here a bit. And besides –' He looked at me. 'Aren't you satisfied it *is* up with humanity? I am. We're down; we're beat.'

I stared. Strange as it may seem, I had not arrived at this fact – a fact perfectly obvious so soon as he spoke. I had still held a vague hope; rather, I had kept a lifelong habit of mind. He repeated his words, 'We're beat.' They carried absolute conviction.

'It's all over,' he said. 'They've lost *one* – just *one*. And they've made their footing good and crippled the greatest power in the world. They've walked over us. The death of that one at Weybridge was an accident. And these are only pioneers. They keep on coming. These green stars – I've seen none these five or six days, but I've no doubt they're falling somewhere every night. Nothing's to be done. We're under! We're beat!'

I made him no answer. I sat staring before me, trying in vain to devise some countervailing thought.

'This isn't a war,' said the artilleryman. 'It never was a war, any more than there's war between men and ants.'

Suddenly I recalled the night in the observatory.

'After the tenth shot they fired no more – at least, until the first cylinder came.'

'How do you know?' said the artilleryman. I explained. He thought. 'Something wrong with the gun,' he said. 'But what if there is? They'll get it right again. And even if there's a delay, how can it alter the end? It's just men and ants. There's the ants build their cities, live their lives, have wars, revolutions, until the men want them out of the way, and then they go out of the way. That's what we are now – just ants. Only—'

'Yes,' I said.

'We're eatable ants.'

We sat looking at each other.

'And what will they do with us?' I said.

'That's what I've been thinking,' he said – 'that's what I've been thinking. After Weybridge I went south – thinking. I saw what was up. Most of the people were hard at it squealing and exciting themselves. But I'm not so fond of squealing. I've been in sight of death once or twice; I'm not an ornamental soldier, and at the best and worst, death – it's just death. And it's the man that keeps on thinking comes through. I saw everyone tracking away south. Says I, "Food won't last this way," and I turned right back. I went for the Martians like a sparrow goes for man. All round' – he waved a hand to the horizon – 'they're starving in heaps, bolting, treading on each other.' . . .

He saw my face, and halted awkwardly.

'No doubt lots who had money have gone away to France,' he said. He seemed to hesitate whether to apologize, met my eyes, and went on: 'There's food all about here. Canned things in shops; wines, spirits, mineral waters; and the water mains and drains are empty. Well, I was telling you what I was thinking. "Here's intelligent things," I said, "and it seems they want us for food. First, they'll smash us up – ships, machines, guns, cities, all the order and organization. All that will go. If we were the size of ants we might pull through. But we're not. It's all too bulky to stop. That's the first certainty." Eh?'

I assented.

'It is; I've thought it out. Very well, then – next; at present we're caught as we're wanted. A Martian has only to go a few miles to get a crowd on the run. And I saw one, one day, out by Wandsworth, picking houses to pieces and routing among the wreckage. But they won't keep on doing that. So soon as they've settled all our guns and ships, and smashed our railways, and done all the things they are doing over there, they will begin catching us systematic, picking the best and storing us in cages and things. That's what they will start doing in a bit. Lord! they haven't begun on us yet. Don't you see that?'

'Not begun!' I exclaimed.

'Not begun. All that's happened so far is through our not having the sense to keep quiet – worrying them with guns and such foolery. And losing our heads, and rushing off in crowds to where there wasn't any more safety than where we were. They don't want to bother us yet. They're making their things – making all the things they couldn't bring with them, getting things ready for the rest of their people. Very likely that's why the cylinders have stopped for a bit, for fear of hitting those who are here. And instead of our rushing about blind, on the howl, or getting dynamite on the chance of busting them up, we've got to fix ourselves up according to the new state of affairs. That's how I figure it out. It isn't quite according to what a man wants for his species, but it's about what the facts point to. And that's the principle I acted upon. Cities, nations, civilization, progress – it's all over. That game's up. We're beat.'

'But if that is so, what is there to live for?'

The artilleryman looked at me for a moment.

'There won't be any more blessed concerts for a million years or so; there won't be any Royal Academy of Arts, and no nice little feeds at restaurants. If it's amusement you're after, I reckon the game is up. If you've got any drawing-room manners or a dislike to eating peas with a knife[2] or dropping aitches, you'd better chuck 'em away. They ain't no further use.'

'You mean—'

'I mean that men like me are going on living – for the sake of the breed. I tell you, I'm grim set on living. And if I'm not mistaken, you'll show what insides *you've* got, too, before long. We aren't going to be exterminated. And I don't mean to be caught, either, and tamed and fattened and bred like a thundering ox. Ugh! Fancy those brown creepers!'

'You don't mean to say—'

'I do. I'm going on. Under their feet. I've got it planned; I've thought it out. We men are beat. We don't know enough. We've got to learn before we've got a chance. And we've got to live and keep independent while we learn. See! That's what has to be done.'

I stared, astonished, and stirred profoundly by the man's resolution.

'Great God!' cried I. 'But you are a man, indeed!' And suddenly I gripped his hand.

'Eh!' he said, with his eyes shining. 'I've thought it out, eh?'

'Go on,' I said.

'Well, those who mean to escape their catching must get ready. I'm getting ready. Mind you, it isn't all of us that are made for wild beasts; and that's what it's got to be. That's why I watched you. I had my doubts. You're slender. I didn't know that it was you, you see, or just how you'd been buried. All these – the sort of people that lived in these houses, and all those damn little clerks that used to live down that way – they'd be no good. They haven't any spirit in them – no proud dreams and no proud lusts; and a man who hasn't one or the other – Lord! what is he but funk and precautions?[3] They just used to skedaddle off to work – I've seen hundreds of 'em, bit of breakfast in hand, running wild and shining to catch their little season-ticket train, for fear they'd get dismissed if they didn't; working at businesses they were afraid to take the trouble to understand; skedaddling back for fear they wouldn't be in time for dinner; keeping indoors after dinner for fear of the back-streets; and sleeping with the wives they married, not because they wanted them, but because they had a bit of money that would make for safety in their one little miserable skedaddle through the world. Lives insured and a bit invested for fear of accidents. And on Sundays – fear of the hereafter. As if hell was built for rabbits! Well, the Martians will just be a godsend to these. Nice roomy cages, fattening food, careful breeding, no worry. After a week or so chasing about the fields and lands on empty stomachs, they'll come and be caught cheerful. They'll be quite glad after a bit. They'll wonder what people did before there were Martians to take care of them. And the bar-loafers, and mashers,[4] and singers – I can imagine them. I can imagine them,' he said, with a sort of sombre gratification. 'There'll be any amount of sentiment and religion loose among them. There's hundreds of things I saw with my eyes that I've only begun to see clearly these last few days. There's lots will take things as they are – fat and stupid; and lots will be worried by a sort of feeling that it's all wrong, and that they ought to be doing something. Now whenever things are so that a lot of people feel they ought to be doing something, the weak, and those who go weak with a lot of complicated thinking, always make for a sort of do-nothing religion, very pious and superior, and submit to persecution and the will of the Lord. Very likely you've seen the same thing. It's energy in a gale of funk, and turned clean inside out. These cages will be full of psalms and hymns and piety. And those of a less simple sort will work in a bit of – what is it? – eroticism.'

He paused.

'Very likely these Martians will make pets of some of them; train them to do tricks – who knows? – get sentimental over the pet boy who grew up and had to be killed. And some, maybe, they will train to hunt us.'

'No,' I cried, 'that's impossible! No human being—'

'What's the good of going on with such lies?' said the artilleryman. 'There's men who'd do it cheerful. What nonsense to pretend there isn't!'

And I succumbed to his conviction.

'If they come after me,' he said – 'Lord! if they come after me!' and subsided into a grim meditation.

I sat contemplating these things. I could find nothing to bring against this man's reasoning. In the days before the invasion no one would have questioned my intellectual superiority to his – I, a professed and recognized writer on philosophical themes, and he, a common soldier; and yet he had already formulated a situation that I had scarcely realized.

'What are you doing?' I said, presently. 'What plans have you made?'

He hesitated.

'Well, it's like this,' he said. 'What have we to do? We have to invent a sort of life where men can live and breed, and be sufficiently secure to bring the children up. Yes – wait a bit, and I'll make it clearer what I think ought to be done. The tame ones will go like all tame beasts; in a few generations they'll be big, beautiful, rich-blooded, stupid – rubbish! The risk is that we who keep wild will go savage – degenerate into a sort of big, savage rat . . . You see, how I mean to live is underground. I've been thinking about the drains. Of course, those who don't know drains think horrible things; but under this London are miles and miles – hundreds of miles – and a few days' rain and London empty will leave them sweet and clean. The main drains are big enough and airy enough for anyone. Then there's cellars, vaults, stores, from which bolting passages may be made to the drains. And the railway tunnels and subways. Eh? You begin to see? And we form a band – able-bodied, clean-minded men. We're not going to pick up any rubbish that drifts in. Weaklings go out again.'

'As you meant me to go?'

'Well – I parleyed, didn't I?'

'We won't quarrel about that. Go on.'

'Those who stop obey orders. Able-bodied, clean-minded women we want also – mothers and teachers. No lackadaisical ladies – no blasted rolling eyes. We can't have any weak or silly. Life is real again, and the useless and cumbersome and mischievous have to die. They ought to die. They ought to be willing to die. It's a sort of disloyalty, after all, to live and taint the race. And they can't be happy. Moreover, dying's none so dreadful; it's the funking makes it bad. And in all those places we shall gather. Our district will be London. And we may even be able to keep a watch, and run about in the open when the Martians keep away. Play cricket, perhaps. That's how we shall save the race. Eh? It's a possible thing? But saving the race is nothing in itself. As I say, that's only being rats. It's saving our knowledge and adding to it is the thing. There men like you come in. There's books, there's models. We must make great safe places down deep, and get all the books we can; not novels and poetry swipes,[5] but ideas, science books. That's where men like you come in. We must go to the British Museum and pick all those books through. Especially we must keep up our science – learn more. We must watch these Martians. Some of us must go as spies. When it's all working, perhaps I will. Get caught, I mean. And the great thing is, we must leave the Martians alone. We mustn't even steal. If we get in their way, we clear out. We must show them we mean no harm. Yes, I know. But they're intelligent things, and they won't hunt us down if they have all they want, and think we're just harmless vermin.'

The artilleryman paused and laid a brown hand upon my arm.

'After all, it may not be so much we may have to learn before— Just imagine this: Four or five of their fighting-machines suddenly starting off – Heat-Rays right and left, and not a Martian in 'em. Not a Martian in 'em, but men – men who have learned the way how. It may be in my time, even – those men. Fancy having one of them lovely things, with its Heat-Ray wide and free! Fancy having it in control! What would it matter if you smashed to smithereens at the end of the run, after a bust like that? I reckon the Martians'll open their beautiful eyes! Can't you see them, man? Can't you see them hurrying, hurrying – puffing and blowing and hooting to their other mechanical affairs? Something out of gear in every case. And swish, bang, rattle, swish! just as they are fumbling over it, *swish* comes the Heat-Ray, and, behold! man has come back to his own.'

For a while the imaginative daring of the artilleryman, and the tone of assurance and courage he assumed, completely dominated my mind. I believed unhesitatingly both in his fore-cast of human destiny and in the practicability of his astonishing scheme, and the reader who thinks me susceptible and foolish must contrast his position, reading steadily with all his thoughts about his subject, and mine, crouching fearfully in the bushes and listening, distracted by apprehension. We talked in this manner through the early morning time, and later crept out of the bushes, and, after scanning the sky for Martians, hurried precipitately to the house on Putney Hill where he had made his lair. It was the coal-cellar of the place, and when I saw the work he had spent a week upon – it was a burrow scarcely ten yards long, which he designed to reach to the main drain on Putney Hill – I had my first inkling of the gulf between his dreams and his powers. Such a hole I could have dug in a day.

But I believed in him sufficiently to work with him all that morning until past midday at his digging. We had a garden-barrow and shot the earth we removed against the kitchen range. We refreshed ourselves with a tin of mock-turtle soup[6] and wine from the neighbouring pantry. I found a curious relief from the aching strangeness of the world in this steady labour. As we worked, I turned his project over in my mind, and presently objections and doubts began to arise; but I worked there all the morning, so glad was I to find myself with a purpose again. After working an hour I began to speculate on the distance one had to go before the cloaca was reached, the chances we had of missing it altogether. My immediate trouble was why we should dig this long tunnel, when it was possible to get into the drain at once down one of the manholes, and work back to the house. It seemed to me, too, that the house was inconveniently chosen, and required a needless length of tunnel. And just as I was beginning to face these things, the artilleryman stopped digging, and looked at me.

'We're working well,' he said. He put down his spade. 'Let us knock off a bit,' he said. 'I think it's time we reconnoitred from the roof of the house.'

I was for going on, and after a little hesitation he resumed his spade; and then suddenly I was struck by a thought. I stopped, and so did he at once.

'Why were you walking about the common,' I said, 'instead of being here?'

'Taking the air,' he said. 'I was coming back. It's safer by night.'

'But the work?'

'Oh, one can't always work,' he said, and in a flash I saw the man plain. He hesitated, holding his spade. 'We ought to reconnoitre now,' he said, 'because if any come near they may hear the spades and drop upon us unawares.'

I was no longer disposed to object. We went together to the roof and stood on a ladder peeping out of the roof door. No Martians were to be seen, and we ventured out on the tiles, and slipped down under shelter of the parapet.

From this position a shrubbery hid the greater portion of

Putney, but we could see the river below, a bubbly mass of red weed, and the low parts of Lambeth flooded and red. The red creeper swarmed up the trees about the old palace,[7] and their branches stretched gaunt and dead, and set with shrivelled leaves, from amid its clusters. It was strange how entirely dependent both these things were upon flowing water for their propagation. About us neither had gained a footing; laburnums, pink mays, snowballs, and trees of arbor vitae,[8] rose out of laurels and hydrangeas, green and brilliant into the sunlight. Beyond Kensington dense smoke was rising, and that and a blue haze hid the northward hills.

The artilleryman began to tell me of the sort of people who still remained in London.

'One night last week,' he said, 'some fools got the electric light in order, and there was all Regent's Street and the Circus[9] ablaze, crowded with painted and ragged drunkards, men and women, dancing and shouting till dawn. A man who was there told me. And as the day came they became aware of a fighting-machine standing near by the Langham[10] and looking down at them. Heaven knows how long he had been there. It must have given some of them a nasty turn. He came down the road towards them, and picked up nearly a hundred too drunk or frightened to run away.'

Grotesque gleam of a time no history will ever fully describe!

From that, in answer to my questions, he came round to his grandiose plans again. He grew enthusiastic. He talked so eloquently of the possibility of capturing a fighting-machine that I more than half believed in him again. But now that I was beginning to understand something of his quality, I could divine the stress he laid on doing nothing precipitately. And I noted that now there was no question that he personally was to capture and fight the great machine.

After a time we went down to the cellar. Neither of us seemed disposed to resume digging, and when he suggested a meal, I was nothing loath. He became suddenly very generous, and when we had eaten he went away and returned with some excellent cigars. We lit these, and his optimism glowed. He was inclined to regard my coming as a great occasion.

'There's some champagne in the cellar,' he said.

'We can dig better on this Thames-side burgundy,'[11] said I.

'No,' said he; 'I am host today. Champagne! Great God! we've a heavy enough task before us! Let us take a rest and gather strength while we may. Look at these blistered hands!'

And pursuant to this idea of a holiday, he insisted upon playing cards after we had eaten. He taught me euchre,[12] and after dividing London between us, I taking the northern side and he the southern, we played for parish points.[13] Grotesque and foolish as this will seem to the sober reader, it is absolutely true, and, what is more remarkable, I found the card game and several others we played extremely interesting.

Strange mind of man! that, with our species upon the edge of extermination or appalling degradation, with no clear prospect before us but the chance of a horrible death, we could sit following the chance of this painted pasteboard, and playing the 'joker' with vivid delight. Afterwards he taught me poker, and I beat him at three tough chess games. When dark came we decided to take the risk, and lit a lamp.

After an interminable string of games, we supped, and the artilleryman finished the champagne. We went on smoking the cigars. He was no longer the energetic regenerator of his species I had encountered in the morning. He was still optimistic, but it was a less kinetic, a more thoughtful optimism. I remember he wound up with my health, proposed in a speech of small variety and considerable intermittence. I took a cigar, and went upstairs to look at the lights of which he had spoken, that blazed so greenly along the Highgate hills.

At first I stared unintelligently across the London valley. The northern hills were shrouded in darkness; the fires near Kensington glowed redly, and now and then an orange-red tongue of flame flashed up and vanished in the deep blue night. All the rest of London was black. Then, nearer, I perceived a strange light, a pale, violet-purple fluorescent glow, quivering under the night breeze. For a space I could not understand it, and then I knew that it must be the red weed from which this faint irradiation proceeded. With that realization my dormant sense of wonder, my sense of the proportion of things, awoke again. I glanced from that to Mars, red and clear, glowing high in the west, and then gazed long and earnestly at the darkness of Hampstead and Highgate.

I remained a very long time upon the roof, wondering at the grotesque changes of the day. I recalled my mental states from the midnight prayer to the foolish card-playing. I had a violent revulsion of feeling. I remember I flung away the cigar with a certain wasteful symbolism. My folly came to me with glaring exaggeration. I seemed a traitor to my wife and to my kind; I was filled with remorse. I resolved to leave this strange undisciplined dreamer of great things to his drink and gluttony, and to go on into London. There, it seemed to me, I had the best chance of learning what the Martians and my fellow-men were doing. I was still upon the roof when the late moon rose.

8

DEAD LONDON

After I had parted from the artilleryman, I went down the hill, and by the High Street across the bridge to Fulham. The red weed was tumultuous at that time, and nearly choked the bridge roadway; but its fronds were already whitened in patches by the spreading disease that presently removed it so swiftly.

At the corner of the lane that runs to Putney Bridge station I found a man lying. He was as black as a sweep with the black dust, alive, but helplessly and speechlessly drunk. I could get nothing from him but curses and furious lunges at my head. I think I should have stayed by him but for the brutal expression of his face.

There was black dust along the roadway from the bridge onwards, and it grew thicker in Fulham. The streets were horribly quiet. I got food – sour, hard, and mouldy, but quite eatable – in a baker's shop here. Some way towards Walham Green the streets became clear of powder, and I passed a white terrace of houses on fire; the noise of the burning was an absolute relief. Going on towards Brompton, the streets were quiet again.

Here I came once more upon the black powder in the streets and upon dead bodies. I saw altogether about a dozen in the length of the Fulham Road. They had been dead many days, so that I hurried quickly past them. The black powder covered them over, and softened their outlines. One or two had been disturbed by dogs.

Where there was no black powder, it was curiously like a Sunday in the City,[1] with the closed shops, the houses locked up and the blinds drawn, the desertion, and the stillness. In some places plunderers had been at work, but rarely at other than the provision and wine-shops. A jeweller's window had been broken open in one place, but apparently the thief had been disturbed, and a number of gold chains and a watch were scattered on the pavement. I did not trouble to touch them. Further on was a tattered woman in a heap on a doorstep; the hand that hung over her knee was gashed and bled down her rusty brown dress, and a smashed magnum of champagne formed a pool across the pavement. She seemed asleep, but she was dead.

The further I penetrated into London, the profounder grew the stillness. But it was not so much the stillness of death – it was the stillness of suspense, of expectation. At any time the destruction that had already singed the north-western borders of the metropolis, and had annihilated Ealing and Kilburn, might strike among these houses and leave them smoking ruins. It was a city condemned and derelict . . .

In South Kensington the streets were clear of dead and of black powder. It was near South Kensington that I first heard the howling. It crept almost imperceptibly upon my senses. It was a sobbing alternation of two notes, 'Ulla, ulla, ulla, ulla,' keeping on perpetually. When I passed streets that ran north-ward it grew in volume, and houses and buildings seemed to deaden and cut it off again. It came in a full tide down Exhibition Road. I stopped, staring towards Kensington Gardens, wondering at this strange, remote wailing. It was as if that mighty desert of houses had found a voice for its fear and solitude.

'Ulla, ulla, ulla, ulla,' wailed that superhuman note – great waves of sound sweeping down the broad, sunlit roadway, between the tall buildings on each side. I turned northward, marvelling, towards the iron gates of Hyde Park. I had half a mind to break into the Natural History Museum and find my way up to the summits of the towers, in order to see across the park. But I decided to keep to the ground, where quick hiding was possible, and so went on up the Exhibition Road. All the large mansions on each side of the road were empty and still, and my footsteps echoed against the sides of the houses. At the top, near the park gate, I came upon a strange sight – a bus overturned, and the skeleton of a horse picked clean. I puzzled over this for a time, and then went on to the bridge over the Serpentine. The voice grew stronger and stronger, though I could see nothing above the housetops on the north side of the park, save a haze of smoke to the north-west.

'Ulla, ulla, ulla, ulla,' cried the voice, coming, as it seemed to me, from the district about Regent's Park. The desolating cry worked upon my mind. The mood that had sustained me passed. The wailing took possession of me. I found I was intensely weary, footsore, and now again hungry and thirsty.

It was already past noon. Why was I wandering alone in this city of the dead? Why was I alone when all London was lying in state, and in its black shroud? I felt intolerably lonely. My mind ran on old friends that I had forgotten for years. I thought of the poisons in the chemists' shops, of the liquors the wine-merchants stored; I recalled the two sodden creatures of despair who, so far as I knew, shared the city with myself . . .

I came into Oxford Street by the Marble Arch, and here again were black powder and several bodies, and an evil, ominous smell from the gratings of the cellars of some of the houses. I grew very thirsty after the heat of my long walk. With infinite trouble I managed to break into a public-house and get food and drink. I was weary after eating, and went into the parlour behind the bar, and slept on a black horsehair sofa I found there.

I awoke to find that dismal howling still in my ears, 'Ulla, ulla, ulla, ulla.' It was now dusk, and after I had routed out some biscuits and a cheese in the bar – there was a meat-safe, but it contained nothing but maggots – I wandered on through the silent residential squares to Baker Street – Portman Square is the only one I can name – and so came out at last upon Regent's Park. And as I emerged from the top of Baker Street, I saw far away over the trees in the clearness of the sunset the hood of the Martian giant from which this howling proceeded. I was not terrified. I came upon him as if it were a matter of course. I watched him for some time, but he did not move. He appeared to be standing and yelling, for no reason that I could discover.

I tried to formulate a plan of action. That perpetual sound of 'Ulla, ulla, ulla, ulla,' confused my mind. Perhaps I was too tired to be very fearful. Certainly I was more curious to know the reason of this monotonous crying than afraid. I turned back away from the park and struck into Park Road, intending to skirt the park, went along under shelter of the terraces, and got a view of this stationary, howling Martian from the direction of St John's Wood. A couple of hundred yards out of Baker Street I heard a yelping chorus, and saw, first a dog with a piece of putrescent red meat in his jaws coming headlong towards me, and then a pack of starving mongrels in pursuit of him. He made a wide curve to avoid me, as though he feared I might prove a fresh competitor. As the yelping died away down the silent road, the wailing sound of 'Ulla, ulla, ulla, ulla,' reasserted itself.

I came upon the wrecked handling-machine halfway to St John's Wood station. At first I thought a house had fallen across the road. It was only as I clambered among the ruins that I saw, with a start, this mechanical Samson[2] lying, with its tentacles bent and smashed and twisted, among the ruins it had made. The forepart was shattered. It seemed as if it had driven blindly straight at the house, and had been overwhelmed in its overthrow. It seemed to me then that this might have happened by a handling-machine escaping from the guidance of its Martian. I could not clamber among the ruins to see it, and the twilight was now so far advanced that the blood with which its seat was smeared, and the gnawed gristle of the Martian that the dogs had left, were invisible to me.

Wondering still more at all that I had seen, I pushed on towards Primrose Hill. Far away, through a gap in the trees, I saw a second Martian, as motionless as the first, standing in the park towards the Zoological Gardens, and silent. A little beyond the ruins about the smashed handling-machine I came upon the red weed again, and found the Regent's Canal a spongy mass of dark-red vegetation.

As I crossed the bridge, the sound of 'Ulla, ulla, ulla, ulla,' ceased. It was, as it were, cut off. The silence came like a thunderclap.

The dusky houses about me stood faint and tall and dim; the trees towards the park were growing black. All about me the red weed clambered among the ruins, writhing to get above me in the dimness. Night, the mother of fear and mystery, was coming upon me. But while that voice sounded, the solitude, the desolation, had been endurable; by virtue of it London had still seemed alive, and the sense of life about me had upheld me. Then suddenly a change, the passing of something – I knew not what – and then a stillness that could be felt. Nothing but this gaunt quiet.

London about me gazed at me spectrally. The windows in the white houses were like the eye-sockets of skulls. About me my imagination found a thousand noiseless enemies moving. Terror seized me, a horror of my temerity. In front of me the road became pitchy black as though it was tarred, and I saw a contorted shape lying across the pathway. I could not bring myself to go on. I turned down St John's Wood Road, and ran headlong from this unendurable stillness towards Kilburn. I hid from the night and the silence, until long after midnight, in a cabmen's shelter in Harrow Road. But before the dawn my courage returned, and while the stars were still in the sky I turned once more towards Regent's Park. I missed my way among the streets, and presently saw down a long avenue, in the half-light of the early dawn, the curve of Primrose Hill. On the summit, towering up to the fading stars, was a third Martian, erect and motionless like the others.

An insane resolve possessed me. I would die and end it. And I would save myself even the trouble of killing myself. I marched on recklessly towards this Titan, and then, as I drew nearer and the light grew, I saw that a multitude of black birds was circling and clustering about the hood. At that my heart gave a bound, and I began running along the road.

I hurried through the red weed that choked St Edmund's Terrace (I waded breast-high across a torrent of water that was rushing down from the water-works towards the Albert Road), and emerged upon the grass before the rising of the sun. Great mounds had been heaped about the crest of the hill, making a huge redoubt of it – it was the final and largest place the

Martians had made – and from behind these heaps there rose a thin smoke against the sky. Against the skyline an eager dog ran and disappeared. The thought that had flashed into my mind grew real, grew credible. I felt no fear, only a wild, trembling exultation, as I ran up the hill towards the motionless monster. Out of the hood hung lank shreds of brown, at which the hungry birds pecked and tore.

In another moment I had scrambled up the earthen rampart and stood upon its crest, and the interior of the redoubt was below me. A mighty space it was, with gigantic machines here and there within it, huge mounds of material and strange shelter-places. And scattered about it, some in their overturned war-machines, some in the now rigid handling-machines, and a dozen of them stark and silent and laid in a row, were the Martians – *dead!* – slain by the putrefactive and disease bacteria against which their systems were unprepared; slain as the red weed was being slain; slain, after all man's devices had failed, by the humblest things that God, in his wisdom, has put upon this earth.

For so it had come about, as indeed I and many men might have foreseen had not terror and disaster blinded our minds. These germs of disease have taken toll of humanity since the beginning of things – taken toll of our prehuman ancestors since life began here. But by virtue of this natural selection of our kind we have developed resisting-power; to no germs do we succumb without a struggle, and to many – those that cause putrefaction in dead matter, for instance – our living frames are altogether immune. But there are no bacteria in Mars, and directly these invaders arrived, directly they drank and fed, our microscopic allies began to work their overthrow. Already when I watched them they were irrevocably doomed, dying and rotting even as they went to and fro. It was inevitable. By the toll of a billion deaths man has bought his birthright of the earth, and it is his against all comers; it would still be his were the Martians ten times as mighty as they are. For neither do men live nor die in vain.

Here and there they were scattered, nearly fifty altogether, in that great gulf they had made, overtaken by a death that must have seemed to them as incomprehensible as any death could be. To me also at that time this death was incomprehensible. All I knew was that these things that had been alive and so terrible to men were dead. For a moment I believed that the destruction of Sennacherib[3] had been repeated, that God had repented, that the Angel of Death had slain them in the night.

I stood staring into the pit, and my heart lightened gloriously, even as the rising sun struck the world to fire about me with his rays. The pit was still in darkness; the mighty engines, so great and wonderful in their power and complexity, so unearthly in their tortuous forms, rose weird and vague and strange out of the shadows towards the light. A multitude of dogs, I could hear, fought over the bodies that lay darkly in the depth of the pit, far below me. Across the pit on its further lip, flat and vast and strange, lay the great flying-machine with which they had been experimenting upon our denser atmosphere when decay and death arrested them. Death had come not a day too soon. At the sound of a cawing overhead I looked up at the huge fighting-machine that would fight no more forever, at the tattered red shreds of flesh that dripped down upon the overturned seats on the summit of Primrose Hill.

I turned and looked down the slope of the hill to where, enhaloed now in birds, stood those other two Martians that I had seen overnight, just as death had overtaken them. The one had died, even as it had been crying to its companions; perhaps it was the last to die, and its voice had gone on perpetually until the force of its machinery was exhausted. They glittered now, harmless tripod towers of shining metal, in the brightness of the rising sun.

All about the pit, and saved as by a miracle from everlasting destruction, stretched the great Mother of Cities. Those who have only seen London veiled in her sombre robes of smoke can scarcely imagine the naked clearness and beauty of the silent wilderness of houses.

Eastward, over the blackened ruins of the Albert Terrace and the splintered spire of the church, the sun blazed dazzling in a clear sky, and here and there some facet in the great wilderness of roofs caught the light and glared with a white intensity. It touched even that round store place for wines by the Chalk Farm Station, and the vast railway yards, marked once with a graining of black rails, but red-lined now with the quick rusting of a fortnight's disuse, with something of the mystery of beauty.

Northward were Kilburn and Hampstead, blue and crowded with houses; westward the great city was dimmed; and southward, beyond the Martians, the green wash of Regent's Park, the Langham Hotel, the dome of the Albert Hall,[4] the Imperial Institute, and the giant mansions of the Brompton Road came out clear and little in the sunrise, the jagged ruins of Westminster rising hazily beyond. Far away and blue were the Surrey hills, and the towers of the Crystal Palace[5] glittered like two silver rods. The dome of St Paul's was dark against the sunrise, and injured, I saw for the first time, by a huge gaping cavity on its western side.

And as I looked at this wide expanse of houses and factories and churches, silent and abandoned; as I thought of the multitudinous hopes and efforts, the innumerable hosts of lives that had gone to build this human reef, and of the swift and ruthless destruction that had hung over it all; when I realized that the shadow had been rolled back, and that men might still live in the streets, and this dear vast dead city of mine be once more alive and powerful, I felt a wave of emotion that was near akin to tears.

The torment was over. Even that day the healing would begin. The survivors of the people scattered over the country – leaderless, lawless, foodless, like sheep without a shepherd – the thousands who had fled by sea, would begin to return; the pulse of life, growing stronger and stronger, would beat again in the empty streets and pour across the vacant squares. Whatever destruction was done, the hand of the destroyer was stayed. All the gaunt wrecks, the blackened skeletons of houses that stared so dismally at the sunlit grass of the hill, would presently be echoing with the hammers of the restorers and ringing with the tapping of their trowels. At the thought I extended my hands towards the sky and began thanking God. In a year, thought I – in a year . . .

With overwhelming force, came the thought of myself, of my wife, and the old life of hope and tender helpfulness that had ceased forever.

9

WRECKAGE

And now comes the strangest thing in my story. Yet, perhaps, it is not altogether strange. I remember, clearly and coldly and vividly, all that I did that day until the time that I stood weeping and praising God upon the summit of Primrose Hill. And then I forget.

Of the next three days I know nothing. I have learnt since that, so far from my being the first discoverer of the Martian overthrow, several such wanderers as myself had already discovered this on the previous night. One man – the first – had gone to St Martin's-le-Grand, and, while I sheltered in the cabmen's hut, had contrived to telegraph to Paris. Thence the joyful news had flashed all over the world; a thousand cities, chilled by ghastly apprehensions, suddenly flashed into frantic illuminations; they knew of it in Dublin, Edinburgh, Manchester, Birmingham, at the time when I stood upon the verge of the pit. Already men, weeping with joy, as I have heard, shouting and staying their work to shake hands and shout, were making up trains, even as near as Crewe, to descend upon London. The church bells that had ceased a fortnight since suddenly caught the news, until all England was bell-ringing. Men on cycles, lean-faced, unkempt, scorched along every country lane shouting of unhoped deliverance, shouting to gaunt, staring figures of despair. And for the food! Across the Channel, across the Irish Sea, across the Atlantic, corn, bread, and meat were tearing to our relief. All the shipping in the world seemed going Londonward in those days. But of all this I have no memory. I drifted – a demented man. I found myself in a house of kindly people, who had found me on the third day wandering, weeping and raving, through the streets of St John's Wood. They have told me since that I was singing some inane doggerel about 'The Last Man Left Alive! Hurrah! The Last Man Left Alive!'[1] Troubled as they were with their own affairs, these people, whose name, much as I would like to express my gratitude to them, I may not even give here, nevertheless cumbered themselves with me, sheltered me, and protected me from myself. Apparently they had learnt something of my story from me during the days of my lapse.

Very gently, when my mind was assured again, did they break to me what they had learnt of the fate of Leatherhead. Two days after I was imprisoned it had been destroyed, with every soul in it, by a Martian. He had swept it out of existence, as it seemed, without any provocation, as a boy might crush an anthill, in the mere wantonness of power.

I was a lonely man, and they were very kind to me. I was a lonely man and a sad one, and they bore with me. I remained with them four days after my recovery. All that time I felt a vague, a growing craving to look once more on whatever remained of the little life that seemed so happy and bright in my past. It was a mere hopeless desire to feast upon my misery. They dissuaded me. They did all they could to divert me from this morbidity. But at last I could resist the impulse no longer, and, promising faithfully to return to them, and parting, as I will confess, from these four-day friends with tears, I went out again into the streets that had lately been so dark and strange and empty.

Already they were busy with returning people; in places even there were shops open, and I saw a drinking-fountain running water.

I remember how mockingly bright the day seemed as I went back on my melancholy pilgrimage to the little house at Woking, how busy the streets and vivid the moving life about me. So many people were abroad everywhere, busied in a thousand activities, that it seemed incredible that any great proportion of the population could have been slain. But then I noticed how yellow were the skins of the people I met, how shaggy the hair of the men, how large and bright their eyes, and that every other man still wore his dirty rags. Their faces seemed all with one of two expressions – a leaping exultation and energy, or a grim resolution. Save for the expression of the faces, London seemed a city of tramps. The vestries were indiscriminately distributing bread sent us by the French government. The ribs of the few horses showed dismally. Haggard special constables with white badges stood at the corners of every street. I saw little of the mischief wrought by the Martians until I reached Wellington Street, and there I saw the red weed clambering over the buttresses of Waterloo Bridge.

At the corner of the bridge, too, I saw one of the common contrasts of that grotesque time – a sheet of paper flaunting against a thicket of the red weed, transfixed by a stick that kept it in place. It was the placard of the first newspaper to resume publication – the *Daily Mail*.[2] I bought a copy for a blackened shilling I found in my pocket. Most of it was in blank, but the solitary compositor who did the thing had amused himself by making a grotesque scheme of advertisement stereo[3] on the back page. The matter he printed was emotional; the news organization had not as yet found its way back. I learnt nothing fresh except that already in one week the examination of the Martian mechanisms had yielded astonishing results. Among other things, the article assured me what I did not believe at the time, that the 'Secret of Flying' was discovered. At Waterloo I found the free trains that were taking people to their homes. The first rush was already over. There were few people in the train, and I was in no mood for casual conversation. I got a compartment to myself, and sat with folded arms, looking greyly at the sunlit devastation that flowed past the windows. And just outside the terminus the train jolted over temporary rails, and on either side of the railway the houses were blackened ruins. To Clapham Junction the face of London was grimy with powder of the Black Smoke, in spite of two days of thunderstorms and rain, and at Clapham Junction the line had been wrecked again; there were hundreds of out-of-work clerks and shopmen working side by side with the customary navvies, and we were jolted over a hasty relaying.

All down the line from there the aspect of the country was

gaunt and unfamiliar; Wimbledon particularly had suffered. Walton, by virtue of its unburnt pine-woods, seemed the least hurt of any place along the line. The Wandle, the Mole, every little stream, was a heaped mass of red weed, in appearance between butcher's meat and pickled cabbage. The Surrey pine-woods were too dry, however, for the festoons of the red climber. Beyond Wimbledon, within sight of the line, in certain nursery grounds, were the heaped masses of earth about the sixth cylinder. A number of people were standing about it, and some sappers were busy in the midst of it. Over it flaunted a Union Jack, flapping cheerfully in the morning breeze. The nursery grounds were everywhere crimson with the weed, a wide expanse of livid colour cut with purple shadows, and very painful to the eye. One's gaze went with infinite relief from the scorched greys and sullen reds of the foreground to the blue-green softness of the eastward hills.

The line on the London side of Woking station was still undergoing repair, so I descended at Byfleet station and took the road to Maybury, past the place where I and the artillery-man had talked to the hussars, and on by the spot where the Martian had appeared to me in the thunderstorm. Here, moved by curiosity, I turned aside to find, among a tangle of red fronds, the warped and broken dogcart with the whitened bones of the horse, scattered and gnawed. For a time I stood regarding these vestiges . . .

Then I returned through the pine-wood, neck-high with red weed here and there, to find the landlord of the Spotted Dog had already found burial, and so came home past the College Arms. A man standing at an open cottage door greeted me by name as I passed.

I looked at my house with a quick flash of hope that faded immediately. The door had been forced; it was unfastened, and was opening slowly as I approached.

It slammed again. The curtains of my study fluttered out of the open window from which I and the artilleryman had watched the dawn. No one had closed it since. The smashed bushes were just as I had left them nearly four weeks ago. I stumbled into the hall, and the house felt empty. The stair-carpet was ruffled and discoloured where I had crouched, soaked to the skin from the thunderstorm the night of the catastrophe. Our muddy footsteps I saw still went up the stairs.

I followed them to my study, and found lying on my writing-table still, with the selenite paper-weight upon it, the sheet of work I had left on the afternoon of the opening of the cylinder. For a space I stood reading over my abandoned arguments. It was a paper on the probable development of Moral Ideas with the development of the civilizing process; and the last sentence was the opening of a prophecy: 'In about two hundred years,' I had written, 'we may expect—' The sentence ended abruptly. I remembered my inability to fix my mind that morning, scarcely a month gone by, and how I had broken off to get my *Daily Chronicle* from the newsboy. I remembered how I went down to the garden gate as he came along, and how I had listened to his odd story of 'Men from Mars'.

I came down and went into the dining-room. There were the mutton and the bread, both far gone now in decay, and a beer bottle overturned, just as I and the artilleryman had left them. My home was desolate. I perceived the folly of the faint hope I had cherished so long. And then a strange thing occurred. 'It is no use,' said a voice. 'The house is deserted. No one has been here these ten days. Do not stay here to torment yourself. No one escaped but you.'

I was startled. Had I spoken my thought aloud? I turned, and the French window was open behind me. I made a step to it, and stood looking out.

And there, amazed and afraid, even as I stood amazed and afraid, were my cousin and my wife – my wife white and tearless. She gave a faint cry.

'I came,' she said. 'I knew – knew—'

She put her hand to her throat – swayed. I made a step forward, and caught her in my arms.

10

THE EPILOGUE

I cannot but regret, now that I am concluding my story, how little I am able to contribute to the discussion of the many debatable questions which are still unsettled. In one respect I shall certainly provoke criticism. My particular province is speculative philosophy. My knowledge of comparative physiology is confined to a book or two, but it seems to me that Carver's suggestions as to the reason of the rapid death of the Martians is so probable as to be regarded almost as a proven conclusion. I have assumed that in the body of my narrative.

At any rate, in all the bodies of the Martians that were examined after the war, no bacteria except those already known as terrestrial species were found. That they did not bury any of their dead, and the reckless slaughter they perpetrated, point also to an entire ignorance of the putrefactive process. But probable as this seems, it is by no means a proven conclusion.

Neither is the composition of the Black Smoke known, which the Martians used with such deadly effect, and the generator of the Heat-Ray remains a puzzle. The terrible disasters at the Ealing and South Kensington laboratories have disinclined analysts for further investigations upon the latter. Spectrum analysis of the black powder points unmistakably to the presence of an unknown element with a brilliant group of three lines in the green, and it is possible that it combines with argon to form a compound which acts at once with deadly effect upon some constituent in the blood. But such unproven speculations will scarcely be of interest to the general reader, to whom this story is addressed. None of the brown scum that drifted down the

Thames after the destruction of Shepperton was examined at the time, and now none is forthcoming.

The results of an anatomical examination of the Martians, so far as the prowling dogs had left such an examination possible, I have already given. But everyone is familiar with the magnificent and almost complete specimen in spirits at the Natural History Museum, and the countless drawings that have been made from it; and beyond that the interest of their physiology and structure is purely scientific.

A question of graver and universal interest is the possibility of another attack from the Martians. I do not think that nearly enough attention is being given to this aspect of the matter. At present the planet Mars is in conjunction, but with every return to opposition I, for one, anticipate a renewal of their adventure. In any case, we should be prepared. It seems to me that it should be possible to define the position of the gun from which the shots are discharged, to keep a sustained watch upon this part of the planet, and to anticipate the arrival of the next attack.

In that case the cylinder might be destroyed with dynamite or artillery before it was sufficiently cool for the Martians to emerge, or they might be butchered by means of guns so soon as the screw opened. It seems to me that they have lost a vast advantage in the failure of their first surprise. Possibly they see it in the same light.

Lessing has advanced excellent reasons for supposing that the Martians have actually succeeded in effecting a landing on the planet Venus. Seven months ago now, Venus and Mars were in alignment with the sun; that is to say, Mars was in opposition from the point of view of an observer on Venus. Subsequently a peculiar luminous and sinuous marking[1] appeared on the unillumined half of the inner planet, and almost simultaneously a faint dark mark of a similar sinuous character was detected upon a photograph of the Martian disc. One needs to see the drawings of these appearances in order to appreciate fully their remarkable resemblance in character.

At any rate, whether we expect another invasion or not, our views of the human future must be greatly modified by these events. We have learned now that we cannot regard this planet as being fenced in and a secure abiding-place for Man; we can never anticipate the unseen good or evil that may come upon us suddenly out of space. It may be that in the larger design of the universe this invasion from Mars is not without its ultimate benefit for men; it has robbed us of that serene confidence in the future which is the most fruitful source of decadence, the gifts to human science it has brought are enormous, and it has done much to promote the conception of the commonweal of mankind. It may be that across the immensity of space the Martians have watched the fate of these pioneers of theirs and learned their lesson, and that on the planet Venus they have found a securer settlement. Be that as it may, for many years yet there will certainly be no relaxation of the eager scrutiny of the Martian disc, and those fiery darts of the sky, the shooting stars, will bring with them as they fall an unavoidable apprehension to all the sons of men.

The broadening of men's views that has resulted can scarcely be exaggerated. Before the cylinder fell there was a general persuasion that through all the deep of space no life existed beyond the petty surface of our minute sphere. Now we see further. If the Martians can reach Venus, there is no reason to suppose that the thing is impossible for men, and when the slow cooling of the sun makes this earth uninhabitable, as at last it must do, it may be that the thread of life that has begun here will have streamed out and caught our sister planet within its toils.

Dim and wonderful is the vision I have conjured up in my mind of life spreading slowly from this little seed-bed of the solar system throughout the inanimate vastness of sidereal space. But that is a remote dream. It may be, on the other hand, that the destruction of the Martians is only a reprieve. To them, and not to us, perhaps, is the future ordained.

I must confess the stress and danger of the time have left an abiding sense of doubt and insecurity in my mind. I sit in my study writing by lamplight, and suddenly I see again the healing valley below set with writhing flames, and feel the house behind and about me empty and desolate. I go out into the Byfleet Road, and vehicles pass me, a butcher-boy in a cart, a cabful of visitors, a workman on a bicycle, children going to school, and suddenly they become vague and unreal, and I hurry again with the artilleryman through the hot, brooding silence. Of a night I see the black powder darkening the silent streets, and the contorted bodies shrouded in that layer; they rise upon me tattered and dog-bitten. They gibber and grow fiercer, paler, uglier, mad distortions of humanity at last, and I wake, cold and wretched, in the darkness of the night.

I go to London and see the busy multitudes in Fleet Street and the Strand, and it comes across my mind that they are but the ghosts of the past, haunting the streets that I have seen silent and wretched, going to and fro, phantasms in a dead city, the mockery of life in a galvanized body. And strange, too, it is to stand on Primrose Hill, as I did but a day before writing this last chapter, to see the great province of houses, dim and blue through the haze of the smoke and mist, vanishing at last into the vague lower sky, to see the people walking to and fro among the flower-beds on the hill, to see the sightseers about the Martian machine that stands there still, to hear the tumult of playing children, and to recall the time when I saw it all bright and clear-cut, hard and silent, under the dawn of that last great day . . .

And strangest of all is it to hold my wife's hand again, and to think that I have counted her, and that she has counted me, among the dead.

Appendix

NOTE ON PLACES IN THE NOVEL

Places in the text are only annotated to explain a particular geographical reference, i.e. the 'Shepperton Bank' as the north bank of the Thames, or a historical event which may have had reference to Wells's theme of disruption and invasion. However, it is important to note that the events of *The War of the Worlds* take place in a particular location (largely the suburbs of London, particularly the town of Woking, Surrey, where Wells was living when he wrote the novel and London itself), and the effect of the story for many of its readers was in the familiarity of its landscape. Only very particular details such as the names of certain public houses or other buildings are fictionalized. The story begins around Woking, about four miles north of Guildford and twenty-three miles south-west of London. The narrator lives in Maybury, the eastern part of Woking, as did Wells during the writing of *The War of the Worlds*. In *Experiment in Autobiography*, Wells says that he 'wheeled about the district marking down suitable places and people for destruction by my Martians' (vol. 2, p. 543). There is now a statue of a Martian tripod in Woking town centre.

The (fictional) astronomer Ogilvy lives in Ottershaw, about three miles from Maybury. Woking is also sixteen miles north-west of Dorking, the location of George Chesney's *The Battle of Dorking* (1871) which sparked off a tradition of 'future-war' and invasion stories in which the flesh of the reading public was made to creep by the destruction of well-known places. *The War of the Worlds* can be seen as the culmination and transcendence of this tradition.

The first Martian landing is on Horsell Common, north of Woking, the second on the golf links between Woking and Byfleet, three miles to the north-east. After removing his wife to Leatherhead, east and south of Woking, the narrator returns to be 'in at the death' and is caught up in the advance of the Martians north through the village

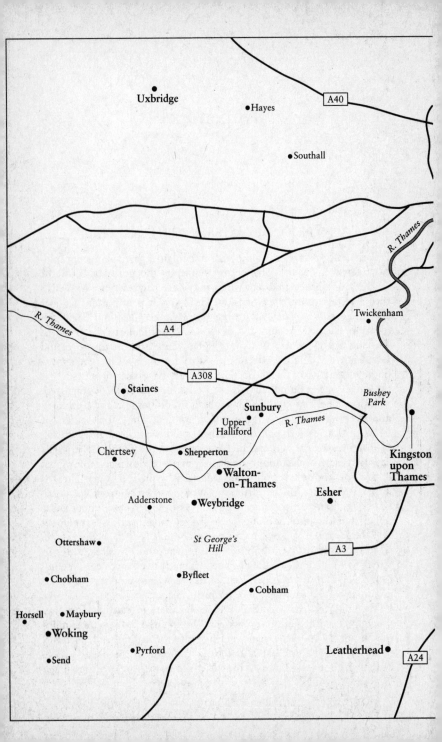

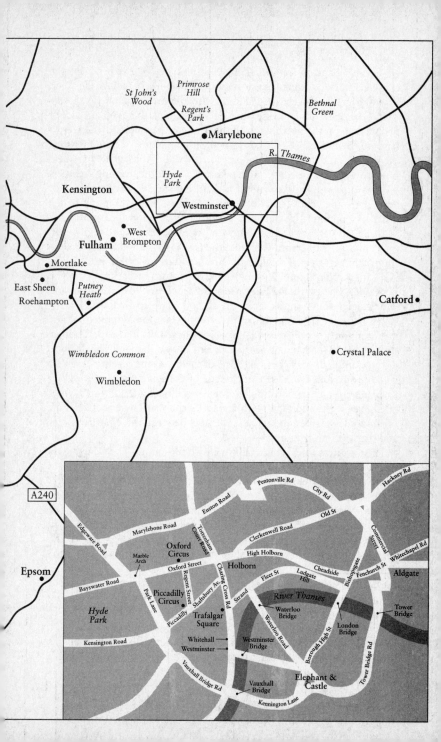

of Cobham and is cut off from returning to Leatherhead by the third cylinder, landing in the region of Pyrford, a village between Woking and Leatherhead. He flees with the artilleryman north-east to Weybridge and witnesses the destruction of that village and of Shepperton on the north bank of the Thames, escaping down-river to land on the north bank opposite Walton-on-Thames. There he meets the curate, and they set off northward to Halliford. The Martians prepare for their advance, and take up a position from St George's Hill, five miles north-north-east of Woking station, to the village of Send, with the central part of the line at Weybridge, pointing to the heart of London. The narrator's brother in London, hearing of the Martian advance from the south-west, witnesses chaos and fugitives in the iconic parts of central London: the Strand (location of fashionable shops and theatres), Trafalgar Square (monuments of Empire such as Nelson's Column) and Westminster (the Houses of Parliament). The Londoners flee north, via Edgware and Barnet, east towards Southend and Shoeburyness on the Essex coast, and south to Deal and Broadstairs. After witnessing the sixth cylinder land at Wimbledon, the narrator's brother with two companions heads off in the direction of Colchester, seventy miles north-east of London, beyond which ports to the Continent are accessible. One of them sees the seventh cylinder, which lands on Primrose Hill, north of Regent's Park in London. They reach Chelmsford and eventually Tillingham, sixty-five miles north-east of London and within sight of the sea. There they embark on a paddle-steamer and witness the duel between the *Thunder Child* and the Martian tripod.

The narrator holes up in Halliford with the curate. Then they travel via Sunbury, Bushey Park, where the fourth cylinder landed, Twickenham, and cross Richmond Bridge, where the Thames is flowing north, in the direction of Kew and the Royal Botanical gardens. Despite the narrator's desire to find his wife in Leatherhead, they are still travelling north and then east, but are now south of the Thames. In Sheen, in the direction of Mortlake (then a small village on the bank of the Thames north of East Sheen) they take shelter in a house where the fifth cylinder lands, trapping them. Following the death of the curate, the narrator remains in hiding and on his emergence sets off westwards towards Kew, but is prevented by a swamp of 'red weed' from going further and retraces his steps to Mortlake, Roehampton and Putney Common, north of Wimbledon, where the sixth cylinder landed. On Putney Hill he meets again the artilleryman. After his disillusion with the artilleryman's survivalist project he crosses the bridge to Fulham and Brompton, witnessing the devastation of fashionable London as he journeys through South Kensington, Hyde Park, Oxford Street, Baker Street, Regent's Park, St John's Wood to Primrose Hill, north of Regent's Park, from where much of London to the Thames and beyond could be seen. It is here he sees the dead Martian (from the seventh cylinder, which landed on Primrose Hill) and observes the catastrophe brought to London, including the damage done to St Paul's Cathedral.

Andy Sawyer

Notes

EPIGRAPH

1. *Kepler (quoted in 'The Anatomy of Melancholy.'):* The astronomer Johannes Kepler (1571–1630) devised laws of planetary motion which remain fundamental to modern astronomy. His *Somnium* ('Dream'), published 1634, speculated about life on other worlds. Robert Burton (1577–1640) quotes Kepler in *The Anatomy of Melancholy* (1621) in the context of this question.

BOOK I

CHAPTER 1

THE EVE OF THE WAR

1. *watched:* In Wells's stories 'The Star' and 'The Crystal Egg' (both 1897) Martians also observe the Earth.
2. *infusoria:* Microscopic organisms.
3. *the older worlds of space:* According to the then prevailing theory of planetary formation, the outer planets formed first. Mars, being further from the sun and smaller, would have cooled and aged faster than the Earth.
4. *the beasts that perish:* Psalm 49:12. (All Biblical references are taken from the Authorized Version.)
5. *Mars:* Named after the Roman god of war, it is the fourth planet from the sun. Known as the 'red planet' from its appearance, it was the setting for fictional civilizations at least as early as Percy Greg's *Across the Zodiac* (1880) and still remains one of the most resonant locations in science fiction.
6. *I scarcely need remind the reader:* Viewpoint in this chapter shifts from the impersonal author to a recognizable character who, like Wells, is a writer with scientific interests producing articles on

'the probable developments of moral ideas' and who lives with his wife in Woking. While there are Wellsian aspects to this character, particularly in his reaction to religion and ideas about future societies, he is not necessarily a reliable narrator. The historical H. G. Wells may be tangentially referred to in this story (see notes for Book II, Ch. 2, 'What We Saw from the Ruined House').

7. *nebular hypothesis*: Immanuel Kant (1724–1804) and Pierre-Simon Laplace (1749–1827) suggested that the planets condensed from rings of gas thrown off by the sun.

8. *inhabitants of Mars*: Camille Flammarion (1842–1925) in *L'Astronomie populaire* (1879) and *La Planète Mars* (1892), and Percival Lowell (1855–1916) in *Mars* (1895) argued that Mars was inhabited by intelligent beings.

9. *bison and the dodo*: The bison or American buffalo was all but exterminated by hunters during the nineteenth century. The dodo, a flightless pigeon-like bird native to Mauritius, was driven to extinction by 1680.

10. *Tasmanians*: Tasmania became a British convict settlement in 1803. By 1876 the native inhabitants had been exterminated by murder, enslavement and disease. In *The Outline of History* (1920) Wells describes the Tasmanians as 'palaeolithic' and describes how poisoned meat was left out for them.

11. *Schiaparelli*: Giovanni Virginio Schiaparelli (1835–1910) observed, during the 1877 opposition (see note 12), 'canali' (channels). Lowell continued his mapping, and argued that they were very likely actual canals, built by Martians.

12. *the opposition of 1894*: Opposition is when the Earth is between the sun and Mars, and the two planets are at their closest. Conjunction is when the sun is directly between Mars and Earth.

13. *Lick Observatory*: Mount Hamilton, California. It was opened in 1888.

14. *Perrotin of Nice*: The Director of the observatory built in 1880 near Nice on the Mediterranean coast of France.

15. *the issue of Nature dated August 2nd*: On that date in 1894 *Nature* reported on a 'A Strange Light on Mars' observed by the astronomer Javelle. The report speculates, not altogether seriously, that the light could be signals from the Martian inhabitants. The fictional 'Lavelle of Java' is clearly an echo of the French astronomer.

16. *Daily Telegraph*: Founded in 1855, it was (and is) an important

Conservative newspaper, in Wells's time selling about 300,000 copies a day.

17. *Ogilvy ... at Ottershaw*: Fictional, but an astronomer of that name features in Wells's short story 'The Star' (1897). Wells mixes real and fictitious names in *War of the Worlds*. Only real names, or fictional versions of real people, are hereafter annotated. For Ottershaw, see p. 181, 'Note on Places in the Novel'.

18. *Punch*: British weekly satirical magazine (founded 1841) noted especially for its cartoons. It was published until 1992, revived in 1996, and ceased publication in 2002.

19. *learning to ride the bicycle*: As Wells himself was doing during the composition of *The War of the Worlds*.

CHAPTER 2

THE FALLING STAR

1. *Denning*: William Frederick Denning (1848–1931), Britain's leading authority on meteorites.

2. *Daily Chronicle*: Established 1877, the major pro-Liberal British newspaper.

CHAPTER 3

ON HORSELL COMMON

1. *'touch'*: 'Tag', or 'tig': children's game in which the person touched chases the other players until he or she touches one, who takes over the chase.

2. *gas-float*: A kind of beacon. The *Oxford English Dictionary* quotes the *Daily News* of 26 May 1897: 'a species of beacon, shaped at the bottom like a ship, and carrying on a lofty pyramid the light, which is fed from a gas cylinder placed in the hull.'

3. *three kingdoms*: England, Scotland and Ireland. (Wales is a Principality.)

4. *basket-chaise*: A light horse-drawn carriage.

5. *Astronomer Royal*: A position dating from 1675, when Charles II appointed the first Director of the Royal Observatory, Greenwich. Wells's 'Stent' is fictional: the actual Astronomer Royal during the dates covered by *The War of the Worlds* was William Christie (1845–1922).

CHAPTER 4
THE CYLINDER OPENS

1. *a big greyish rounded bulk*: Wells's description of the Martians is based upon speculation about how life could evolve on a low-gravity, arid world like Mars, but also owes much to his essay 'The Man of the Year Million' (see note 5 for Book II, Ch. 2) in which he considers how humanity could evolve into a being in which the brain develops, the lower limbs atrophy and the digestive system loses the ability to cope with solid food.
2. *Gorgon*: In Greek mythology, the three Gorgons (Medusa, Stheno and Euryale) had writhing serpents for hair.

CHAPTER 5
THE HEAT-RAY

1. *The Heat-Ray*: The *Oxford English Dictionary* cites *The War of the Worlds* as the first use of this term to describe a futuristic weapon.

CHAPTER 7
HOW I REACHED HOME

1. *electric lamps*: A number of inventors worked on electric light in the late nineteenth century. London's first public electric lighting using 'carbon arc lamps' was erected in 1878. Sir Joseph Wilson Swan (1828–1914) demonstrated electric lamps in Newcastle, England in 1879 and in the same year the American Thomas Alva Edison (1847–1931) produced a long-lasting light bulb. In 1882, Thomas Edison's Electric Light Company opened a power station in London.
2. *Times*: Established 1788, Britain's leading daily newspaper, and still published.
3. *argon*: Inert gas discovered in 1894 by Lord Rayleigh (1842–1919) and William Ramsey (1852–1916).

CHAPTER 8
FRIDAY NIGHT

1. *Trenching on Smith's monopoly*: Infringing the right of the W. H. Smith company to sell newspapers and books on railway stations.
2. *hussars*: Light cavalry.
3. *Maxims*: An early machine-gun patented 1884 by Sir Hiram Stevens Maxim (1840–1916) and adopted by the British Army in 1889.
4. *Cardigan regiment*: Army regiment named for Cardiganshire, Wales, but in this instance based in Aldershot, a garrison town in Hampshire about ten miles from the events of the story.

CHAPTER 9
THE FIGHTING BEGINS

1. *Horse Guards*: One of the British Army's elite regiments.
2. *'fishers of men'*: Matthew 4:19: 'And he saith unto them, Follow me and I shall make ye fishers of men.'
3. *Oriental College*: About half a mile east of Woking station. Formerly the Royal Dramatic College, the buildings were converted into a centre for distinguished visitors from India.
4. *her cousins*: other references make them the narrator's cousins.
5. *Spotted Dog*: in reality the 'Princess of Wales', near Wakeford.
6. *dogcart*: a small open cart, originally with seats constructed and positioned so as to form a box for sportsmens' dogs (*Oxford English Dictionary*).
7. *'my bit of a pig'*: Either the landlord is selling an actual pig to the stranger and so he and the narrator are talking at cross-purposes, or he is using one of the several slang meanings of 'pig' as 'property'.

CHAPTER 10
IN THE STORM

1. *articulate ropes*: Jointed steel cables.
2. *College Arms*: The real name of the public house.

CHAPTER 11

AT THE WINDOW

1. *Potteries*: The 'Five Towns' after Arnold Bennett (1867–1931): the pottery-making region of Staffordshire, now making up the city of Stoke-on-Trent: Burslem, Fenton, Hanley, Longton, Stoke-upon-Trent and Tunstall. Although there are six towns, Bennett's novel *Anna of the Five Towns* (1902) omitted Fenton. Wells spent three months in the area in 1888.
2. *ironclad*: Warship protected by thick plates of iron or steel. The term came into general use in the 1860s, during the American Civil War.
3. *pillars of fire*: Exodus 13:21, 'And the Lord went before them by day in a pillar of a cloud, to lead them the way; and by night in a pillar of fire.'

CHAPTER 12

WHAT I SAW OF THE DESTRUCTION OF WEYBRIDGE AND SHEPPERTON

1. *theodolite*: An instrument used in surveying for measuring angles.
2. *heliograph*: A signalling apparatus using a mirror to reflect sunlight.
3. *''luminium'*: Aluminium; first produced in 1825, but expensive to produce until electrolysis was perfected in 1886.
4. *sabbatical*: It was Sunday, so they were dressing for church.
5. *Shepperton side*: The north bank of the Thames, as is the 'Middlesex Bank' (Ch. 13). The 'Surrey side' is the south bank.

CHAPTER 13

HOW I FELL IN WITH THE CURATE

1. *the earthquake that destroyed Lisbon*: 1 November 1775, when 50,000 people died and the city was devastated.
2. *'Sodom and Gomorrah!'*: Cities destroyed for their sinfulness as recounted in Genesis 19.
3. *'The smoke of her burning goeth up for ever and ever!'*: An echo of Revelation 19:3. Many of the curate's subsequent utterances

are also quotations or slight misquotations from the Book of Revelation.

CHAPTER 14
IN LONDON

1. *crammer's*: Institutions designed to prepare students for examinations such as University entrance.
2. *St James's Gazette*: A Conservative paper (published 1880–1905) with a leaning towards literary interests.
3. *theatre trains*: Trains timed to return London theatre-goers to their homes in the suburbs.
4. *Sunday Sun*: London's first popular halfpenny evening newspaper, it was established 1891, and relaunched with a new series from 1893–1908.
5. *'hand-book' article in the Referee*: London weekly paper, published 1877–1928, with an emphasis on sport, humour and the arts.
6. *Foundling Hospital*: A home for illegitimate children in Bloomsbury, founded in 1739 by Thomas Coram (1688–1751).
7. *'lungs'*: Areas of open parkland.
8. *omnibuses*: At this time, like 'cabs', horse-drawn.
9. *Epsom High Street on a Derby Day*: The Epsom Derby, held in June, is the most important event in the horse-racing calendar. In other words, swarming with people.

CHAPTER 15
WHAT HAD HAPPENED IN SURREY

1. *St George's Hill*: About five miles north-east of Woking station. In 1649, it was the site of the Digger settlement led by Gerrard Winstanley (1609–76).
2. *evening star*: Venus.
3. *greater Moscow*: The Russians frustrated Napoleon's invasion in 1812 by setting fire to Moscow, forcing the French to make a humiliating retreat.
4. *kopjes*: Small flat-topped hills, as in South Africa (Afrikaans).
5. *carbonic acid gas*: Carbon dioxide.
6. *four lines in the blue of the spectrum*: See the contradiction in the Epilogue.

CHAPTER 16

THE EXODUS FROM LONDON

1. *pony-chaise*: Light carriage.
2. *thirty pounds in gold*: In coin: gold sovereigns worth one pound sterling.
3. *East End*: London's poor working-class district. The driver of the cart is speaking with a strong East London accent.
4. *'Vestry'*: A committee 'vested' to provide services.
5. *'Lord Garrick . . . the Chief Justice?'*: The Lord Chief Justice is the second-highest Judge of the Courts of England and Wales (after the Lord Chancellor) and presides over the Criminal Division of the Court of Appeal. The Lord Chief Justice during the period *The War of the Worlds* was written and published was Lord Russell of Killowen (1832–1900).

CHAPTER 17

THE 'THUNDER CHILD'

1. *home counties*: The counties neighbouring London: Middlesex, Essex, Kent and Surrey (sometimes also Sussex and Hertfordshire).
2. *Goths and Huns*: The Goths, a Germanic tribe, ravaged Europe during the third to fifth centuries AD. The Asiatic Huns, led by the feared Attila, invaded Europe in the fifth century.
3. *Pool of London*: The dockland area of the River Thames reaching upstream to London Bridge: the heart of London's maritime trading.
4. *lightermen*: The operators of 'lighters' or barges that unload ships of their cargo.
5. *Committee of Public Supply*: An echo of the 'Committee of Public Safety' of the French Revolution.
6. *Waltham Abbey Powder Mills*: Waltham Abbey in Essex is sixteen miles north of London. The 'powder-mills' had produced gunpowder since the seventeenth century.
7. *electric boats*: William Woodnut Griscom invented an electric motor suitable for marine application in 1879, and by the 1890s electric boats were used for pleasure boats and light naval craft.
8. *rained down darkness upon the land*: Genesis 19:24, 'The Lord rained upon Sodom and upon Gomorrah brimstone and fire';

Exodus 10:22, 'and there was a thick darkness in all the land of Egypt'. See also Matthew 27:45.

BOOK II

CHAPTER 1

UNDER FOOT

1. *destruction of Pompeii*: The Roman city of Pompeii, near Naples, was overwhelmed by hot ash and lava on the eruption of Vesuvius in 79 BC.

2. *semi-detached villa*: Small suburban houses (two houses sharing a common wall). More socially desirable than rows of joined 'terraced' housing.

3. *coloured supplements*: Coloured reproductions of works of art given away with newspapers and used for decoration in poorer households.

CHAPTER 2

WHAT WE SAW FROM THE RUINED HOUSE

1. *one of the first pamphlets*: Wells was not impressed by the illustrations, by Warwick Goble (1862–1943), for the original magazine serialization of *The War of the Worlds* in *Pearson's Magazine*.

2. *Professor Howes*: George Bond Howes (1853–1905), was assistant to T. H. Huxley at the time of Wells's education under him and wrote the introduction to Wells's *Text-Book of Biology* (1893).

3. *fresh-water polyp*: 'Polyp' is a general term for small tentacled animals, but Wells is probably referring to the Hydra (Hydrozoa).

4. *Tunicates*: A group of small marine animals (Urochordata) including sea-squirts and kinds of plankton, a sub-group of the phylum Chordata (Vertebrates or backboned animals). The free-swimming young have nerve cords along their backs which are lost in adulthood, so they are seen as transitional between invertebrates and vertebrates.

5. *a certain speculative writer*: Obviously named H. G. Wells, whose 'The Man of the Year Million' appeared in the *Pall Mall Gazette* (9 November 1893) and on 16 November 1893 in the *Pall Mall Budget*, a weekly which reprinted items from the *Gazette*. It was parodied in *Punch* (25 November 1893). Wells's description of

the Martians in *War of the Worlds* is similar to his picture of evolved Humanity in this article.

6. *'teacher and agent of the brain'*: In 'The Man of the Year Million' the 'Professor' refers to the hand as 'the teacher and interpreter of the brain'.

7. *Red Weed*: In 'The Crystal Egg' (1897) Wells describes the expanses of water on Mars lined with 'dense *red* weeds' (his emphasis). Percy Gregg's novel *Across the Zodiac* (1880) speculated that Martian vegetation was orange. The French astronomer Camille Flammarion (see note 8 to Book I, Ch. 1) argued that the dominant colour of Martian vegetation could be red, thus explaining the planet's colour. His *L'Astronomie populaire* was translated into English in 1894 and was read by Wells.

8. *Philips*: Philips appears to be one of Wells's fictional 'authorities'.

9. *hastily compiled pamphlet*: In context, another joke reference to the original serialization of *War of the Worlds*, but David Y. Hughes and Harry M. Geduld, in their critical edition of the novel, point out that the serial does not refer to Martian communication in this way.

10. *telepathic theory*: The term 'telepathy' for thought transference was coined in 1882 by Fredric W. H. Myers (1843–1901) of the Society for Psychical Research. Wells had published a hostile review of a book on thought transference in *Nature* (6 December 1894).

11. *road-skates*: Roller-skating was popular until overtaken by the bicycle craze in the 1890s, but Wells may be using the word 'skate' in a more general sense: 'a device with a set of rollers or wheels on which something moves' (*OED*).

12. *Lilienthal*: The German inventor Otto Lilienthal (1848–96) constructed and tested gliders until his death following a crash.

13. *sticks*: Shooting-sticks, i.e. pistols.

14. *the wheel is absent*: The Martians do, however, use 'discs' and curved bearings. The civilizations of South America had no knowledge of the wheel as a tool. Unlike the Martians, they succumbed to invasion. Some writers have since speculated about wheels found as part of natural biology: examples are in Philip Pullman's *Amber Spyglass* (2001) and James White's 'Vertigo' (1968).

15. *friction bearings*: Parts placed between moving parts of a machine to reduce friction. Wells describes them as 'curved' but they may not be what we call 'ball-bearings'.

CHAPTER 4

THE DEATH OF THE CURATE

1. *'The wine-press of God'*: Revelation 14:19, 'the great winepress of the wrath of god'.
2. *'Woe unto this unfaithful city!'*: An echo of numerous Biblical lamentations, for example Revelation 18:10: 'Alas, alas, that great city, Babylon'; Revelation 8:13: 'Woe, woe, woe to the inhabiters of the earth'; Isaiah 1:21: 'How is the faithful city become an harlot!'
3. *split-ring*: Ring on which keys are attached.
4. *Briareus*: In Greek mythology, a giant with a hundred hands.

CHAPTER 6

THE WORK OF FIFTEEN DAYS

1. *Putney*: A district of London south of the Thames and about seven miles west of the city centre. In October/November 1647 Putney Church was the site of the 'Putney debates' between the New Model Army and the Levellers, chaired by Oliver Cromwell.
2. *cankering*: Festering, corrupting; with an implication of 'cancerous'.

CHAPTER 7

THE MAN ON PUTNEY HILL

1. *'They've lost one – just one'*: That witnessed in Book I, Ch. 12. In fact, the Martians have lost at least two tripods: the narrator's brother witnessed the destruction of a second in Book I, Ch. 17, but neither the artilleryman nor the narrator know this.
2. *'eating peas with a knife'*: A sign of lower-class origins, as is dropping the 'h'.
3. *'funk and precautions'*: Cowardice.
4. *'mashers'*: Fashionable young men, dandies, often seducers of young women.
5. *'poetry swipes'*: 'Swipes' is watery beer, and the implication is that poetry is 'wet' as in effete or useless.
6. *mock-turtle soup*: Soup (usually from a calf's head) made in imitation of turtle soup.

7. *old palace*: Lambeth Palace, the official residence of the Archbishop of Canterbury.
8. *arbor vitae*: Evergreen shrubs.
9. *Circus*: Piccadilly Circus, the centre of London's theatre-going area, and a location of vice and revelry.
10. *the Langham*: The Langham Hotel, mentioned again in the next chapter.
11. *'Thames-side burgundy'*: Although wine was produced in the south-east of England on an experimental basis during the nineteenth century, the narrator may be referring to weak imported wine from London wholesalers.
12. *euchre*: A game of cards for two to four players in which the object is, as in whist and many other card games, to take 'tricks'.
13. *parish points*: They played for the parishes of London as stakes, rather than for money.

CHAPTER 8

DEAD LONDON

1. *a Sunday in the City*: The City of London is a business district with few residents. On Sundays it would be (and still is) quiet.
2. *mechanical Samson*: Samson, the hero of the Israelites whose story is told in Judges 13–16, tore down the temple of the Philistines with his bare hands.
3. *destruction of Sennacherib*: The destruction by the Angel of the Lord of the army led by Sennacherib, King of the Assyrians, as told in II Kings 35–7, and the subject of Byron's poem 'The Destruction of Sennacherib'.
4. *Albert Hall*: In South Kensington, part of a range of museums and cultural institutions planned by Queen Victoria's consort Prince Albert (1819–61) after the Great Exhibition of 1851. It opened in 1871 and remains one of London's major concert halls.
5. *Crystal Palace*: Constructed in Hyde Park for the Great Exhibition of 1851 and reopened at Sydenham Hill in South London in 1854. It was destroyed by fire in 1936.

CHAPTER 9
WRECKAGE

1. *'The Last Man Left Alive!'*: A line from the poem by Thomas Hood, (1799–1845) 'The Last Man' (1824): 'and there I stood,/ The LAST MAN left alive,/To have my own will of all the earth'.

2. *Daily Mail*: Founded 1896 by Alfred Harmsworth, Lord Northcliffe (1865–1922) and still published today. Its cheap price and popular approach soon gave it a circulation of over half a million.

3. *advertisement stereo*: Newspaper advertising often took the form of repetitions of a single slogan. (In printing, 'stereotype' is a block or set of fixed type for reproducing impressions.)

CHAPTER 10
THE EPILOGUE

1. *luminous and sinuous marking*: Possibly the invading Martians on Venus are signalling home. If so, as well as the wheel they have not discovered radio.

A.S.

FOR THE BEST IN PAPERBACKS, LOOK FOR THE

In every corner of the world, on every subject under the sun, Penguin represents quality and variety—the very best in publishing today.

For complete information about books available from Penguin—including Penguin Classics, Penguin Compass, and Puffins—and how to order them, write to us at the appropriate address below. Please note that for copyright reasons the selection of books varies from country to country.

In the United States: Please write to *Penguin Group (USA), P.O. Box 12289 Dept. B, Newark, New Jersey 07101-5289* or call *1-800-788-6262.*

In the United Kingdom: Please write to *Dept. EP, Penguin Books Ltd, Bath Road, Harmondsworth, West Drayton, Middlesex UB7 0DA.*

In Canada: Please write to *Penguin Books Canada Ltd, 10 Alcorn Avenue, Suite 300, Toronto, Ontario M4V 3B2.*

In Australia: Please write to *Penguin Books Australia Ltd, P.O. Box 257, Ringwood, Victoria 3134.*

In New Zealand: Please write to *Penguin Books (NZ) Ltd, Private Bag 102902, North Shore Mail Centre, Auckland 10.*

In India: Please write to *Penguin Books India Pvt Ltd, 11 Panchsheel Shopping Centre, Panchsheel Park, New Delhi 110 017.*

In the Netherlands: Please write to *Penguin Books Netherlands bv, Postbus 3507, NL-1001 AH Amsterdam.*

In Germany: Please write to *Penguin Books Deutschland GmbH, Metzlerstrasse 26, 60594 Frankfurt am Main.*

In Spain: Please write to *Penguin Books S. A., Bravo Murillo 19, 1° B, 28015 Madrid.*

In Italy: Please write to *Penguin Italia s.r.l., Via Benedetto Croce 2, 20094 Corsico, Milano.*

In France: Please write to *Penguin France, Le Carré Wilson, 62 rue Benjamin Baillaud, 31500 Toulouse.*

In Japan: Please write to *Penguin Books Japan Ltd, Kaneko Building, 2-3-25 Koraku, Bunkyo-Ku, Tokyo 112.*

In South Africa: Please write to *Penguin Books South Africa (Pty) Ltd, Private Bag X14, Parkview, 2122 Johannesburg.*